THE
TAKEN
CHILD

BOOKS BY MARIA FRANKLAND

Last Christmas

I Let Her In

The Bridal Party

MARIA FRANKLAND

THE
TAKEN
CHILD

Bookouture

Published by Bookouture in 2024

An imprint of Storyfire Ltd.
Carmelite House
50 Victoria Embankment
London EC4Y 0DZ

www.bookouture.com

ISBN: 978-1-83525-007-5
eBook ISBN: 978-1-83525-006-8

For my gorgeous niece Thea, who gave me the inspiration for this story.

PROLOGUE

Dusk is falling as I rush from the building. I can't sit idly, waiting, terrified. I need to be out there, helping them find him. Toby's fear of darkness haunts my thoughts. The other children mocked him for bringing a nightlight. They're now safe in their homes, but my little boy... An innocent life has already been lost here today, and now my son is at risk. If the same person who was responsible for what happened earlier has also taken Toby, he's in terrible danger.

I see the rhythmic flash of blue lights, an ominous dance in the twilight. Voices pierce through the woodland, disorienting me. The dread in my stomach deepens with every step.

'Find.' A distant shout stops me in my tracks.

Find? What does that mean? A vice is squeezing all air from my lungs. I can't believe this is happening.

I push myself on and sprint towards the voice. Toby's life unfolds like a rapid slideshow in my mind, from the day he entered this world to his tentative first steps. Images of his innocence, his school uniform engulfing him, his arms around my neck, his gap-toothed grin, all intensify my desperation.

Please God, keep him safe. Please, don't let anything happen to him. I'll be a better mother, I promise. I'll do anything.

But there's no sign of him.

ONE

LEONIE

'Find your partner,' Catherine, our headteacher, urges, her voice cutting through the din of not only the children but their parents as well. She waves her arms around like an air hostess. 'When you've found them, go and line up with your adult.'

It's the first time I've seen her in jeans and a T-shirt. Even on teacher training days, she usually dresses as though an education authority inspector could arrive at any moment. Which is the norm at our school.

'Quickly and quietly, please!' she calls, her voice strained.

'We need to get this moving.' She nudges me and I notice the stress etched deep into her forehead. 'We're already behind schedule.' She raises her voice again, though this time, it's laced with further exasperation. 'If the parents could just stand aside while we get the children into their allocated seats please.'

Mia, my teaching assistant, rolls her eyes – a silent acknowledgement of our shared frustration. We're all only too aware that everything with Catherine has to be just so. Right down to where everyone will sit on the coach. Rather than allowing the kids to sit wherever they want, we've got a seating plan to adhere to.

As soon as Mia saw it, she said, *who knows what the rest of the trip's going to be like?*

I try to catch David's eye as he lines his group up, longing for that frisson of excitement his attention always gives me. But he's not looking back at me – instead, he's speaking to Jeanette, one of the parent helpers, as she lines her group up next to him. She's not *only* a parent helper – she's also the daughter of our chair of governors so we've really got a snake in the grass this week. In more ways than one.

Something gives way within me as I notice the way she returns David's gaze and shakes her mane of dark hair behind her back as she laughs. She's dressed more appropriately for an evening out with her wedge heels and summer dress, and I'm surprised that Catherine hasn't remarked on it.

I pull myself together and quickly check to see if Catherine has noticed me watching them. She hasn't – but judging by her pursed lips and narrowed eyes, Kirsty, the other parent helper, *has*. For a moment, she looks as though she's going to say something to me but must think better of it as she busies herself with her son instead.

'Hang on a minute,' David calls out. 'Who's been messing with these lists? Toby, you should be in *my* group.'

'He's with *me*,' Kirsty calls back, looking from David to Catherine with anguish in her eyes.

'No, he's not. Toby – get yourself over here now.'

'Can't I just stay with Mum?' Toby edges closer to her as she puts her hands on his shoulders. 'And I want to be with my friends.' His voice wobbles as he looks at his dad. Poor kid. It breaks my heart to see him being so torn between them.

Catherine marches over and gives David a look as if to dare him to persist with this. 'Let's just leave things as they are, shall we? The groupings are just a way of us being organised.' She smiles across at the parents who, clearly, are expecting a row to ensue between him and Kirsty. After all, it wouldn't be the first time.

But to my surprise, after a final glare at Catherine, David appears to relent and carries on gathering his group around him. Catherine watches him for a few moments before returning to what she was doing.

'I was so looking forward to this,' I say to Mia as I continue to watch Catherine, David and Kirsty, just in case. '*Was* being the key word here.'

'I know what you mean,' she replies in a low voice as our groups line up in front of us. 'But look – me and you can still make the best of it. The activities at the centre look amazing and we've got each other for company, haven't we?'

'I know.' I can't exactly tell her that it was *David's* company I really wanted. With the prospect of spending three days and two nights around each other, I was fit to burst with excitement. Until Catherine announced her attendance.

'I hope you haven't got any ideas about him while we're there.' She must have read my mind as she jerks her head in David's direction. 'Catherine will be watching you both like a hawk.'

'You'd think we were having an illicit affair, the way she spies on us.' I sigh. However, at least it probably explains why David's been keeping his distance from me this morning.

'Right everybody.' Catherine claps her hands three times. Her voice, shrill and businesslike, cuts through me like a knife. I hope I don't lose it with Catherine over the next three days – that could be disastrous. Or with either of the parent helpers for that matter.

A hush descends over the children as they stand to attention and clap back at her. 'Can we all please listen?' She sweeps her gaze over them. At the age they're at, some of them are nearly as tall as her now. It's nice to see them all in their own clothes, an array of colours and patterns. It doesn't happen often. Oldale Primary serves such a deprived catchment area that we like to make things easier for the parents by insisting on a uniform, and we have plenty of spare stocks for those who are struggling.

'Yes Miss Fox,' the children chorus like robots. Yet their parents continue chatting. As Catherine extends a steely gaze to them, one by one they fall silent, a couple of them pulling amused faces at one another. I know exactly how they feel. I might be an experienced teacher, but each time Catherine summons me to her office, I feel like she's going to expel me.

'Miss Hudson, if you could be taking a few photographs of the children as they're boarding and then seated on the coach.' Catherine's bun, a tightly wound crown, sits close to the top of her head like a symbol of authority. She waves her arm towards Mia as if she's dismissing her.

'As if I've got a choice,' Mia mutters.

'Miss Johnson, you and Miss Hudson look like sisters,' Abigail remarks as she walks behind us onto the coach.

'Thank you.' Mia flushes, yet looks delighted, as though she's been given a huge compliment.

Abigail's not the first pupil to make this observation. Mia's started using the same hairdresser as me – not just the salon, but the actual stylist too. We're roughly the same shape and size and she's even started to dress more like me. Bootcut trousers and patterned blouses for work, and even today, it's as if she's had a sneak peek at the clothes I laid out last night. Jeans, a brightly-coloured T-shirt and sandals. Hers is pink and mine green but other than that, we're dressed nearly the same. Eerily so. Perhaps I'll have to find a new hairdresser.

'I'd like to sit with my daughter if you don't mind.' Jeanette's foot is already on the step into the coach as her daughter trails behind. I look back to the door and watch Catherine's reaction. Hopefully, she'll put Jeanette in her place, despite whose daughter she is.

She does. 'You're sitting with Mrs Naylor.' Catherine reaches for her shoulder and for a moment, I think she's going to physically tug her back. She quickly lets go but her action's enough for Jeanette to return to the pavement, looking daggers at her.

'I came on this trip to spend time with my Jessica, *not* to sit with Kirsty.' The look on Jeanette's face is a picture as she puts her arm around her daughter. 'Sorry, no offence.' She shoots Kirsty an apologetic look then looks towards David as though he might support her. Thankfully, he doesn't.

'None taken.' At least Kirsty's dressed more appropriately for the trip in shorts, T-shirt, Converse and her hair in a high ponytail. She barely looks old enough to be the mum of an eleven-year-old, only months away from high school. I guess she's not out to impress anyone like Jeanette seems to be. And there can be no prizes for guessing exactly who *she's* out to impress. She knows David and I have a thing going now but it doesn't seem to be enough to persuade her to butt out.

'May I remind you how many other parents wanted to be part of this trip?' Catherine's jaw is set in a firm line as though daring Jeanette to argue with her any further. I wouldn't put it past her to send Jeanette home and give her place to one of the other parents who were coveting it. I wish.

I'd leave it if I were you, I would have warned her if she were anyone else. Being on the wrong side of Catherine isn't a good place to be. But since it's her, I hope she continues to argue.

Jeanette and Kirsty eventually take a seat together, neither of them looking too happy about being told what to do, but starting to chat with each other nonetheless. Hopefully Jeanette's waging war on Catherine, but if she is, she's confiding in the wrong person. Catherine and Kirsty have been friends since they were at school together.

Mia leans towards me. 'I'm surprised at the two of *them* being put together. What do you think the rationale is there?'

'I'm past caring.' I shrug. I might have helped David organise this trip but it seems I've now been delegated to the back of beyond. We're under Catherine's control now.

I might have known Catherine would sit David next to her. She'll know it's her best chance of keeping me and him as far apart from each other as possible.

'Miss Hudson.' Catherine twists in her seat. 'If you could just take a photograph from the front before we set off.' There isn't even a please.

Mia flashes a smile at her before turning to me and rolling her eyes again. She does that a lot when Catherine's around. We all do.

'Finally,' Mia says as the coach's engine roars to life. The gentle sway of the vehicle signals our departure, as we leave our school gates behind.

The familiar red-brick walls of Oldale Primary now blur with the parents waving goodbye to us. 'Make sure you give your grown-ups a wave everyone,' I call to the children around me. 'Boarding the coach has been more stressful than *any* of the planning and risk assessing we've had to do in the lead-up.'

'That's because you've been working with *David*.' Mia's voice has a mocking edge as she says his name.

'At least it's going ahead,' I say, ignoring my teaching assistant's sarcasm. 'No thanks to bloody Nancy.' A vision of our chair of governors' disapproving face swims into my mind. 'I'm surprised she hasn't wangled her way onto the trip as well.'

'What was her problem anyway? You never said.'

'*We should wait a while longer before embarking on a trip like this.*' I mimic her high-pitched voice. '*I have a bad feeling in my gut about it.*'

'Shhh.' Mia nods towards the front of the coach to where Catherine's left her seat and is making her way up the aisle.

'Are we all clipped in correctly?' She checks each child in turn. 'Good. That's good. Well done. Are you excited? Me too.'

'God help anybody who moves,' I mutter as she gets closer to us.

She smiles at Kirsty as she passes her.

'The chosen one.' It's Mia's turn to mutter. It's true. Kirsty's the only adult on this trip who's in favour with her.

'She didn't smile at us, did she?' I check Catherine's already well past us before nudging Mia. I wouldn't want her to hear what I really think of her. Mia laughs.

As I crane my neck towards the front of the coach, I'm able to see that David's messing on his phone. I stare at the back of his dark head, again wishing I was the one sitting next to him.

Bending forwards, I rummage in my bag for my own phone, just in case he's texting me while Catherine's out of her seat. Hopefully, he's as fed up as I am about her being here and putting a dampener on everything.

But if nothing else, at least this trip has given me the chance to legitimately work with David in a way that Catherine *or* Nancy can't object to while we've been organising it.

'Don't let Catherine catch you on that in front of the children,' Mia hisses as she looks around. 'Oh, it's OK, she's busy talking to Kirsty. Surprise, surprise.'

'If only Nick had been able to come,' I say, thinking of David's teaching assistant. 'I can't believe we've got Catherine to contend with for the entire time instead.'

'And if only *any* other name had been drawn in that school assembly, other than Kirsty's.'

'I nearly fainted when that scrap of paper was waved in the air.'

Why didn't you choose another one? we'd all asked afterwards, but as was so rightly said – with the eyes of the school and many of the parents on that all-important draw, Kirsty's name couldn't exactly be dropped back in just because she happens to be *David's ex-wife*, could it?

❧

I remember when we met.
When you made me feel like I was everything.

TWO

LEONIE

'Did you see my mum crying?' Gracie, who's sitting behind me, says, as Catherine heads back to the front of the coach. 'I told her not to. *How embarrassing.*'

Abigail, sitting beside her, giggles. '*My* mum reckons she's going to have a party while I'm gone and she's got the house all to herself.'

I suppress a smile. If I ever become a mum, I imagine I'll be of the partying variety rather than the crying type when sending my child off for a school residential. I wouldn't be one of the parents vying for the parent helper places either. But then, I've never known that kind of desperation to get away when affording any other sort of holiday feels impossible.

'You've got to feel sorry for Toby.' I nudge Mia and nod in the direction of where he's sitting. 'With *both* his parents here. Especially with how things have been between them.'

'I know. He's a lovely lad, isn't he? It's sad to see him so utterly torn all the time. And anyone can tell that he prefers to be with his mum.' As if he senses us discussing him, his tousled strawberry blonde head turns around, offering us a smile before he acknowledges his mother and turns back to his friend.

'Poor kid,' I remark as he returns his attention back to Sam, who's sitting next to him. 'He must be so mixed up with it all.'

'Have you and Kirsty spoken this morning?' Mia tilts her head to where she's sitting, and as though she's sensed us talking about her, she turns and glances our way.

'Not really. I'm never sure what to say to her, if I'm honest.' It's true. David and I seeing each other was always going to be awkward and I've never directly broached it with her. But hopefully, as far as she, and especially Catherine are concerned, anything between me and David has fizzled out.

'She keeps staring at you.' Mia taps my arm. 'Have you noticed?'

'Give over,' I reply. 'We're supposed to all be adults here.'

'*Jeanette's* not the most ideal second helper either.' Mia lowers her voice. 'She'll only have come along to fawn over David anyway.' She turns to look at me, and I know she's trying to read if I'm jealous after what she's just said.

'What about her husband?' I stare at Jeanette's glossy chestnut brown head. She's more glamorous than the rest of us women here put together. She certainly wouldn't be seen with paint all over her face and a pencil stabbed into her ponytail like I seem to spend most of my days.

'I can't imagine she'd let a small detail like *having a husband* stop her,' Mia whispers. 'She was all over David last year, according to Nick. Then it was off for a bit, then it was back on. And now, who knows?'

'You've already told me all this – more than once.'

It's wearing how Mia takes any and every opportunity to put David and everything to do with him down. I know she's envious of the time and energy I've given to getting to know him but I can't help it if she feels like that.

'I don't know what all the mums see in him,' she continues. 'I mean, I know he's good-looking but he's so arrogant with it.'

'You don't know him like I do,' I reply. 'And if you must know, he gets fed up with them flirting with him all the time.'

'Only because of all the warnings he's had about mixing work with—'

'Alright Mia, give it a rest.' I must raise my voice too much, as I manage to attract the attention of the other adults and all four turn to look at us, Jeanette with a raised eyebrow and David with a wink which, I can't lie, does make me feel better. I can't help but notice that now Catherine's moved away from their seat, Jeanette's got her phone in her hand. I just hope it wasn't *her* that David was texting.

I fix my gaze on the passing scenery beyond the window. The vibrant colours of the countryside blur as the coach speeds along the country road. We've left Oldale well behind us and we're now onto the country road towards Ilkstone Crag. Flashes of bright sunlight flicker through the endless woodland. With a headache suddenly threatening, I twist the nozzle above my head for the air conditioning. A stale scent fills the air, a mix of bus interior and lingering traces of the bygone snacks.

'Great.' I wrinkle my nose against the odour and twist it around again. 'It's not working.'

'You might have warned me how twisty the roads are.' Mia grimaces as well.

'I just hope the kids are all dosed up with anti-sickness pills.' I shudder. 'You know I don't do vomit.'

'It's just as well you've got me then, isn't it?' She reaches over and pats the top of my hand.

As if anyone would volunteer to clean something like *that*. One of the things I'll say for Mia though is she'll cheerfully roll her sleeves up and muck in. She'll happily do anything I ask of her, which is everything I could want from a teaching assistant.

'This is going to be such a fun adventure for us,' she says. 'I've always said we don't do enough together outside school.'

I haven't got the heart to tell her this *is* technically still school.

'So, you and David – what *is* going on there?' Mia lowers her voice and separates her face from the rest of the coach behind a curtain of her hair. 'I thought it was all over – but judging by the way you keep looking at him...' Her question trails off.

'Shhh.' I turn from the window to meet her eye. 'You know it's not something I can talk about. Definitely not *here.*'

'No one's going to hear what we're saying above this racket.' The children at the back have started singing. I can only hope their noise will meet with Catherine's approval. She might have made a better head in the Victorian era, when *children were seen and not heard.* 'But yes, I've noticed you watching him like a lovesick puppy several times today.' There's a definite edge to her words.

'I've done no such thing,' I retort, feeling uncomfortable at how many people seem to be watching me so closely at the moment.

'I get the feeling,' Mia continues, 'that Catherine's disapproval of you and *David* has more to do with her being friends with Kirsty, than about you being distracted from your job. But either way, it doesn't change anything, does it?'

'Look – can we not talk about David please?' I lower my voice this time.

'Are you still planning to go for that promotion when it's advertised?' A note of sadness creeps into her voice. She's told me several times that a large part of her would hate for me to be successful when I apply, as it will be the end of us working together.

'Of course I am.'

'I just think' – she sniffs – 'that Catherine will want to keep you as a class teacher rather than promote you to be her deputy.

She's more likely to bring someone in from the outside, I reckon.'

'Let's just wait and see, shall we?' I reply. I avert my eyes from the window. I don't know what's worse, the flashing sunlight between the trees or the nasty overhead lighting on this coach.

'The next three days are certainly going to be interesting, aren't they?' Mia laughs. 'But don't worry, I've got provisions for us.' She points at the bag by her feet.

'What do you mean?'

'Gin in a tin of course – for our consumption only, mind.'

'Blimey – don't let Catherine catch you with those.'

Mia picks her bag up and pats it in an almost protective fashion. 'I'm surprised she hasn't carried out a bag search – especially after that briefing. *No alcohol will be permitted.*' She does such a good impression of Catherine's voice that I can't help but laugh.

'Me too.' I shake my head. 'It's the first residential I'll have been on where we can't have a glass of wine or two to unwind with in the evening.'

'She probably got this job straight from being a sergeant major in the army.'

I laugh again amidst the sound of children's voices and the rumble of the coach. Looking at the back of Catherine's head, she would definitely fit the bill.

'Can you think of three worse chaperones for this trip than the head from hell, David's ex and Nancy's daughter?'

'No,' I reply drily, unable to return her smile. 'I really can't.'

∾

I remember our first falling out.
But the making-up seemed worth it.
At least that's what you said.

THREE

CATHERINE

'It's good to sit back and have a breather, don't you think?' I nearly fall into my seat as the coach rounds the corner. David shifts his leg to his own side as I straighten myself up.

'Why did you swap Toby into Kirsty's group?' His jaw is set in a firm line and I can tell from his tone that he's far from happy.

'It wasn't the *only* change I made. I was just balancing the boys and girls out some more.'

'Oh come on Catherine – I'm not that daft.'

'Fine. I thought it would be nice for Toby to be with his mum for a change. You have him all the time, don't you?'

'That wasn't your call and I've asked you before to—'

'Let's not make this into something it doesn't need to be,' I cut in. The last thing I need is an argument with David. 'You'll still get lots of time with him, but honestly, you saw his face when Kirsty was calling her group's names, didn't you? He positively lit up.'

'I'm still not happy. I really think—'

'I'm glad you got the message back there anyway. Especially

with the two parent governors who were hanging around. *And* Amelia's mum.'

'What about her?' At least David seems to be moving away from the subject of Toby and whose group he is or isn't in.

'Her husband writes for the local rag, doesn't he? We need to make a point of being extra nice to each other in front of her – and *to* her.' I give him a knowing look. '*Keep your enemies close* as they say.'

'A Year Six teacher having custody of his son is hardly front page news.'

'I'm not saying it is, but after all the bad press from last year, we don't want to offer any further angst for them to get their claws into, do we?'

He doesn't reply but instead, stares out of the window. We lapse back into silence.

I turn and glance up the coach again, the sunlight streaming through the windows, creating a dance of dust particles in the air.

'It's such a responsibility we have – bringing all these children away from their usual routine and onto this sort of residential, don't you agree?' I sip my lukewarm coffee from my thermal cup. I've been trying to drink it since seven o'clock this morning but keep forgetting it's here. 'It brought it home to me when all the parents were waving us off.'

'What do you mean – *this sort of residential*?' David's eyes, dark already, look even darker as he turns to me.

'Well, it's not exactly your run-of-the-mill treasure hunts and den building sort of a trip, is it?'

'Yes, I'm fully aware of that.'

This was the main factor to encourage me that the trip was worth persuading the governors to give their approval for. They, in turn, were bowled over by David's energy and enthusiasm for the amazing time the children would have and the team-building opportunities it would present. As always, he was very convincing when he gave his presentation to them. But with the exception of myself and Nancy, David could probably convince most people of anything once he turns on his charm.

'We're also lucky to be the first school to try it all out,' he adds, as though he's trying to persuade me all over again.

'I can't deny that it's been great for us to have more positivity among the parents again.' I cast my mind over the three assemblies we've held in preparation for it.

I could add here, *especially after the negative attention this school's had over the last couple of years.* But I don't.

'I can't believe how many of them wanted to come.' He smiles. 'It was the mention of them being so *fully* involved in all the activities that did it, I think.'

'I think it's more about many of them not being able to afford a break of their own. The chance to have some *quality* time with their children.'

'Perhaps.' David sniffs as though he wishes my suggestion had been his.

'So we've got even more of a responsibility to make sure they all have an unforgettable experience.'

'Their backgrounds aren't *that* deprived.' He shakes his head.

'How can you say that?' I keep my voice low. The last thing I would want is for one of the children to hear me. 'There are so many of them who wouldn't even get a hot meal every day if it wasn't for school dinners. The reason we had so many parents seeing them off is because so many of them are out of work.'

My phone's ringtone rises above the rhythmic hum of the coach engine. I bend down and tilt the screen towards me.

'Gosh, we've barely left the school and Nancy's calling me.'

'Already?'

'All the more reason that we can't allow *anything* to take our attention away from the children's welfare while we're here.'

David gives me a strange look. 'As if we would. Besides, it's not as though there aren't qualified instructors who will be fully supervising it all,' he says.

My phone rings off and then starts again straight away. 'Aren't you going to answer it?' He nods towards my bag.

'I'll ring her back when we've settled in at the centre.'

If Nancy thinks I'm going to be answering the phone to her morning, noon and night while we're away, she's very much mistaken. The boundaries need to be set from the off.

'Is everything OK?' David looks at me in the piercing way he looks at everyone, his gaze carrying the weight of the concern he's so capable of exuding. I can see why people are so won over by him. The way he looks and listens to what others have to say has a way of drawing them out of themselves and making them feel like they are the most important people around.

'Of course. Why wouldn't it be?'

'Blimey this is some coach ride.' David turns to the window. 'I don't remember it being this jerky and bumpy when we drove up in the car.'

As the coach ascends, the silhouette of craggy peaks begins to emerge in the distance. Hopefully, we're not too far away now.

I glance back to check for green faces and my gaze meets Kirsty's. We smile at each other.

'Do you think you and Kirsty will be OK while we're here?' I turn back to David.

'In what respect?'

'In every respect. It can't be easy for you both after the court case and everything. But I'm sure that as a potential deputy head applicant, your conduct won't be anything less than professional towards her.'

'If she's OK with me, I'll be OK with her. As long as she respects that *I'm* the one who has custody of Toby now and doesn't keep trying to muscle in outside of the group activities.'

Like anyone needs reminding of *that*.

**As time went on,
I began to learn what made you angry.**

FOUR

CATHERINE

Nancy was apoplectic about Kirsty's name being drawn to be here on the trip. I *can* see why she might think it's less than ideal. However, Kirsty's over the moon to be spending extra time with Toby – and she more than deserves it.

I glance around at her again. After Jeanette's initial reluctance to sit with her, they're now animatedly talking.

'You should watch yourself around Jeanette as well,' I say. 'I see she's still harbouring that ridiculous crush on you.'

She and Leonie seem to eye each other like competitors for the same prize. Perhaps Jeanette becoming more friendly with Kirsty will convince her to avert her attention back to her *own* husband. Another reason why Nancy's on my back. *Make sure you watch Jeanette and David*, she's implored of me. Three times in as many days.

'She's just being friendly, that's all. If Jessica wasn't moving into my class next year, she wouldn't give me the time of day.'

'Well don't ever forget whose daughter Jeanette is.' I give him a knowing look.

He turns away from me as if to say, *subject closed*.

'What's the plan when we arrive?' I glance at my watch.

'My contact at the centre, Harry, is meeting us off the bus.'

'So he's someone you know personally?'

'I used to. Anyway, he's going to give us a tour and then either he or the centre manager will give a welcome talk for—'

'Whoa!' A collective shout and a few screams erupt from behind me as the driver slams on at a junction.

He mouths *sorry* back at me into his mirror before setting off again.

I scowl back at him via his rear-view mirror. The coach's jolt serves as a stark reminder of our responsibility for the children's safety.

It's on the tip of my tongue to demand that he pays more attention to his driving. But this isn't the time to tell him that. He needs to keep his focus on the road.

'I can't believe he nearly overshot that junction.' David shakes his head with a mixture of disbelief and relief etched across his face. 'That could have been disastrous.'

'I can't imagine him making any more mistakes like that.' My grip tightens on the rail in front of us, a silent plea for the driver's focus. 'Anyway, what were you saying?'

'Oh yes – we'll give them time to get unpacked, have lunch, and then...' Reaching into the bag at his feet, he tugs out a battered folder.

I notice his trainers as he reaches down, which are strange to see. He usually wears shoes so shiny he can probably see his face in them. He leafs through some pages before pulling one out. 'This afternoon we're starting with raft building and canoeing.'

'When's the zip wire?' A shiver, more pronounced than I'd like, rips through me as I ask. The thought of the zip wire sends a chill down my spine and not for the first time.

'Ah, the big and exciting one.' David's face breaks into a wide grin. 'That's tomorrow. Toby's been going on about it for weeks.'

'Dad!' Right on cue Toby calls out from where he's sitting a few seats behind us.

I twist in my seat to look at him. 'I think you mean *Mr Naylor* when we're in school, young man.'

'But we're not in school Miss Fox.' Annie Thorpe giggles from the seat behind me. I avert my gaze to give her one of my looks as her friend nudges her.

'Sam feels sick,' Toby continues, his voice carrying an edge of desperation. 'Really sick. He's... Ugh. Too late.'

David and I glance at each other. Great. Here we go. Normally, when one child is sick, they all follow suit. I turn in my seat again. 'Miss Hudson?' I call up the coach to where Mia's sitting, seemingly oblivious to what's going on a little further up there as she chats with Leonie. 'Miss Hudson?'

Her head jerks towards me, her usual lack of friendliness written all over her face.

'Would you mind seeing to Sam please? It sounds as though he's been sick.'

She nods. Although she doesn't look happy about it, she knows this sort of thing is an unofficial element of a teaching assistant's job description, falling under *any other tasks or responsibilities deemed necessary by the class teacher or the headteacher*. She rises from her seat.

A collective of 'ughs' and 'let's sees' and 'I feel sick toos' erupts from the children and I find myself trying not to breathe through my nose in case the smell drifts here, to the front of the coach. I check my watch again.

'How much longer have we got to go?'

'You sound like one of the children.' David pulls a face. 'Ten minutes or so, I think.'

'Thank goodness for teaching assistants – that's all I can say.'

David drops the folder back into his bag. 'That's one part of the job I'm very glad we can delegate.'

Kirsty appears beside me in the aisle, looking skinnier than ever in her tight jeans.

'Is everything OK?' I ask her.

'Can Toby swap places with Jeanette and sit next to me?'

'He's fine where he is.' David replies without even looking at her.

'I want him sitting next to me, that's all *David*. Not next to some boy who's throwing up.'

'Sit down Kirsty.' He still doesn't look at her.

'We'll be there in a few minutes.' I smile. 'Just sit tight. Don't worry, you'll have plenty of time to spend with him over the next three days.'

David stares back out of the window, clearly aware of how guarded he needs to be in what he says when he's around me.

Which is very guarded indeed.

~

I needed you more and more.
At times you seemed to like that.
Until you didn't.

FIVE

MIA

'It's alright Sam – we're nearly there now – we've just passed the sign.' I wrap his clothes in a plastic bag and give him some water. 'Some fresh air will help you to feel better.'

'Is he OK?' Kirsty calls out. Then I hear her saying to Jeanette, 'I hope it's just travel sickness and not some bug.'

'Me too,' Jeanette replies. 'As if we want to be all swimming in vomit for the next three days.'

Leonie gives me a sympathetic smile as I retake my seat next to her.

'If *you'd* asked me to deal with Sam, I wouldn't have minded as much.'

'Does Catherine really irk you *that* badly?'

'She just has a way of getting right under my skin.'

'What do you mean?'

'Well, on the surface she seems pleasant enough, doesn't she? What with her perma-smile and her homely rosy cheeks.' I stare down the coach at the back of her head. She can probably sense my gaze boring into it.

'We're all aware that there's a sharp edge to her – and I have tried to warn you about it!'

'I know. I guess I had to feel it for myself to believe it.'

'You should never have argued with her like you did.' Leonie gives me a look that's a cross between protectiveness and *I told you so*. 'Especially in front of the entire staff meeting.'

'I felt like one of the children that day. You should have seen the look she gave me when she mentioned the need to *schedule a meeting to discuss the renewal of my fixed-term contract*.' I put on my best Catherine impersonation in the hope it will make Leonie laugh again. It does.

I smile back at her. I like to make Leonie laugh.

'She was probably just reminding you who's in charge. Though it makes you wonder what she's so defensive about.' Leonie follows my gaze to the back of her head.

'I did ask Nick if Catherine forced him to say he couldn't come on the trip but he wasn't giving anything away. But I could tell by the look on his face that I'd hit a nerve.'

'Just be careful Mia. I'd hate to see her try to oust you.'

I want Leonie to reassure me with how she'd put her own neck on the line if it came to it, or even how much she'd miss me if I *was* forced out of Oldale, but she doesn't say anything else.

'I feel like she's watching me all the time now,' I continue, still hoping for a promise of support or a word of encouragement that *all will be well*. 'I need this job – I can't lose it.'

What I don't add to Leonie is that my wage only just covers my bills and services my debts. Without it, even for just a few weeks, I really *am* in trouble. I wish I could talk to her about the mess I've made of my finances. She's only a few years older than me but is far more experienced and knowledgeable in life. She's got everything and *is* everything that I want for myself.

But I wouldn't want her judgement and the last thing I'd want is for her to think anything bad about me. Especially if she knew that all my new clothes and even the expensive colour and cut at the hairdresser's has gone on my credit card.

As the months of this school year have gone on, I've found

myself imitating her style. From the way she wears her hair in a low ponytail or a side plait, to some of her mannerisms, like how much she waves her hands around as she speaks. Perhaps this is inevitable because we spend so much time together – maybe it's not even a conscious copying.

David even commented on it recently when I went into his classroom for his register.

'I thought you were Leonie when I first glanced up,' he'd said, frowning. Then later I'd heard them laughing about it together. I haven't been able to stop thinking about it since and I've often wondered firstly why he was frowning and secondly what was so funny about my clothes and hair being similar to hers.

The coach winds its way through the rocky landscape, and as we approach Ilkstone Crag, a weathered sign emerges, perched on the side of a rugged rock. Surrounding it, tulips, once vibrant but now faded, nod in the breeze. A renewed excitement buzzes from the children as the coach curls up the sweeping drive towards the main building.

'Look.'

Leonie and I exchange wide-eyed glances as the distant figure on the zip wire comes into view. The towering structure, framed against the clear blue sky, fills me with awe. 'Blimey – it looks much higher than it did in the pictures.'

'I can't wait to give it a whirl.'

'It's no wonder so many of the parents wanted to come. I'm going to try *everything* while we're here.'

'We might as well.'

'I take it the kids won't be riding that one then?'

'Gosh no.' Leonie laughs. 'There's a far smaller one for them.'

'Stay in your seats until you're told to get up,' Catherine hollers from the front of the coach as we crunch onto the gravel in front of the sprawling brick building with solar panels on the roof.

I have to admit, as I take in the sleek glass windows which reflect the surrounding nature, that it looks exciting here. I remember my own Year Six residential, fifteen years ago now – we only stayed for one night and the highlight of the trip was trudging up some hill in torrential rain. No thank you.

'Who's he?' I nod in the direction of the muscular, dark-haired man approaching the door of the coach. 'Does he work here?'

The bus doors whoosh open and everyone watches as David descends the steps to meet him.

'That's Harry. David knew him when they were younger,' Leonie says, her voice conveying some kind of authority and almost *ownership* of David, which I find really irritating. I don't usually get irritated by Leonie – only when she's hankering after David.

'Is that why we're the first primary school to be able to come here?'

'I guess so.'

'I never want to get married,' Leonie says suddenly in a hushed voice.

'What's brought this on?' I turn to her in surprise.

'I've just been watching Kirsty.'

'Why?'

'She looks so damn miserable all the time. I can't imagine going to all the trouble and expense of getting married only to end up at each other's throats like they have.'

'Never mind about Kirsty. We'll have a great time, won't we?' I nudge her. 'I've got nail polishes and face masks in here too.' I pat my bag.

'Have I ever told you any of the horror stories David's shared with me about all their wrangling?' She continues to watch David talking Harry through a page he's holding in front of him.

'He got the lot in the end though, didn't he? The house, the money, the custody? As my brother said when he and his wife split – *the winner really does take it all.*'

Harry's now running his finger down a piece of paper he's showing to David. I wish they'd hurry up. I want to get off this bus that stinks of vomit and stale food.

'Yeah.' Leonie lowers her voice. 'I just hope Kirsty's not here with an agenda about David, because if she is, she'll have a fight on her hands.'

Kirsty twists in her seat and narrows her eyes at Leonie, making me wonder if she's heard anything – whether she has any idea we're talking about her.

~

I'd have done anything for you.
But then you knew that,
didn't you?

SIX

MIA

David waves from the side of the coach and Catherine gets to her feet at the front, seemingly poised to convey her next instruction.

'We're going to unload our bags children,' Catherine begins with her usual irritating smile plastered across her face. 'Then you're going to stay in your groups as you're shown to your rooms. You can leave your bags on your beds until we've had a look around and then time will be given later to unpack.'

'Be sure to thank the driver as you're leaving the bus,' Leonie calls as the children start leaving their seats. I catch glimpses of their expressions as they reach into the overhead lockers for their belongings – an array of wide eyes and excited smiles.

Once off the coach, Toby makes a beeline for Kirsty and tugs at her arm. 'I can stay in *your* group, can't I Mum? Dad won't make me change, will he?'

She looks over to where he's now talking to Jeanette as if being careful before she replies. 'Don't you worry,' she says. 'You're sticking right with me.'

A smile lights up his face but disappears as quickly as it

arrived when he notices David watching their exchange. It's evident from the look on his face that not having Toby with him has seriously angered him but, with Catherine around, there's not a lot he can do.

My room is *next door* to Catherine's. 'Whose idea was this?' I hiss at Leonie as the children go in their sixes to their dorms. 'Was it so *you* didn't have to be next to her?'

I bet her room is next to David's but I don't say anything.

'There's only six rooms for the adults,' she replies as she nudges me towards it. 'We all had to go *somewhere* and be next to *someone*, didn't we? Stop moaning – at least you've got an en suite.'

'I want the top bunk.' A screech erupts from one of the dorms as I let the door close behind me. My room welcomes me with a fresh scent, a blend of laundered sheets and the subtle fragrance of a cleaning product. It's surprisingly pleasant in here – certainly better than the bedroom in my flat. I stride to the window, throwing it open to reveal the ongoing climbing and abseiling activities on the rocks. We couldn't have picked a better few days to be here. Sunshine always lifts my mood.

As instructed by Catherine, I round my group of children up from their dorm and we head for the Asquith room, where we've been told to expect the welcome talk. Ours is the last in – the other children are already seated in their groups on the tiled floor where the sunlight is casting its patterns over them. Everything looks shiny and new, and a whiff of fresh paint hangs in the air. Catherine gives me a look as if to say *about time* but she's too busy speaking to someone to allow me to interrupt her conversation.

My gaze falls on Leonie, who's standing at the far end of the room with David. My hackles rise as soon as I notice and I make a beeline for her.

'Who are the kids that are already here?' I ask in a breezy voice as I try to wedge myself between them.

She follows my gesture to the window before stepping to the side so she's even *closer* to David than before. 'They're from the local high school and have been here since Monday – but as far as I know, they're going home today.'

'They are.' David addresses me rather than Leonie. 'So how are *you* finding it so far Mia?'

We don't have much to do with one another outside the context of me delivering his register or when he's asking me to cover his playground duty. But when I do these things, he has a knack for making me feel as though I'm doing something really important. At times, I *can* see why everyone falls for him, including Leonie. I wouldn't be so bothered if their relationship didn't take her away from *me*.

'Erm, it's great. I'm really glad I was able to be here.'

I always feel uncomfortable when David looks at me directly – he's got such a piercing gaze that it makes me wonder what he's *really* thinking. I glance to the other side of the room where Catherine, Kirsty *and* Jeanette all seem to be eyeballing us.

'So we'll have the place to ourselves then, will we?' I step around the other side of Leonie. 'It's going to be *great*.'

'We hope so.' Leonie nudges David. 'We've worked hard to pull this all together, haven't we?'

She turns further into him, as though trying to exclude me as much as possible from continuing any sort of conversation with them.

'Miss Hudson?' says Amelia as she sidles up to me. 'Can I get a drink?'

'Just a second.' I nod towards the front of the room as Harry clears his throat in readiness to speak.

He's changed out of the clothes he was wearing when we arrived and is wearing clothes similar to David's – combat shorts and a T-shirt. He's quite a good-looking man and I steal a glance at Leonie to see if she might have noticed this too but her eyes seem stuck on David. He, however, seems to have his attention focused on Harry.

Several voices still persist. Leonie's being one of them.

'Settle down please.' Catherine casts her frown around the room, resting her eventual disapproval on Leonie before turning her attention to me. 'Get another photograph,' she mouths as the remaining couple of people quieten themselves.

'So, I'm going to run through the programme for the time you're spending with us,' Harry begins in a surprisingly expressionless voice. 'Which is today, tomorrow and Friday.'

The children jiggle around on the floor in excitement. This is what they've been waiting for. I listen peripherally as Harry lists the activities and the safety training that will be given before each one. I already know about all this from our staff meeting.

'Ultimately,' Catherine interjects, 'you're here to enjoy some fabulous new experiences and to look out for each other, as well as staying safe at all times.'

The children nod earnestly. Catherine's manner is definitely softer when she's addressing the children than it is with staff.

Harry's moved on to talking about something else. His gaze is dark to the point of being brooding and I wonder how much work he's done with children of this age. He hasn't smiled once at them.

'All meals will be served in here,' he says. 'And your bedtime will be at nine o'clock.'

The children's response is a mix of *awws* and *yesses*. Clearly, nine o'clock will be late for some of our children and not so late for others.

As he finishes speaking and the children's noise returns to its usual levels, I catch some snippets of their comments.

He's a scary man, isn't he? – Is he allowed to tell us off? – Is he in charge of Miss Fox? – Do you think he looks mean?

Overhearing them, I feel a twinge of sympathy for Harry. The kids have barely given him a chance before making their assumptions. They say *kids are cruel* and they certainly can be. As he leaves the room, I can only hope he hasn't heard them.

'As I was saying,' David's voice echoes from behind me. He and Leonie have moved even further away. 'About your mini-me.'

I feel the weight of Leonie's glance so I look towards the front while making an effort to keep my expression as though I haven't heard them. I've already been told from one of the other teaching assistants that David's referred to me as Leonie's *mini-me*. What I'm really interested in is how she'll reply. I twist to face the other direction but my ears are trained on their conversation.

'Miss Hudson?' Sam appears at my side.

'Just a second Sam. We just need to listen a little longer.' What I mean is *I* just need to listen a bit longer.

'Stop calling her that – you know how much it winds me up.' Leonie makes more of an attempt at lowering her voice than David did. I can't believe they're talking about me when I'm so close by.

Catherine's looking over us all as though she's got something else to say.

'Ah give over. It's funny,' David continues. 'How does it feel to have someone moulding themselves into a carbon copy of you?' I can no longer see them both but I can imagine the smirk on his face.

'Creepy, if you must know. I can't stand it. Even the kids are commenting.'

'Well tell her straight then.'

'How can I? I still have to work with her, no matter how weird she might be. Anyway—'

Catherine claps and the children clap back at her.

I feel like I've been winded. When I first had my hair done

and asked Leonie what she thought, she said it looked nice. But all the time she's been laughing at me with David behind my back and calling me creepy and weird. Tears stab at my eyes and I blink them away. I can't cry, I won't cry. What reason would I give for it if someone was to say, *What on earth is the matter Mia?* I don't know what's hurt me more, what Leonie actually said to David or the fact that she's talking about me in the first place. I avert my attention to the rocks in the distance. *Get a grip, get a grip.*

But I'm really struggling with this. And I really don't know what I'm going to do.

'Children,' Catherine begins in a highly pitched voice. 'I'm going to give you fifteen minutes to get settled into your dorms and wash your hands ready for lunch.'

At the word *lunch*, my own belly rumbles. Breakfast seems like a long, long time ago. I might be able to think more clearly once I've eaten. And at least I'll be on my own table with my group of children rather than having to face Leonie. Fresh tears stab at my eyes at the prospect.

I need to pull myself together. Maybe what Leonie said was a one off. Perhaps she was just saying those things to impress David in some way. Though, one thing is for certain. I definitely need to try harder to prise them apart – once and for all.

~

**The lower I got,
the more you seemed to despise me.**

THE INVESTIGATION

DI GILBERT

'I've been told you're ready for me.'

I glance up as our latest interviewee strides in. The staff room, a cramped space adorned only with a kettle and a pair of nondescript, plasticky sofas, lacks the invite a retreat from the children might be expected to offer.

'Have a seat.' I gesture at the sofa facing us. 'I'm DI Bradley Gilbert. I'm in charge of the investigation into what's happened today, and this is my colleague Sergeant Chris Parkins. As we mentioned before, we need to take a witness statement from everyone.'

My eyes meet Chris's, and an unspoken understanding passes between us. No words are exchanged, but we both recognise the arduous task that lies ahead – a marathon of interviews with children, teachers, and all the other adults here. The gravity of the situation hangs heavy in the air.

'I'm happy to help in any way I can, although I don't know how much I'll be able to help you. I only saw what the others did.'

I shield my eyes from the mid-afternoon sunshine as I reply.

'It's not just about the *accident* itself, it's also about the lead-up to what happened.'

'OK.'

As soon as the words have left me, I'm aware of my emphasis on the word *accident*. The last thing I want at this stage is to give any hint that we're considering all options.

'From the experience I've had with my own kids,' Chris says, 'aren't these residential trips usually just offered to children in their *final* term of primary school? Yet there are some nine-year-olds present.'

'There were thirty-six places and the Year Six class is smaller than that. So the remaining places were offered to the Year Fives.'

'I see. Can I ask how the additional children were chosen?' I gesture in the direction of the rocks. 'I imagine *all* the Year Fives wanted to come.'

'Their names went into a draw.'

'In a similar way to how the two parent helpers were selected?'

'That's correct.'

'Were you present at the draw?'

'I was.'

'What were your thoughts at that moment? After the parent helpers were drawn, I mean.'

I try to keep my tone neutral. A teacher and his ex-wife where their split has been toxic and messy attending a school residential sounds like a recipe for disaster to me, but it's not my opinion that's important here.

'That it could be a tricky situation but the bottom line is that we're all here for the children.'

Such diplomatic and well-chosen words.

'Do you *normally* attend school trips?'

'When I can.'

'Did *you* personally know where the safety equipment for the activities was being stored?'

'No – that side of things had nothing to do with me.'

'Can you recall whether the rucksack containing your harness was labelled with *your* name?'

'Yes – it was. It had been fitted to me the day before. Why's that important?'

'Every bit of information is important if we are to piece together exactly what happened up there.' Chris looks up from his notepad.

'Starting with,' I say, 'any hostilities you know of between the adults that were present.'

Their eyes betray a flicker of unease and the atmosphere in the room seems to tighten.

'Gosh,' comes the eventual reply. 'Where do I start?'

SEVEN

LEONIE

Catherine seems to have welded herself to David's side since the moment we left school this morning – even ensuring he and his group are seated on the table next to her and her group for lunch. I can't imagine it's for any reason other than to keep me away from him. I've only managed to speak to him once.

As for me and my group, we have, of course, been delegated to the far corner of the room. I keep trying to catch David's eye but he's not looking this way. It's probably because we've both been given the hard word from Catherine.

'Are you excited Miss Johnson?' Abigail asks as I pass a bowl of soup to her.

I give her the largest smile I can muster. 'Of course I am. We're going to have such a wonderful time.'

When we found out about Catherine coming along at the staff meeting, he joked afterwards that if the only opportunity we'd get for time together was in the middle of the night, then we'd have to settle for that.

'Can I have some more bread please Miss Johnson?' Gracie looks up from her soup.

'Me too,' asks Abigail.

'That's right – you get it all eaten up,' I tell them, my heart sinking as I notice David and Jeanette smiling at each other from their opposite ends of the room. 'We're going to need lots of energy this afternoon.'

The air is heavy with the slurps of vegetable soup and the clatter of spoons against bowls. A sweet smell is emanating from the kitchen – it could be waffles. However, I'm struggling to get much down today. I can't seem to quell the sense of foreboding that's intensifying in the pit of my stomach, and it's not just to do with David.

I can always sense when someone's staring at me and as I glance up, Mia looks away. She's got a similar look on her face to the one she has every time Catherine tells her to do something which makes me wonder if they've had words again. After a few moments, our gazes catch and this time she scowls before dropping hers again. I'll try and talk with her after lunch and see what the matter is this time.

My gaze flits to the table next to ours, where Jeanette's surreptitiously texting under the table. At least she's finally managed to stop making eyes at David. It's pathetic – utterly pathetic. And I am *too* for feeling so jealous about her. After all, it's *me* he's seeing now, not her. At least I hope it is. I guess I just feel dumpy and mousy in comparison.

'I wouldn't let Catherine catch you doing that,' I say.

She jumps and then frowns at me. 'It's not as if I'm getting paid for helping on this trip.'

'On your head be it then.'

'Do we have to stay with our groups the *entire* time?' Jeanette slides her phone into the pocket of her cardigan.

'As far as I know we do.' She doesn't normally talk to me so her question is a surprise.

I'm aware of how cool my tone is towards her, but I can't help it. She must know about my involvement with David through the parent grapevine, yet her open flirtation with him in front of me persists. He's moved on from whatever was going on between them but clearly, she can't accept it.

'It seems quite unreasonable that they're travelling, eating, sleeping and doing *all* their activities in their groups,' she continues. 'Can't they be mixed up – at least a little?'

What she probably means is *can't she and David be mixed up a little?* 'You need to take that up with Miss Fox.' I jerk my head towards Catherine, who's no longer at her table but is now talking with Kirsty at hers.

David's also moved his attention to Catherine and Kirsty with a look I can't decipher. Like me, he's probably wondering what they're so engrossed in conversation about. It's an allegiance that makes me extremely uneasy. My line manager and my boyfriend's ex-wife. That's if I can call him my *boyfriend.* Until the last few days, maybe I could. But now I'm not so sure.

Since they're distracted, I rise to my feet, never one to pass up an opportunity. 'I'll be back in a minute children,' I tell my group before sidling around the edge of the room towards David, the rubber soles of my plimsolls squeaking against the polished floor.

Noticing my approach, he rises from his chair too.

'Can I have a word please Mr Naylor?'

'Of course.' He responds with a mock bow, stepping away from his table. The room is bustling, providing a cover for our conversation. In any case, there's no law saying I can't converse with my colleague about school trip matters. No matter how much Catherine, Jeanette, or anyone else wants to keep us apart.

'It's not quite what we planned here, is it?' I dab my fingers against the corners of my mouth. I should have double-checked I'd been tidy with that soup before heading over here. Knowing me, I've probably slopped it all over my lovely new white top. But I won't look down and draw attention to it if I have.

'I guess not.' I can't quite read his expression or his voice.

He's always been impossible to read. This, whether I knew it at the time or not, was part of the initial attraction.

'Do you remember what we were saying about the middle of the night?' I shuffle from foot to foot, feeling somewhat awkward about making such references amidst a room full of children.

'Of course I do.' He looks at me intently, clearly wondering what I'm going to say about it.

'Well, I'm in the bedroom next to you.'

'But I've got Kirsty on my other side.' He pulls a face. 'It's hardly conducive to—'

'So what? She'll be asleep.'

'Now we're here with my ex-wife about, I don't really know if I'll be able to bear three days of being around her.'

So he's changing the subject away from my 'middle of the night' proposition.

'She's certainly making her presence felt.' I turn to glance over at her and Catherine. They don't seem to have noticed my movement across the dining room. Yet.

Only Mia's watching us but when she sees me looking at her, she looks away again. I'm not sure if she's in some sort of mood with me. I get the impression that to keep her happy, my attention should have *her* at the centre of it. Whatever's up with her though, she needs to get over it.

'I gave myself a good talking to this morning.' David runs his fingers through his hair and I find myself longing to do the same. 'I wasn't going to let it rattle me. But that's easier said than done.' He sighs. 'The fact that we're all constantly having to refer to her as "Mrs Naylor" is getting under my skin as well.'

I glance towards her. She's finished talking to Catherine and is now saying something to Toby. She reaches to him and ruffles his hair. Not that I'm going to say anything but he looks happier than he has in a long time.

'I'm not surprised – especially now you're divorced.' I shake my head, regretting for the millionth time that I didn't meet him before Kirsty did. I know the aftermath of their divorce has left him cautious about commitment, which is why things have been going so slowly between us.

'You do realise that the two of us are being watched the whole time and not just by Catherine. We need to be careful here Leonie.' He thrusts his hands into the pockets of his shorts as he nods towards her.

I turn to look over my shoulder; Mia's still staring and now Jeanette is as well. It seems like they don't have anything better to do than to gawp at us.

'What is it with you and her?' I try to keep my voice light and airy. The last thing I want is to sound jealous. Unless there's something to be jealous of, that is. 'Is anything still going on between the two of you?' I drop my gaze. I'm probably watching him far too intently as I wait for his reply.

'Jeanette's married,' he replies, as if that makes any difference to some people. It certainly doesn't to *her*, from what I've heard.

'So what's the story? I mean, look at her.' I look across the room, expecting her still to be watching us but she's back on her phone, texting beneath the table. 'She's always flirting with you. And if you don't mind me saying—'

'She's had a thing about me for a while, that's all.' He lowers his voice. 'Ever since her eldest daughter was in my class. I might have reciprocated a time or two but that's all in the past.'

'You've never told me that before. *Reciprocated!* What's that supposed to mean?'

'Oh come on Leonie. Do I have to spell it out for you?'

Shit. How did I not know this? No wonder I can feel the daggers firing from her eyes into my back at every turn. 'How long ago?'

'A while now. Look – do we have to discuss this? *Here?*'

'But nothing's actually going on with you now – is that what you're saying?'

'No it isn't.' David laughs. 'Besides, have you seen the size of her husband?'

I don't laugh; this isn't amusing in the slightest. 'You're saying that as if her husband is the only thing getting in your way.'

'Hang on a minute.' His face seems to darken as he notices Toby on his feet, chattering with the other children on his table with his arm around Kirsty's shoulders. They're clearly enjoying each other's company which will, no doubt, annoy David to no end. I'll never know the full extent of what went on between them, nor do I want to. I only know that none of it was pretty.

'Toby, get back in your seat now please.' David's voice is stern.

His smile fades as he lets go of his mother, and drops back onto his chair. I glance over at my table. Two of my children are flicking bread at each other. I give them my strictest stare but neither of them seem to notice. However, I'm sure Catherine will have seen them and I'll probably be in for the high jump later.

Just like I always am.

~

The first time you hit me,
I was so shocked,
I couldn't even cry.

EIGHT

LEONIE

My attempt to talk to David is abruptly cut short by Catherine's three-clap sequence, casting a silent spell over the room. It feels deliberate, designed to prevent any further conversation between the two of us. Some of the children are still eating – she didn't need to stop them yet.

David shuffles back, seemingly distancing himself from me. I want to ask him more about Jeanette but the moment appears to have passed.

'Carry on with your lunch children,' Catherine begins with her beaming smile. I can see why Mia refers to it as a *perma-smile*. 'But while you're still eating, I need your listening ears.'

It winds me up how she speaks to our classes and if I were standing closer to her, she'd probably have seen me roll my eyes. Many of the children are going up to high school soon, yet she addresses them as if they're still in Year One.

'After lunch, we're going to split into two teams of eighteen children,' she announces. 'Team One will be my group, Miss Hudson's and Mr Naylor's groups and you will all be canoeing. In Team Two, we'll have Miss Johnson's group, *Mrs* Naylor's and Mrs Smith's and you will all be raft building.'

I hate the emphasis she puts on the *Mrs* when she refers to Kirsty. If *me* and David were to ever get married, I wonder if she'd finally let go of his name.

'Awww.' Clearly not everyone's happy with their allocated activity and would rather do the other one.

'At three o'clock, we'll be all getting together for drinks and snacks before swapping over.'

'Yesss.' This time, a hiss of appreciation.

I can't believe Catherine's put me with Kirsty and Jeanette. Why couldn't I have been with Mia and David for the afternoon? All possibility of being able to keep my distance from Kirsty and Jeanette has gone out of the window. As the only paid member of staff, I'll have to take the lead with them.

A titter of conversation rises among the children.

'When you've finished eating,' Catherine continues, 'you'll visit the...' Her last words are lost in a wave of children's chatter.

'I'd better get my lot sorted,' says David, glancing over at his table. 'Chin up Leonie.' He squeezes my shoulder as he passes me. 'It could be worse, you know.'

'Have you dried your hands? Good girl. Go and wait over there. Yes. Behind Matilda. That one's empty. That's it. Hurry up now.'

I lean against the cool, tiled wall. Jeanette, confidently playing the role of a teacher, orchestrates the children with an air of authority and often seems to carry herself with aspirations beyond her station. She might enjoy getting them to fall into line at the toilet but she wouldn't last five minutes with a medium-term plan and a behaviour chart.

She certainly wouldn't be sporting those impeccably manicured nails and designer heels. I mean, who wears heels like those for a school residential?

Really, it should be me taking charge of the children as we

get ready for the raft building. However, she seems to be enjoying her new-found role directing them so much that I'll happily leave her to it. Besides, I don't want to get any closer to the obscene-smelling air-freshening blocks that are wafting from the toilets. I can smell them even out here, in the cloakroom.

'You might want to change your shoes.' I point at them. Then I immediately hate myself for sounding so catty. Being around the women I've suddenly found myself surrounded by seems to be bringing out the worst in me. Usually, I don't have a bitchy bone in my body. On countless occasions, I've even found myself feeling sorry for Kirsty since I started this job. I often see the hunger in her eyes as she watches Toby and even I can see how fiercely they love each other.

'Miss Johnson. Can I get something from the dorm?' Abigail lands in front of me, breaking my train of thought.

'Go on. Be quick though. We're going outside in a minute for the safety briefing.'

I watch as she skips away, wishing I had her lightness of step. I barely notice as Kirsty appears beside me, shaking her mane of hair behind one shoulder. 'I thought you and David weren't seeing each other anymore.'

I swing around and look at her. It's the first time we've spoken today. Since we assembled in the school car park, I've caught her staring at me several times. Now we've been forced together for the afternoon, we've *got* to speak to each other. *Thanks for this Catherine.*

'I, erm, we're not.' She's straight for the jugular, I'll give her that. I look towards Jeanette to see if she's listening in. 'What makes you think that?'

'I noticed you before.'

'We were talking – we're colleagues, after all.' My voice is flat and I hope it conveys my sentiment – *do one.*

'It looks like more than that to me,' she persists.

'If I *was* still seeing David.' I stand up straighter and glance around the cloakroom. No one's around so I'm safe to continue. 'It has *nothing* to do with anyone else.'

'Take it from someone who knows, Leonie.' Her eyes narrow. 'You really need to be careful.'

'Is that supposed to be some kind of threat?' My retort is sharp, a mix of defiance and irritation. But the moment I open my mouth, everything falls silent and my words seem to bounce from every wall. Then, to my horror, I notice Catherine striding across the foyer. Of course, she's heading right towards us. *Me and my big mouth.*

'What on earth is going on here?' Catherine's voice pierces the air, sharp and authoritative.

Oh my God. Even the children are staring at us now. Why the hell did I rise to Kirsty's bait? David's warned me what she can be like.

'Nothing,' I mumble. Feeling the weight of Catherine's scrutiny, I instinctively straighten up, my eyes darting around, searching for an escape from the uncomfortable situation. 'We're just getting the children ready, like you asked.'

'From what I can see, it seems to be *Mrs Smith* who's getting them ready.'

She looks from me and Kirsty, to Jeanette, who smiles her lipsticked smile and shrugs her shoulders.

'You might want to change your shoes Mrs Smith.' She waves her hand towards Jeanette's feet.

'Yes Miss Fox. I was just about to.' At least that's wiped the smile off her face.

Mia appears in the foyer and in the hope of a sympathetic look from her, I try to catch her eye but she looks away again with what looks like anger in her eyes. I've definitely done something to upset her. Maybe it's when I turned away from her earlier in favour of continuing my conversation with David. I let a long sigh out. It's a known fact throughout the teaching profession that school residentials are notorious for backstabbing, sniping and one-upmanship – but isn't that supposed to be amongst the children?

We've barely arrived and I've had enough already. I'm really not sure how I'm going to get through these next three days.

~

The bruises would always fade,
but your taunting insults lingered.

NINE

CATHERINE

Now replete from my lunch, I could happily stretch out on this plush grass where we're surrounded by the invigorating scent of pine, and have a snooze. But duty calls.

The centre manager, Frances, finishes speaking and invites Harry to demonstrate the life jackets to the children. He marches to the front and grabs a jacket from the box.

'If you can't make your life jacket feel *snug*, then it's too big,' Harry explains in rather a flat voice. Amidst the children's eager anticipation, I expect Harry to exude more enthusiasm. Instead, there's an almost edgy impatience about him, which makes me wonder what might be going on for him.

'And if you can't comfortably put it on and fasten it, it's too small,' he says, as he demonstrates with the jacket he's now wearing.

'We'll come around and check you all,' Frances says, her blonde curls bobbing around her face as she rises to her feet. She might be darkly dressed, in combat trousers and a loose fitted T-shirt, but she's got a happy twinkle about her, far more suited to working with children.

I shield my eyes from the sun and look across the lake to

where Leonie's group are having their own briefing with two of the other centre staff.

Observing her stiff body language and her deliberate distance from Kirsty and Jeanette, it's evident that an air of discontent envelops her. I don't know exactly what transpired between them in that cloakroom but it seems like I'll have to have a word. I can't have an unhappy atmosphere spoiling things for the children.

From the snippet I heard as I approached them, Kirsty might have been about to go too far in whatever she was saying to Leonie – a scenario I warned her against from the moment we knew she was coming on this trip.

'Can you help me Miss Fox?' Sam appears beside me with a light tap on my arm, his beaming face full of colour again after his earlier sickness.

'Of course I can.' I tug at his life jacket and then tousle his hair as he leaps back to the others. I love the lot of them, but Sam's one of my favourites. Like so many of our children, he has such a difficult home life and yet he's a little darling.

'Do you have children of your own?' Frances is watching me as I start checking a couple of the other children's life jackets.

I shake my head. 'What do I need children of my own for? I've got a school full of them.'

She laughs and heads to where all our canoes are lined up and waiting.

'Mr Naylor,' I call to David, whose shoulders look rigid with tension as he fixates on Kirsty and Toby. 'Can you just check Rory and Amelia's life jackets, please?' He looks as though he needs the distraction.

Despite what he might be feeling, it's lovely to see Kirsty and Toby enjoying each other's company so much. She's shown incredible resilience, emerging from the dark clutches of depression and alcoholism. She's been through hell and no one could be prouder of her than I am. Now she has managed to get her act together, she really shouldn't be so shut out of her son's life and if there's anything I can do to make a difference, I'm more than happy to do it.

David's still not taking his eyes off Kirsty and their son. He's probably thinking that it should be *him* helping him into his life jacket and spending quality time with him while we're here – which had never been my plan, once I knew she was coming.

'I've never rowed before,' Mia says as we're directed to the full-size canoes.

'Paddled,' David corrects her.

She blushes.

The children are lining up along the decking with Frances and Harry, looking as excited as I've ever seen them. I have no doubt they'll all be talking about this trip for a long time after we've returned to school next week.

'I'm not sure if I'll be able to do it.' She tugs a boat from the line.

'You'll soon get the hang of it.' David winks at her. 'I'll show you how.'

'We're going to demonstrate paddling to the children once we're all in,' Frances calls, her voice carrying across the excited chatter of children.

I chuckle. 'There you go Mia.'

The mournful look she gives me suggests my tone might have been disparaging.

'I only meant to help you learn how to paddle, that's all.' I duck into my own life jacket. 'Smile Mia. You might find that you enjoy it once you get going.'

She forces a smile as she drags her canoe towards the water. I don't mean to be derogatory but those who don't know me well always take my dry sense of humour too personally. This is another reason for the staff room conversations to suddenly dry up whenever I get within spitting distance. But it's fine – after all, I didn't accept this job to make friends.

～

You threw me out,
you reeled me in,
and I let you.

TEN

CATHERINE

'Are you counting us *again* Miss Fox?'

Sam's right. It does seem like I'm counting them for the thousandth time already since we convened this morning. But I can't seem to help myself.

'Stand by your canoes children,' Frances calls over the top of their heads.

I might have the reassurance of the lake not being very deep, *and* the fact that the children can all swim but still I worry. After all, if anything untoward were to happen, my head would be first on the chopping block.

Additionally, I'm grappling with the weird sense of unease I've had – ever since David first mooted this trip at the staff meeting. It's a feeling that's only gained in strength as we've got closer to this half-term break. It feels as though I've got so much to prove and so much to lose – all at the same time.

'That looks like fun.' Abigail points across the lake at the children who've begun building their rafts.

'I think this will be the most fun.' I pull my most excited face back at her. 'But don't worry, we'll be having our turn at what they're doing after the break.'

. . .

It's years since I paddled a canoe but I'm relieved to find it's like riding a bike – once mastered, never forgotten. Despite the pressure at school, the rhythmic paddling seems to be washing away the strains. Surprising myself, I find relaxation settling in.

'I'll get you back for that,' I laugh as Jacob accidentally splashes water into my face.

Being out here on this sun-dappled lake surrounded by the shrieks of happy and excited children is very freeing and just what I needed.

'They're doing alright, aren't they?' I call across to David, whose sullen mood appears to have lifted, thank goodness.

Most of the children seem able to move their canoes to varying degrees of success and for those who are struggling, Frances and Harry are milling around to help them.

'How do you do it? I really can't do it!' Unfortunately, the same paddling praise can't be heaped onto poor Mia. 'I'm just going around in circles.' She looks over at Harry as if willing him to come and help her. Hmmm, I know that look.

'It's easy Miss Hudson.' Sam sails up beside her. 'Watch Mr Naylor if you want to see how to do it.'

All eyes turn to David, which, no doubt, he'll be pleased about.

'The kids seem in awe of your Year Six teacher.' Frances draws her canoe up beside mine and nods in David's direction as he deftly weaves in and out of the others, clearly enjoying us all watching him.

'I've never seen a teacher so hero-worshipped by the kids, especially the boys,' I reply. It's true. Everyone's so eager to please him and win his approval. And I'm not just talking about the children.

'Is he the only male teacher at your school?'

I nod. 'They're a rare breed.'

'I know,' she replies. 'Which is why we snapped Harry up when he offered to work with us as a volunteer.' She nods in his direction.

'So he's new here then?' That could explain his demeanour. Perhaps he just needs time to settle in and to feel more comfortable in dealing with children.

'Fairly,' she replies. Then she leans into my boat. 'Between you and me' – she lowers her voice – 'the teacher from the last group of high school students we had said he reminded her of Heathcliff. Apparently, they're studying that text at the moment. She said she might want to borrow him!'

I laugh.

Then as though he can feel our attention on him, he stares back, moving his gaze from me to Frances.

'Aren't you brilliant? You've done this before,' I look away and call to one of the boys as he sails past me.

'Look at me Miss Fox,' shrieks one of the girls, her ponytail swinging out behind her.

'And me,' shouts another.

'You're all *brilliant* paddlers.' I beam at them as they look back at me. Gaining the approval of the head must be nearly as validating as the approval from the 'cool' Year Six teacher. 'Are you getting the hang of it yet Mia?'

She seems to be happy drifting now and has become more interested in watching what's going on on the other side of the lake rather than in trying to master her canoe.

'You need to keep an eye on your own group,' I remind her. 'Never mind what's going on over there.' Sometimes, when I'm speaking to Mia, I almost feel like I'm addressing one of the children.

She scowls and heads towards Jacob. It's been a positive move to separate her from Leonie this afternoon – she needs to find her *own* way with the children, without her sidekick.

'You look like you're enjoying this Miss Fox,' David calls

from the other side of a group of children. The complimentary and charming side of his persona has returned.

'Thank you,' I call back, perhaps a little too stiffly. I expect his professionalism but I can do without his false friendliness.

'She definitely must have done this before,' Frances agrees.

'Just wait until we get her on that zip wire tomorrow,' David says.

'I haven't said I'm definitely going to do it yet,' I reply.

'Ah, you've got to. What do you say children?' He laughs.

'Yes Miss Fox – we're all going to have a go.'

'You can always ride the smaller one with us.'

As I lean back in my canoe, I'm suddenly enveloped by a huge shiver. Which in the heat of this glorious June day is most unexpected.

∾

I was warned you'd keep on going
until you'd torn me apart.
But I never listened.

ELEVEN

MIA

'Thankfully you're a better teaching assistant than a rower.' Catherine laughs as we stack our life jackets back on the decking. I even feel dowdy beside her today as I compare her summery top with its sparkly motif against my two-pound special from Primark Essentials.

I never know quite how to take Catherine. I steal a glance at her to ascertain whether she's being nice or sarcastic. Her smile, as always, is fixed firmly in place and I can't detect any traces of malice within it.

'I hoped I might get the hang of it eventually,' I reply. 'I think I'm saving myself for the zip wire instead.'

'Yes – I'm sure you'll enjoy that.' It's clear from her tone that she's not looking forward to it. 'Unlike me.'

I smile, grateful for what seems like her genuine attempt at conversation. Perhaps she's OK outside work.

It's gorgeous here. Green, spacious and a far cry from concrete Oldale. I wish we were staying here for longer than we are. As I follow Catherine around the banks of the lake to join the others for our break, I scan the group to see where Leonie is.

However, my attention's drawn to Harry and I'm taken aback to notice him offering Kirsty his hand.

'Do Harry and Kirsty know each other?' As I'm asking the question, I realise they must do if he's an old acquaintance of David's.

'Why do you ask?' Catherine eyes me with an air of suspicion.

'It seems out of character that he's helping her, that's all.' *That's right Mia. Speak first, think later.* What I've just said is totally out of turn.

'What makes you say *that*?'

'I don't think he's been so helpful to any of the other staff, that's all. He left me twirling in circles when we were in the canoes.'

However, it's not exactly difficult to see why he might be helping *Kirsty* up from the raft. With that luxurious head of hair and green eyes that are too large in her face, she exudes something I never will. It's always been the same old story – I'm flat-chested, scrawny and generally pointless, no matter how hard I try to copy Leonie's hair and clothes. It's as though I'm only destined to observe other women while wishing I was like them. I don't think I'll ever be comfortable in my own skin.

'Why don't you just concentrate on getting some brilliant photos of everyone while they're enjoying their snacks?'

She turns towards one of the centre staff who's laying drinks and biscuits on the picnic tables. 'Thank you!'

She's hellbent on keeping me in my place, Catherine is. *Do this Mia – do that Mia.*

I shuffle away from her and head in Leonie's direction before David thinks about doing the same.

'Cheer up Mia!' As I reach her, she throws her arm around my shoulder and squeezes it. It feels amazing to be hugged, albeit briefly. The anger I've had seething within me after overhearing her call me weird earlier dissipates somewhat. I can never stay mad at her for long.

What, or should I say, *who,* has averted her attention from me now? Oh, I should have known.

'You were pretty good at that canoeing malarkey.' She smiles at David, the sunlight catching the strands of her hair making her look even prettier than she already is.

'Cheers.' David smiles back at her and then at me. 'We enjoyed it, didn't we Mia?' He winks and Leonie's face falls slightly. My stomach twists with excitement from receiving the wink, and also with someone feeling envious of *me* for a change. And she deserves it after talking about me earlier.

'Erm, I wasn't very good though.' I flush and step away from David, who's landed right beside me. I need to get better at reading people. His friendliness since we arrived on this trip makes me wonder if he fancies *me* all of a sudden. Maybe being a *mini-*me of Leonie isn't such a bad thing after all. I shake the thought away. He's hardly going to pay me any attention when he's got Leonie and Jeanette already vying for his attention.

'How was the raft building?' He turns to Leonie. She gestures to two planks of wood that are attached to an empty barrel. Everything else has capsized around it.

'Hopefully, I'll be better at paddling.' She laughs.

'Toby, over here.' David waves at his son.

Toby, Kirsty and two other boys are tucking into their biscuits. He says something to his mother and then sidles up beside David.

'You can stay in your mother's group for *today.*' David rests his hand on his shoulder. 'But tomorrow you're back with me, where you *should* have been all along.'

'But Miss Fox said—'

'I don't care about what anyone else says – *I'm* your father. You see your mum on Sundays and that's it. Like I said, you're back with *me* tomorrow.'

Toby's bottom lip trembles as if he's been told off.

I've often noticed Kirsty hanging around at the school gates. She comes with her sister while she drops her Year Three daughter off. Leonie's often commented about the hungry look in her eyes as she watches Toby racing around in the playground with his friends. David's tried to have her banned from the gates but he clearly can't control *everything*.

'Toby, I've poured you a drink,' she calls from the table, beckoning him back to her. 'And you need some more sun cream on.'

'Can I go back to Mum?' Toby's face is somewhere between guilt and apology. I don't know how recent their divorce was but I hope things get easier for him. At least they're fighting over who *wants* him. When I was a child, my parents fought over *not* wanting to look after me.

'Mr Naylor, would you mind helping me?' Jeanette thrusts a bottle of sun cream at David, turns her back and lifts her hair.

Leonie's eyes narrow, her frown betraying a mix of annoyance and suspicion. The tension is palpable as David's hands linger on Jeanette's shapely neck. I wouldn't put it past Leonie to throw Jeanette into that lake while they're out on the canoes.

However, having observed Jeanette's flirtatious antics, I can't help but admire her confidence. It's a trait I've always lacked, and it definitely sets her apart from the rest of us.

'Are we ready to go team?' David offers his hand to tug me to my feet – still slippery with sun cream. As I rise from where I've been sprawled on the grass, Leonie's watchful eyes have moved to me.

'Toilets again first please children.' Catherine stands from one of the picnic tables, brushing biscuit crumbs from her shorts. She appears more relaxed than I've seen her look in ages. 'After that, we're good to go with the second part of the afternoon.' She offers Frances a thumbs up as if she's trying to be cool all of a sudden.

'Are you feeling more enthusiastic about *this* activity Miss Hudson?' Catherine turns and calls as we approach the doors of the building.

'Perhaps I won't make such a spectacle of myself this time,' I reply. 'Anyone can fasten a few pieces of wood together, surely?'

She laughs and Leonie gives me a strange look. I seem to be making her as jealous by being friendly with Catherine as I was when David was talking to me. Another person's jealousy is such a new occurrence. And I quite like it – especially after what she was saying about me before.

~

I could no longer recall
the person I was
before I met you.

TWELVE

MIA

'I can't wait to build a raft.' Sam skips along at the side of me as we return to the edge of the water. 'Will we be staying in our groups Miss Hudson? Will you be helping us build it?'

I smile back at him. 'Of course.'

We circle Harry as he demonstrates knot tying and talks about the factors and aids which will ensure buoyancy. The shadow beneath the peak of his cap makes his eyes even darker – eyes that appear to be resting more on David than the children as he speaks – as if he's seeking his approval for what he's imparting.

'Right, back into your sixes,' Frances calls when Harry stops speaking. 'Let the battle of the raft builders begin.'

'Can you get this to go tighter?' Amelia's huffing and puffing as she tugs at some string. I reach over to help her, leaning in at the same time as Harry crouches beside David.

'If you're still on for that pint later.' His voice is low but loud enough for me to hear it.

David looks up and glances in Catherine's direction, presumably to make sure she's not listening in to them.

'I was thinking about 9 p.m., when the kids have gone to bed.'

'Nice one. I'll meet you by the main gate, shall I?'

'Yup.' Harry returns to his feet and our eyes lock for a moment before he heads over to Catherine's group. It sounds like they're arranging to go to the pub. I can't imagine Catherine would be happy. Not when she's banned everyone from bringing alcohol.

I think of my plans with Leonie and excitement flutters in my belly. It'll be so nice to spend time with her that doesn't directly involve work. Other than the staff Christmas party, it will be the first time I've been able to have a drink with her. At least now, I know David will be out of the way as well.

Finally, we're all assembled at the side of the lake with our rafts, waiting for further instruction.

'You're going to paddle out as a relay,' Harry begins, sounding about as enthusiastic as if he were about to go for root canal treatment. He should be in a better mood now that he's got a drink at the pub scheduled. 'Two at a time to the marker.' He points at the buoy bobbing near the centre of the lake. 'Then you'll paddle back here and swap over with two more of your teammates.'

A ripple of excitement washes over the children.

By its third outing, ours is still holding up. 'Look at our raft.' I nudge Catherine. 'I'm astonished with it.'

'Look!' Amelia screams with laughter as the last two of Catherine's team end up in the water.

She and Sam are laughing so much that they nearly fall off *our* raft.

'And now for the judging,' Frances says. 'Emma?' She calls

out to a girl leaving the staff quarters just at the right moment, it would seem. 'Would you like to come and do the honours.' She gestures towards what's left of our rafts.

Emma, looking like something out of *Baywatch*, at least compared to me, struts at the edge of the lake as she inspects each raft. I glance at David to see if he's watching her. Of course he is, which is something I can drop into conversation with Leonie later.

'We need scores for appearance, function and whether each raft looks as though it could last for even more sailings.' Frances presses her hands together with what could be excitement.

Harry slinks back to the picnic tables, watching on as though all this is beneath him.

'In third place is this one.' Emma points to the raft built by Catherine's team. 'It clearly won't endure another sailing, will it?'

Laughter echoes from us all.

'Booo.' Catherine points her thumbs downwards and her group follow suit.

'Second place goes to this rather interesting-looking vessel.' She points at ours. I don't know whether to feel complimented or offended as she emphasises the word *interesting*. 'But however it might look, at least it seems to be functional. And lastly, for the way it looks, functions *and* endures, the winner of the raft competition is *this* one.'

We all clap as David rises to his feet and brushes off the grass which is clinging to his legs. Then he runs circles with his children all running after him as they cheer. It's difficult not to be amused as they act like they've just won the World Cup.

Of course David's group won. I've only known him for a matter of months but it's obvious that no matter what the event or occasion, if there's a position to be had, he *always* has to win.

. . .

'The children seem pretty tired.' I'm at Leonie's side as we crunch along the gravel path which guides us back from the lake. It winds beneath a canopy of arching trees which cast dappled shadows over our faces.

'Yeah, I think the afternoon's flattened them out for now. But it'll be a different story once they've eaten, you watch.' She laughs.

'I just wish we could all eat together – that it could be a bit more free and easy, instead of rules and the groups and all that.'

'That's Catherine for you.' Her voice is airy as she nods to where Catherine's striding ahead of us, deep in conversation with Kirsty. Ahead of them, David's walking with Jeanette, his hands thrust deep into his pockets. I'll have to see what Leonie thinks about the two of them later.

'You watch,' she says. 'She'll have some sort of team-building exercise for us to do after the children have gone to bed.'

'Blimey, I hope not.'

~

My self-esteem was on the floor.
You had me right where you wanted me.

THE INVESTIGATION

DI GILBERT

There's a tapping on the door. I don't know why they're knocking; after all, they've already been summoned and know they're expected in here.

'Come in.'

'Have a seat.' Chris gestures at the recently vacated seat facing ours.

My eyes linger on the shiny kettle in the corner, a silent temptation in the dimly lit room. I could do with an influx of caffeine. However, that might be a step too far, since we've so many people to speak to this afternoon.

'I'm just getting some water Sarge.' My mouth is too parched to conduct this meeting without one.

Our interviewee confirms their name, date of birth, address, and their understanding of why they've been called in to speak to us.

'This is not a formal interview,' Chris says. 'So as such, this conversation won't be recorded and you are free to leave at any time.'

What I won't be adding every time he says this is that if anyone *was* to try and leave, we'd be duty-bound to do whatever it took to prevent them, under the circumstances. After all, someone is *dead* and by choosing not to answer our questions, they'd be deliberately obstructing a police investigation.

'Can you describe your relationship to the deceased for us please?'

'We didn't have *any* relationship. Not directly anyway.'

'What about the other adults that are here?' I shoot back.

'What do you mean?'

'I mean, is there anyone *you* know better than the others?'

'Not especially. My focus here has been on the children throughout the few days they are here. What's that got to do with what's happened though?'

'It's so my colleague and I' – I gesture to Chris – 'can put together a statement of events based on your experiences and recollections in the time since you arrived at this facility.' Frustration simmers within me; each question feels like extracting teeth from an uncooperative mouth. We don't seem to be getting anywhere so far.

'My recollections of last night are extremely hazy, to be honest. I'd had a few drinks.'

'Why don't you tell us what you *do* recollect then.'

'It's difficult to say. There was quite a lot going on.'

'Such as?'

'Well clearly, there's history between several of the adults here. There was some sniping from what I understand, people going into each other's rooms or whispering in quiet corners. School staff in the centre staff quarters – just lots of people all over the place instead of getting some sleep.'

The rundown we're given of everyone's whereabouts makes for interesting listening. No one seemed to be where they were supposed to be.

'We have information that *you* were seen outside the equipment store.'

'Who told you that?'

The door to the centre bangs periodically in the distance but there's none of the usual noise that would be expected from a large group of children out there.

'What were you doing?'

'I don't remember being out there, to be honest.'

'You're seriously telling me you *don't remember*?' I stare back. I don't like being lied to. If this carries on, we'll be finishing this conversation at the station.

'I had a lot going on last night. Things I can't go into.'

A low growl emanates from my stomach, and I press a hand against it, a mix of hunger and unease churning within me.

'Then I would suggest' – Chris glances up from his notebook – 'that you let us have these *things*. Is it necessary to once again remind you that someone has lost their life out there today?'

THIRTEEN

LEONIE

'Mr and Mrs Naylor sitting in a tree. K-I-S-S-I-N-G.' The rhythmic chanting of the Year Six girls permeates the air as they sway in the basket swing. Instantly, my hackles rise.

'Girls, that's quite enough of that.'

'Aww Miss Johnson,' Amelia moans, disappointment etching her face as I halt the swing, nearly slipping on the bark chippings in my haste. 'We were going well high then.'

'Find a different song to sing please.' My voice is snappy but I can't help it. 'One that doesn't use the names of teachers *or* parents.'

'But Mr and Mrs Naylor are Toby's mum and dad, aren't they?' Jessica speaks now. 'So they must have been kissing *some* time.'

'Toby's parents are *not* together anymore,' I explain to the girls, emphasising the word *not*. 'Which is why you should find another song to sing.' I'm probably saying far too much to this impressionable group of nine- to eleven-year-olds but the words have left me before I give myself a chance to think about them.

Meanwhile, Catherine's hovering like a red kite ready to

swoop onto a mouse. It's only a matter of time before she sticks her beak into what I'm doing over here.

So I move away from the children and head towards where Mia's sitting, absently watching the children from her perch on a bench. Before long, Catherine will, no doubt, order her to get up and *mingle with the children like she's being paid for.*

Give her a few minutes of peace, I say. She looks deep in thought but judging from her expression, whatever her thought is, it isn't a happy one.

'You OK?' I sit beside her.

'What?' She startles at first but then moves up as though making way for me. 'Yeah – I'm just watching the kids.'

'You sure?' I was in two minds wondering if she looked miserable or even angry for a moment.

She looks thoughtful, as if deliberating whether to divulge what's on her mind. 'I'm fine,' she eventually says.

'Really? Because if you don't mind me saying so, you've been a bit off this afternoon. Is everything OK?'

'Oh, erm – yes, I guess so. Look, if you must know, I was just churning over my money situation.' Her voice wobbles in a similar way to when she's giving me an excuse for why she's late in a morning. I get the impression she's using her *money situation* as a smokescreen for something else entirely.

'Well, it's been a long month.' I laugh, the sound blending with the children's chatter and the squeak of swings. Not that I've got a great deal to laugh about. David and Jeanette are once again engrossed in conversation at the edge of the playground while she makes eyes at him and keeps touching his arm as they speak.

Mia doesn't laugh back. Her expression remains sombre, a stark contrast to the light-heartedness around us.

'I'm sick of being on my own in life,' she says. 'Of never being able to trust anyone.' She twists in the seat and looks at me properly for the first time since I've sat down with her.

'What do you mean?'

She stays silent but it's clear something's really bugging her.

'If you think things are difficult for you, think what life must be like for poor Kirsty.' I nod in her direction as she watches Toby.

'I thought you didn't like Kirsty?'

'It's not that I don't like her – it's just that things are awkward with her being David's ex. But I'd have a heart of stone not to feel any sympathy towards her.'

'Didn't she bring what happened on *herself*?' Mia stretches her legs out and I'm struck by how white they are. At least we've moved the subject away from whatever's up with her.

'I guess so, *at the time*.' My gaze flits to Toby as he waves from the top of the slide to his mum. Her face lights up.

Then he looks uncomfortable as his eyes fall on David, who's watching this exchange.

'Perhaps my sympathy is more with Toby than anyone.'

'I know David's a good dad,' I begin. 'But I think he could soften towards Kirsty somewhat. Anyone can see how much Toby needs her and wants to be with her.'

'To know she's caused losing him through her own behaviour must be soul destroying,' Mia concedes.

'You'd think David would increase Toby's contact to entire weekends rather than just Sundays wouldn't you?' I say.

'You'd think he'd like the break for himself too.'

'I reckon it's all about David *proving* himself.' I look over at him, pleased to see that he's no longer talking to Jeanette and is now standing with Catherine.

'Over what?'

'His own father walked out when he was young so he's set his stall out to be everything *his* never was.'

'He's said that to you?' She sounds surprised.

'Not exactly but I'm good at reading between the lines.'

'Mia – if you could go and see to the girls.' Catherine points across the playground. She strides to a bench across the way from ours, kicking bark up as she goes. 'Over there please.' She wags her finger. 'One of them has fallen.'

'Duty calls, I guess.' Mia shuffles away and towards the crowd of girls who've gathered around a whimpering Amelia.

'And have you taken many photographs while they've been playing?' Catherine calls after her.

It wouldn't have killed Catherine to have taken care of Amelia's fall since she's the one who saw it. But as I've heard her say before, *why have a dog and bark yourself?* Charming.

'Come and be "it" Mum.' Toby calls from amongst his huddle of friends. 'We're playing hide and seek in the trees.'

As quickly as she sat down, Kirsty rises back up from the bench. With an eager look on her face, it seems she can't get to her feet fast enough.

'No – you stay where you are. *I'll* go.' David starts after her.

Catherine jumps up, quicker than I've ever seen her move and blocks his path. 'Just let Kirsty spend some time with him.'

'She's spent *enough* time with him,' he protests, trying to step around the side of her. 'After *you* swapped the groups around.'

Toby looks over, clearly worried by the exchange. He can probably sense that his father is annoyed.

'She's not doing any harm is she?' Catherine juts her chin out, almost defiantly.

'I'm the one with custody – the person who has parental responsibility.'

'It's not as if you can't keep an eye on him from where you are. But it's just as important for him to spend time with his mother, you know.'

'With all respect Catherine, you know I'm more than happy to take instruction as a member of your staff.' David's nostrils flare.

I hold my breath as he continues. *Go on, let rip,* I think to myself, which isn't like me. I don't want him to get into trouble, not really, but I can't ignore that he's my *direct* competitor for the same promotion. He could be my *only* competition for it. Him having a go at Catherine can only strengthen my chances of being successful.

'But you becoming involved in dealings with my son and ex-wife is another thing altogether.'

Catherine opens her mouth to retort but David gets back in there before her.

'So I'd like you to restrict your opinions to matters relating to the school only, if you don't mind.'

His words might seem considered but I can see from the thin line of his lips and the clench of his jaw that Catherine has rattled him. She has indeed overstepped the mark between what's her business and what isn't – even I can see that.

'May I remind you that we're here in our capacities to act in the children's best interests. Our *professional* capacities.' Catherine's veiled threat hangs in the air as she stands up straighter. 'So if I think you're being unreasonable Mr Naylor, I'll say so.'

Oooh, she's calling him Mr Naylor. She's rattled too.

She glances from me to Jeanette, evidently becoming aware that we're watching them. David follows her gaze before muttering about needing to check on something as he strides away.

I approach the staff room, its door ajar, the distant sounds of children showering and getting into their night clothes filling the corridor. As I get there, it's evident from their shrill voices that Jeanette and Kirsty have beaten me to it.

All I wanted was five minutes to myself. Five minutes to give myself a good talking to before I go wading in with David and making a fool of myself.

Curiosity gets the better of me and I pause at the door to see if I can catch what they're talking about.

'It looks as though Leonie's beginning to see the light from where I'm standing,' Kirsty says.

'So they're definitely still seeing each other?'

'Of course they are. Toby sees her sneaking in and out of the house all the time.'

I swallow. I can't believe Toby's seen me.

'I don't know what David sees in her.' Jeanette's voice hardens. 'She's well, very *plain*, isn't she?'

Unlike you, you mean. Bitch. This would be an *excellent* moment to make my presence felt but for now, I'll carry on listening.

'Oh give over – how plain someone is or isn't is neither here nor there, the fact is that—'

'Have you mentioned what's still going on to Catherine?'

'She already knows.'

'Wait until I tell my mother.' Her voice is full of glee and I can almost imagine her rubbing her hands together.

She clearly doesn't care how ridiculous she sounds. *Wait until I tell my mother.* I knew as soon as her name was drawn for this trip that we'd have a backstabber in our midst.

'What did Catherine have to say about it?'

'Not a lot, to be honest. But she generally keeps things close to her chest, doesn't she?'

'My mum doesn't want Leonie getting that deputy headship, you know. She reckons she's not fit for it. Has Catherine said anything to *you* about it?'

'Why are you so interested? Oh, I get it. You won't be wanting him to get promoted. You'll be hoping for Jessica to move into his class in September, won't you?'

'He's a good teacher, that's all.'

It's taking all I've got not to just burst in there and disrupt their little tête-à-tête.

'All that matters to Catherine right now is getting Oldale out of *significant weakness* status and keeping it open,' Kirsty says. 'She works damn hard for those kids.'

'Who needs to watch soap operas with all the drama we've got going on around us?' Jeanette laughs. 'Honestly, it takes me out of my dreary existence as soon as I step through those school gates.'

'Anyway, back to what we were on about before...'

'David and Leonie?'

I stride into the room and they both swing around to look at me, their eyes wide with shock.

~

The lower I became,
the more power you took.

FOURTEEN

LEONIE

Their expressions when I burst in are almost amusing.

'How long have *you* been standing there?' Jeanette arches an eyebrow.

'Who says I have?'

This is how Catherine must feel when she sweeps into the staff room at school. Unless she's that thick-skinned she doesn't realise. Sometimes I wish I could care about the opinions of others as little as she seems to. Life would be far easier for me that way.

'Have you not read this sign?' I widen the door.

They both stare at me.

'It says *staff* room. Which is something neither of you are.'

'Catherine said—'

'I don't care what *anyone* said.' I stride towards the kettle and slam my palm against the switch.

Kirsty steps towards me. 'Look, Leonie, I—'

'If I want to have a confidential conversation about school matters with one of my colleagues,' I begin, 'I don't want *parent helpers* listening in. Therefore, take your drinks elsewhere please.'

'I don't see any *colleagues* waiting to have a conversation with you.' Jeanette's top lip curls.

'Mia will be here in a moment actually. So if you don't mind.' I point towards the door as though dismissing my pupils.

Jeanette slams her cup into the sink and looks at Kirsty as if to make sure she's following her.

'Give us a minute Jeanette.' Kirsty nods at her. 'I'd just like a word with Leonie.'

'What is it you can't say in front of *me*?' Her face is like thunder. She'll just be concerned about what gossip she could be possibly missing out on.

'Please.'

'You haven't heard the last of this.' She turns on her heel and stomps off down the corridor. Presumably that comment was directed at me.

'What is it?' My tone sharpens as I turn from the kettle.

'I need to talk to you about David.'

'No, not this again. I've told you before that my relationship with your ex is none of your business.'

'So there is still a relationship?' She fixes me with her clear green eyes. There's no malice in them – I bet there's more in mine at this moment.

'I'm not discussing it with *you*.' I continue making my drink.

She doesn't move a muscle. 'I'm concerned for you, that's all. You've no idea what David's really like.'

'I'll be telling him about you cornering me like this. He needs to know.' My voice bounces around the sparse room.

'If I was in your shoes, *I'd* want to know.'

'But you're not anymore, are you?'

'If I knew then what I know now. Look.' She steps closer to me, her eyes still not leaving mine.

'Leave it will you. You've no right—'

'I can't *force* you to listen to me but when you're ready to hear the truth, you know where to find me.'

'Don't hold your breath.'

'Just be careful Leonie. You don't know what he's capable of.'

'Just leave me alone, will you? I mean it.'

Kirsty's footsteps die away along the corridor. My cup wobbles in my grasp as I sip my tea, trying to calm myself before I go back out there.

'What on earth have you said to Jeanette?' David saunters in and my stomach flips in the way it always does when he comes into my presence. 'Your ears must be burning, that's all I can say.'

'I'm not interested in what they think of me – they're nothing but a pair of witches.' I throw myself onto the couch, hoping he'll follow suit and sit beside me. I need to let him know that Kirsty's hellbent on causing trouble between us. However, and I can't put my finger on it – something seems to be stopping me from divulging what she's just been on about.

'Why's she so upset then?'

'Because I pointed out that this is a *staff* room, not a parent helper room.'

'Good for you.' He grins as he walks towards the cupboard. 'Anyone who puts Kirsty in her place gets extra brownie points from me. Are you having one?' He waggles a cup in the air.

'I've got one thanks.' I point to the steaming mug I've left on the draining board.

This looks promising. If David's making himself a drink, perhaps he's going to stick around for a few minutes.

'I'd much prefer something stronger than tea if the truth be known. Maybe we can sneak out together later?' *This is such a good idea. Why didn't I think of it before?* As soon as the kids are settled and everyone's in their rooms, we could go. Yes, there'd be ructions if we got caught. We'd just have to make sure we weren't.

'I've already got something arranged.' He passes my cup.

'Really? Like what?'

It better not involve Jeanette. Not that he would tell me if it did. He reckons that whatever was going on with them is in the past but I don't know if I believe this.

'I'm going for a pint with Harry as it happens.' He drops a teabag into his cup.

'Harry?'

'I've told you we used to know each other, haven't I?'

'You mentioned something when we came to do the risk assessment.'

'Yeah – well obviously, with *you* there, we didn't get much chance to catch up, did we?'

'Well pardon me for existing.'

'I didn't mean—'

'Harry doesn't look like someone who'd accept an invitation for a drink from *anyone* if you ask me.' I wrap my fingers around my mug as though trying to comfort myself with its warmth. I'm gutted.

'*He* invited *me*, if you must know. What are you on about anyway?'

'It's just that – is he always so edgy? He's like a coiled spring ready to snap.'

'You hardly know the man, to be fair.'

'I know enough to see that he's far from being an excited staff member who loves spending time around energetic kids.'

'He's probably stressed – reading between the lines, I think he's trying to prove himself here so he gets taken on properly. Which is probably why he's invited me for a pint or two with him – to pick my brains.'

'So it's *two* pints now, is it? Have you checked if this is OK with Catherine?'

'Erm, grown man alert.' He has the nerve to wink at me.

'We're supposed to be *in loco parentis* while we're here. You wouldn't go out and leave Toby on his own at night, would you?'

'A moment ago, you were inviting me for a drink.'

'That's different.' Though I know really that it isn't. But I'm disappointed. This trip hasn't turned out anything like I thought it would.

'Hardly. Anyway, there's another five adults here. One man down is hardly going to make any difference. Besides, they'll all be in bed soon. So I trust you'll cover for me?' His beseeching look reminds me of Toby.

'It's gone totally wrong, all this, hasn't it?'

'All what?'

'Us.'

The children's excited noise echoes along the corridor. I can't stay in here much longer. Jeanette's probably squealing to Catherine by now that I've kicked them out of here. Any minute now, she'll be bursting in here, hoping to catch us at something. The chance would be a fine thing.

David rests the kettle onto its cradle and turns to face me. 'Look Leonie, about *us...*'

Uh oh. I don't like the sound of this.

'What we had was fun. But that's as far as it went – for me, anyway.'

Had. Went. Past tense words. 'I thought we had more than that.' The last thing I want to sound is needy but I really believed we had something, me and David. 'Why didn't you say something before?'

He shrugs. 'I'm sorry. What else can I say?'

'So what's been the point in all the sneaking around we've been doing? I've quite literally put my career on the line for you.'

Bloody Catherine and her stupid ban on staff relationships.

I don't care what her reasons are for it. She's breaking us up. She's to blame for this.

'I never wanted anything heavy – you knew that all along. I've got Toby to think of.'

'I guess I hoped, in time, you'd...' My voice trails off.

He shakes his head, his fringe wobbling with the movement. 'There was never a chance of that. Not after all the angst and drama I had when I was with her.'

'So that's it then? I'm getting punished for your relationship with Kirsty.' Tears stab at the back of my eyes. I was not expecting this at all. 'Or is this something to do with Jeanette?'

'Jeanette?' He laughs. 'No Leonie. It was just fun I was after.' His voice is bordering on nonchalance. 'That was all. And it *has* been fun, hasn't it?'

'I can't believe this. Can't we just—?'

'I need to go and get ready.' He stirs his tea and drops his spoon into the sink, sipping from his cup as he heads to the door. 'I'll catch you later.'

'Hang on a minute. We can't just leave things like this.' I feel sick.

'Don't make a scene Leonie. We've still got to work together.'

'Can't we talk about it?'

'There's nothing to talk about. Now, if you could just let me past.' He shifts from one foot to the other.

'How can you be so bloody heartless?' I choke on my words, the room echoing their impact. The lump in my throat feels like the Rock of Gibraltar, solid and constricting. But there's nothing I can do other than step to the side so he can leave.

So there I have it. I bring the flat of my palm crashing onto the teabag he's left on the counter, exploding wet tea leaves all around.

Torn between the urge to weep or scream, I take some deep

breaths. Before long, people are going to wonder where I am, so I need to pull myself together.

With tears blurring my vision, I pace the staff room, its institutional magnolia walls closing in on me as the boards creak beneath the rhythm of my footsteps. I don't know what to do. I should go and help with the children but I can't face anyone right now. Being so unceremoniously dumped is gnawing at my edges.

Eventually, I settle on the sofa and drop my head into my hands. If I don't pull myself together, and sharpish, I'm in danger of allowing some man to drag me from being the strong, career-minded woman I've always fought to be, and into some simpering version of myself.

Perhaps that's his plan. He's already given me the impression that he'll do anything to secure the job we're both going after. He's been at Oldale far longer than me and won't want to lose face. Nor does David Naylor ever lose anything without a fight.

So I've got two choices here – I can hang around, hoping that in time, he'll come to see me as more than a workplace distraction.

Or – I can put some distance between us and fight for that deputy headship – using whatever means I can.

Starting by making Nancy aware that something's probably still going on between Jeanette and David. Followed by letting Catherine know that he's planning to bugger off to the pub with Harry.

～

I'd watch the back of your head,
wondering what on earth could be going on in there.

FIFTEEN

CATHERINE

My sandals land with a thud on the wooden floor. I plump up my pillows and shuffle back on the single bed, expecting the same comfort I'd find on my bed at home. However, it's rock hard.

I should be out on my garden patio with my feet up really, relaxing while it's half term. Instead, I'm here, burdened with the responsibility of overseeing adults I should have been able to trust without me.

A heavy sigh escapes me as my gaze drifts towards the window. I can hardly complain. After all, I knew exactly what I was getting into when I took this job. I've got to turn this school around no matter what it takes – those children, and their families, are counting on me.

The breeze carries in what could be the final birdsong of the day. Dusk itself casts a sombre hue across the landscape. All is still, as if the very air is holding its breath. However, it's a different story inside the building as the whelps and yelps echo from both the girls' and the boys' dormitories. I'll give them another half hour to settle down before I go along with the hard word. It's a big day for them tomorrow so they'll need to be well rested for it. As will I.

I stretch my legs along the bed. All the women here have lovely painted toenails but with my job, I barely have time to shower and brush my hair, let alone paint my nails. I reach for the book I wasn't sure I'd have the chance to even pick up, let alone read. But even headteachers of troubled schools deserve a few quiet moments to themselves. At least when I escape into a book filled with as much drama and angst as the one I'm reading at the moment, my own existence feels far more tolerable and mundane when I emerge back into it.

I haven't even read two pages when the shrill ring of my phone slices into my newly found tranquillity. My heart sinks. It's Nancy. For a split second, I'm tempted not to answer it, but she'll only persist until I do, especially since I haven't spoken to her since this morning. I've often asked her to leave a message if she ever reaches my voicemail but she completely ignores this. I should *never* have allowed her to have a direct line to my mobile.

'Nancy, how are you?' I raise the phone to my ear, bracing myself for the inevitable.

'I thought I'd have had a full progress report from you by now.' She's straight to the point, I'll give her that. She's never one for the norms and niceties of a telephone conversation like hello or goodbye.

'There's nothing much to report if I'm honest,' I reply. 'Only that day one's gone without a hitch.'

'That's *not* what I've been hearing.'

'Who from? *Jeanette?*' I should have known she'd be reporting back to her mother with any titbits of gossip.

'An anonymous message actually. It came through some kind of service.'

'Saying what?'

'That if Jeanette doesn't leave David alone, whoever it was from will be letting my son-in-law know.'

'Oh for goodness' sake. When did you get that?'

'Not so long ago, but never mind that. You're supposed to be keeping an eye on everything Catherine.'

'Of course I am. Look, it's got to be Leonie. Who else would send something like that?'

'It doesn't seem like her style to be honest. From what I've heard from Jeanette, she's far more abrupt and forthright than that.'

'Have you been in touch with Jeanette?'

'Not for a few hours. So where are they now?'

'Who?'

'Jeanette, of course. And David.'

'I'm not sure.' Perhaps I should have lied and said I can see one of them from my window. Nancy used to tear her hair out over Jeanette's 'thing' with David but like me, she thought that was in the rear-view mirror and there was only Leonie to keep an eye on things with.

'Where are you? It seems very quiet there.'

'I'm just in my room, having a moment or three to myself. It's been a long day.'

'So David, for all you know, could be in Jeanette's room as we speak; he could be—'

'The children are still very much awake,' I cut in. 'So I imagine they'll be milling around the dormitories with the others, helping to settle them down.'

'Never mind having *a moment or three to yourself* Catherine.' Her voice rises. 'You should know where he is. Not only is my daughter around him but there's his ex-wife and Leonie and we know—'

'It's all under control.' I keep my voice low and even, hoping she'll follow my lead.

'It's an accident waiting to happen if you ask me.'

'What is?' It's becoming a struggle to keep the exasperation from my voice.

'The mix of adults you've got there. It should never have been allowed. Kirsty included.'

'She and Toby are enjoying some extra time together actually. Like I keep saying, there's nothing to worry about.'

'Anything could be going on once you fall asleep. Maybe I should have come along and—'

'*No* Nancy.' My voice is firmer now. She'll be suggesting next that I stay awake all night to keep watch over everyone. Either that or she'll force *herself* on us. 'Nothing untoward is going to take place on this residential...'

'Are you OK? You've gone quiet.'

Something's moving at the top of one of the rocks. I jump up and rush to the window. *Why would someone be up there now?* It's nearly dark – it can't be safe.

'Sorry. I thought I saw something, that's all.'

'What?'

'Just someone outside. But it could have been a trick of what's left of the light.' I rub my tired eyes and look again but can't make out if anyone's really up there or not.

'Anyway,' I sigh. 'I'm going to go now Nancy.'

'Hang on a minute – is *Jessica* enjoying herself?'

'All the children are.' *Thanks for asking,* I stop myself from saying.

'So everything's alright? The activities have all been safe?'

'Of course they have.'

'What are they doing tomorrow?'

'Rock climbing, abseiling and the zip wire.' I load an enthusiasm I'm not feeling into my voice.

'Don't remind me.' I can almost visualise Nancy dropping her head into her hands. 'Please, please, make sure you double and triple-check everything.'

'The instructors are all qualified to high heaven. Nothing's going to go wrong. The children will be perfectly looked after.'

As I say this, I almost say in my mind, *famous last words.* This is the effect Nancy has on me – she's even putting me on edge.

'The school can't withstand another crisis, as you know.' The tension continues to mount in her voice.

'Then please, with all respect Nancy, allow me to get on with it.'

'I just hope he and Leonie have dotted every I and crossed every T for this trip.' There's a finality in her voice which hopefully means I can get her off the phone shortly. 'And that you all don't bring any more negative press to the school.'

'You've got to stop worrying Nancy. You'll drive yourself mad. And me.'

'You don't know David as well as I do. You need to remember that. And so does my gullible daughter. I've warned her about him until I'm blue in the face. And if my son-in-law was to ever—'

'We can't control everything. And sometimes the more we try to come between people, the more we push them together.'

'She swore to me that it was all over between her and David. But this message I've had definitely suggests otherwise. Are you going to speak to Leonie?'

'I'm going to observe the situation between them all first. Only *then* will I do something about it. In the meantime, this trip is about the children.'

'I really think—'

'How's your own half-term going Nancy?'

'Well, in between worrying about whether I'm going to suddenly hear of a calamity at Ilkstone Crag,' she says, her voice softening, 'Georgina wanted to stay with me while Jeanette and Jessica are away.'

'So just enjoy your time with her.' I stare out into the dusk again. I'm satisfied there's nothing to see or worry about out there so I tug the curtains across the window. 'I'll drop you a text tomorrow to set your mind at rest after day two.'

'Never mind a text,' she replies. 'I'll give you a call tomorrow evening. Please keep an eye on Jeanette for me Catherine. She's got so much to lose if she's picked back up with David Naylor again.'

'Yes Nancy. Goodnight Nancy.' I hit the end call button and drop my phone onto the bed. 'Honestly.'

Worrying about a calamity. She's completely overreacting. What does she imagine is going to happen? David could sleep with Jeanette, or one of the others, or all of the others. He could start a fight with Kirsty, or one of them could decide to ride the zip wire at midnight – so what? She's completely disturbed the tiny bit of me time I thought I'd carved out for myself.

∼

At times, I saw glimmers of the person you used to be.
That's who I chased.
That's what kept me with you.

SIXTEEN

CATHERINE

No sooner has my phone landed than it beeps again. It's Leonie. How strange. She's only ever messaged me once since we've worked together and that was to let me know she was going to be off sick from work.

David's on his way out to the pub. I thought you should know.

It *must* have been her who messaged Nancy given the proximity in which the two messages have been sent. But if it *is* her, why is she being transparent with one number and not with the other? And why's *Leonie* of all people telling me? Perhaps it's some kind of decoy.

Aside all that, David is *not* going to the bloody pub. I'm too wired to think of settling back into my book so I slip my sandals back on and head towards the door. What's he playing at?

Striding through the narrow corridor, I approach the exit door just in time to spot him leaving. A moment or two later and I'd have missed him. I catch a glimpse of a bulging wallet protruding from the back pocket of his jeans and his phone in the other.

'Just hang on a minute.' He stops in his tracks and turns to face me, looking somewhat sheepish.

Leonie must have been telling the truth.

'Are you going somewhere?'

'I'm, um, just nipping across to see Harry.' He gestures in the direction of the staff quarters, his leather jacket crinkling as he moves his arm.

I glance through the window, half expecting to see one of the women waiting for him. But there's nobody there. It's nearly dark outside, the last of the sunlight disappearing behind the craggy peaks, casting an eerie glow on our surroundings.

'You look more like you're going to the pub.' I catch a whiff of his overpowering aftershave, its sharp scent lingering in the air. 'And you smell like it too.'

'*The pub?* Don't be daft. What gives you that idea?'

'Don't lie to me. Leonie's informed me of your plans.' I probably shouldn't be divulging my source but I'm not going to pass up an opportunity to drive more of a wedge between the two of them. His expression darkens. I've got no idea why she's told me what he's up to but, no doubt, *he'll* probably have a reasonable idea.

'Alright, I'll be honest with you, shall I?'

I resist the urge to say *that'll be a first.*

'You're right.' He throws his arms in the air. 'I was sneaking out for a quick pint with Harry. You know, at that pub we passed before we pulled in.'

My face probably says it all, for David suddenly stands up straighter. The children are still going strong in their dormitories and I can hear Leonie's voice in the distance. 'Right,' she begins, to whichever group she's telling off. At least *she's* doing what she's supposed to be doing.

'You're supposed to be the head of key stage two. And yet, you think it's acceptable to—'

'Look Catherine.' He steps back inside and looks both ways

along the corridor. 'Can we have a word about all this – in private please?'

'All *what*?'

'I just want to put the record straight.'

'All I want is for you to take off your jacket and do the job you're being paid to do.'

'I won't take up much of your time.'

Despite my reservations, I'm intrigued. If there's something useful for Kirsty in whatever he's planning to say to me, I can't let the opportunity slip away. 'We'll go to the staff room, shall we?' I gesture in its direction.

A 'chat' might also present the opportunity to reaffirm some boundaries as well as to check through the schedule and safety procedures for tomorrow. I can't have Nancy accusing me of not doing my job properly.

'Kirsty and Jeanette are in there,' he replies. 'So shall we?' He points back along the corridor towards my bedroom door.

'I don't think so.'

I try the doors into the dining room and then the Asquith room but they've both been locked for the night.

'We'll go outside.'

'When you were just saying we need to remain in the same building as the children?'

I hesitate. It's probably unwise to allow him into my room – especially given his reputation. But five minutes can't hurt. 'OK then.' I start back along the corridor while knowing that Nancy would have a complete meltdown if she could see me now. But there's nowhere else to talk, not in private.

I'm also curious to learn what the situation is between him and Leonie and why she would be texting me.

The door closes softly behind us. 'What is it then?'

He lowers himself onto the edge of my bed, the mattress creaking beneath his weight. 'I think it's time we talked frankly about things.'

It feels decidedly strange having him here in the room in which I'll be getting showered, undressed and sleeping. But then it would probably be strange no matter which man it was. Colleague or otherwise.

≈

You made me doubt every aspect of myself until I didn't know myself anymore.

SEVENTEEN

MIA

'Did you hear that?' Leonie raises a finger to her lips.

'What?'

She steps towards her door and cups her hand against it. 'It sounded like Catherine.' Her floaty summer dress clings to her shape, showing the faint line of her underwear. I wish I'd changed as well now, instead of turning up at her door in the same shorts and T-shirt I've been wearing all day.

'Doing what?'

'I'm not sure.'

'Ah, she'll just be on at the kids. They're still in full swing, aren't they?' I want her attention to be on me while we're together in here, not on whatever's going on out there. What I overheard her saying is still at the back of my mind though. No matter how hard I try, I can't seem to shake it away. But I don't want to spoil our time together this evening by dwelling too much on it. But I haven't let it go. I can't let it go.

'I guess so.' Her face breaks into a smile. 'You can't blame them though – they're so excited about tomorrow.'

'Me too. Cheers.' I lean forwards from my chair and tap my

tin against hers. We simultaneously raise them to our lips and I wipe at the trace of lipstick I leave on the edge of mine.

'I'm so ready for this.' Her face clouds over.

'Why – what's up?'

She blows a long breath out. 'Oh, I might as well tell you – it'll probably do me good to talk to someone. It's David. He was a complete arse to me earlier.'

'What do you mean?' I like the sound of this. And I like even more that whatever it is, Leonie's confiding in *me*.

'Miss Johnson?' We turn our heads in the direction of the tapping on the door as a small voice trembles behind it.

Leonie places her drink behind the curtain, strides towards the door and throws it open. 'What is it, Casey?'

'Amelia says she feels sick,' she stammers, her eyes wide with anxiety. 'And I'm missing my mum. I think I want to go home.'

'I'll be back in a minute.' Leonie glances at me before disappearing into the corridor with Casey in tow.

Now alone in the room, I take another sip from my can, the soft glow of the bedside lamp casting a warm ambience over the floral curtains and Leonie's neatly arranged belongings. Her make-up and toiletries are lined up in a row, exactly like her desk at school. Her clothes are hung on the rail whereas I haven't even unpacked anything.

Everything about her exudes femininity and perfection and I can't help wondering for the millionth time what her home is like, having never been invited there.

I spray her perfume onto my wrist and raise it to my nose. I rest the bottle back on her dresser, its elegant design catching the soft glow of the lamplight. Then I pick up her lipstick and apply it over my own, rubbing my lips over each other in the mirror. I turn the lipstick over in my palm. Cherry Kiss. I'll have to treat myself to the same one.

It's oddly intimate to notice her toothbrush and a box of

tampons through the gap in her en suite door. Part of me wants to find out if she's actually on her period now – as I am. Not because I'm *weird* like she was saying this morning, but because I've read somewhere that females who become close and spend lots of time together become so in sync that they even menstruate at the same time.

I have a funny relationship with Leonie which I often struggle to make sense of. I look up to her like I've never looked up to anyone before, yet she also evokes a jealousy within me and the anger I felt when I heard her talking about me this morning was more intense than anything I've ever known. I don't know whether this stems from wanting to *be* her, or from wanting to have what she's got and is capable of. Which is more than I could ever dream about.

The door is flung open again, jolting me from my musings. Leonie wrinkles her nose as she re-enters the room. 'Have you sprayed something?'

'Just a squirt of your perfume – I've seen it advertised and have been meaning to test it. You don't mind do you?'

'Erm, no.' But she looks taken aback. I hope she doesn't realise that I've applied her lipstick too. It depends on how much notice she takes of me; after all, I was wearing a light pink shade on my lips when I arrived in her room. At least it sounds like she won't be running back to David and talking about me again. Not if what she's started to tell me is what I hope it's going to be.

'Are they alright – the children, I mean?'

'Yeah.' Leonie sighs as she resumes her position perched at the end of the bed. 'Amelia's eaten too many of the sweets they've sneaked in but she's had a drink of water and seems to have settled down.'

'What about Casey?'

'I've tasked her with keeping her eye on Amelia.'

'That should keep her mind off wanting to go home at least – she likes an important job to do.'

No matter what crap and gossip has flown around school about the adults, I love the kids we work with. This is my first ever teaching assistant post and I've become so attached to them that it will break my heart when our Year Fives move up to David's class.

'It's a good thing I went in when I did – Jessica and Courtney were about to come to blows over a bloody hairbrush. I've warned them there'll be no activities tomorrow if they carry on.'

'She's a so-and-so, that Jessica.'

'And usually the instigator.'

'Well she is Jeanette's daughter, what do you expect?'

Leonie pulls a face.

'Go on anyway,' I say. 'You were telling me about a certain Year Six teacher being an arse.'

She hesitates as if deliberating what or how much to divulge to me now she's had the chance to get herself back in check.

'You know you can trust me.' I sit beside her on the bed. 'Whatever you tell me won't go any further.'

Her shoulders slump. 'Oh, I don't know Mia.' Her tone changes. 'One minute he was all over me, then suddenly I've become nothing but a bit of fun. He said as much in the staff room earlier. Then it was literally thanks and goodbye.'

'*Really?*'

'Yep. It's all off.'

'Well, you were warned about his reputation from the word go.'

'Aww come on Mia. There's nothing worse than an *I told you so.*' It's unusual to see Leonie so downtrodden. 'I suppose I've been trying to ignore what's been staring me in the face all along.'

'Which is?'

'That he doesn't care about me – not one bit. The only person David Naylor cares about is *himself*. I'm just another of his conquests – albeit probably a more fun one because we were warned off each other from the start. The forbidden fruit and all that. But then so is *Jeanette*.'

'Jeanette?'

'Yeah, you must have noticed them cosying up the entire time we've been here.'

'A little – but—'

'Well, anyway, I might be upset about it *now* but deep down, I *have* come to my senses about the whole thing.' A strange look enters her eyes.

'You have?' Hopefully, she's going to say that from now on, she intends to stay single and focus on her teaching role and her friends. Namely me.

'I've finally realised David's not worth the risks I've been taking.'

'In what way?' I sit up straighter. This sounds ominous.

'Well, I'd never get that deputy headship if I were to carry on seeing him. And I want it so badly.'

Something twists in my gut. Over my dead body do I want her to get that job. I wish I could tell her how unhappy it would make me if we were no longer working so closely together. Who knows which teacher I could end up being put with? I could even get placed into David's class.

'I'm going to speak to Catherine tomorrow. Make sure she believes it's over between me and David.'

'So it *definitely* is? What if he changes his mind?' Suddenly, I'm unsure which is the lesser of the two evils here.

She stares down at the can in her hands. 'He won't be changing his mind when he finds out what I've just done.'

'What?'

'I've just squealed on him to Catherine. He was sneaking off to the pub with Harry.'

'You haven't.' I clutch at her arm as though I've just heard the most salacious piece of gossip ever.

She pulls a face. 'Why should he go buggering off to the pub when the rest of us have all these kids to take care of? He's really not bothered about anyone else apart from himself, is he?'

'You're hardly what I'd call a snitch Leonie.' I laugh. 'I'm surprised at you.'

'That's not all either.'

'What do you mean?'

'I thought Nancy might like to know what her precious daughter seems to be up to as well. If he thinks he can dump me and then pick up where he left off with Jeanette...'

Her face is as serious as I've ever seen it. 'I *really* want that job and nothing's going to stand in my way of it, especially David Naylor.'

'But you don't know who else might apply for it.'

Leonie shakes her head. 'By the time Catherine's seen what I'm made of, she won't even *consider* giving it to anyone other than me.'

'It could be someone she already knows – someone she'll feel more loyalty towards. The two of you haven't exactly seen eye to eye, have you?'

'Perhaps getting Kirsty on side might help.' It's as if Leonie's speaking to herself rather than to me.

'What do you mean?'

Leonie sips from her can. 'I've actually been wondering about some of the things she says about him, to be honest. Kirsty, I mean.'

'Such as?'

'It's just that – well, David's been revealing his negative traits more and more to me over the last few weeks. Especially earlier, in the staff room. No one's ever dumped me so callously before.'

'What do you mean, negative traits?'

'Well, he *always* has to be right, doesn't he? And he'll shoot anyone down who dares to disagree with him.'

'You're right there. And he has to win at *everything*.'

'No matter who he treads on in the process. But really Mia, it's far more than just that.'

She traces her feet along the pattern of the rug and I notice her manicured pink toenails. I wish my feet were as pretty as hers and a sudden pang of inadequacy grips me as I stare at my well-worn sandals and the chipped varnish on my own toes.

'I'm getting a sense of something darker,' she continues. 'Obviously, I've only known him since September but...' Her voice trails off.

'Go on.'

'It's like he's got such a tight lid on himself all of the time. As though he could turn at any moment but manages to stop himself. Like he's got some sort of internal battle going on just to keep control of himself.'

'I think I know what you mean.'

'I keep seeing something in his eyes, and there's that edge to his voice which worries me.' Her expression is a cross between misery and contempt. 'Have you ever noticed the way he stiffens up when someone dares to challenge him?'

'To be fair, I don't study him like you do.'

It's you I study – you I want to be. Maybe with David out of the picture, Leonie will come to see me differently. Anyway, if I was that creepy and weird, she would hardly be here now, confiding in me. I look towards the window and stare at the shapes in the darkness beyond it as I wait for her to continue.

'I've even been thinking seriously about all that gaslighting stuff Kirsty accused him of. You must have heard about it?'

'*Everyone* has. Anyway...' I blow out a breath. 'I *never* thought I'd see the day where you'd be siding with Kirsty.'

I really don't like it either. Leonie *did have* strong negative feelings towards her and I don't like the thought of them softening.

'I'm *not* siding with her, no matter how persistent she's becoming.'

'*Persistent?*'

'I was a right cow to her and Jeanette earlier – I even sent them packing from the staff room. Jeanette might have deserved it but Kirsty didn't.'

'And?'

'Kirsty insisted on staying behind to talk to me. And to be honest, I was intrigued.'

'What did she say?'

'The usual, mainly. She wanted to give me the lowdown on David again. I wouldn't get into it with her though – I told her that I'm perfectly capable of working things out for myself.'

'I agree. You hardly need to be joining forces with *her* of all people.'

We turn towards the door as there's another knock at it. 'Miss Johnson.' It's a boy's voice this time.

'I'm sorry Mia. Do you mind if we try again tomorrow night?' Leonie walks towards the door. 'We're not going to get a minute's peace.'

'I can wait here for you – it's fine.'

'No really, we're *both* going to have to see to these kids. Have you heard them all through there? I don't know where Catherine is or what she's doing. I'd have thought she'd be reading them the riot act by now.'

'Can't we come back here afterwards?' I'm trying not to sound too keen but I was so looking forward to getting at least a couple of uninterrupted hours with Leonie.

'I'd prefer to leave it until tomorrow night if you don't mind.'

'But why?'

'I don't know.' Her shoulders droop. 'I guess I'm just not very good company tonight. I need to get my head straight.'

'But I can help you with it all.'

'No, really Mia. It's been nice of you to give up your free time but I'd prefer to be on my own after we've sorted these kids. Speaking of which...'

She rests her fingers on the handle as a thud echoes from the girls' dorm.

'I trust you've got more where that one came from?' She points at her can.

I pat my shoulder bag then I plunge my feet back into my sandals, trying to hide my disappointment behind a curtain of hair. I don't know what I'm going to do with myself for the rest of the evening. The prospect of hours stretching ahead without Leonie's company tugs at the core of my being.

Leonie closes the door again, her eyes darting with a hint of uncertainty. 'Keep everything I've said about you-know-who under your hat, won't you?'

'That goes without saying,' I reply. However, I like being in *the know*.

It certainly gives me more leverage.

~

You'd tell me black was white
and night was day
and I'd believe you.

EIGHTEEN

MIA

Crunching along the gravel path, I pause at the view in front of me. The night sky is velvet-blue and as clear as I've ever seen it, all lit up with a crescent moon. The entire scene mirrors its beauty in the still waters of the lake. It's just a shame I'm on my own, as usual, with no one to enjoy it with.

I resume my journey, the gravel path crunching beneath my shoes with each step until I find myself at the picnic tables where we were sitting at snack time.

I reach into my bag. This is the perfect spot for another gin.

'What are you doing?' The voice behind me makes me jump. Instinctively, I curl my fingers around the can and lower it to the side of my leg. Harry emerges from the shadows, his cap casting a veil over his features.

'I erm...' Just as I am when David speaks to me, I can't seem to articulate my words. Bloody hell – what's wrong with me?

'What have you got there?' His jacket rustles as he points.

'Um – it's just an energy drink.' I slide my bag right in front of it, hoping he won't see what it is. The last thing I need is for him to go squealing to Catherine. I can't trust anyone here and as Leonie showed this morning, not even her.

Harry knows David, so he'll no doubt be aware of Kirsty being a recovering alcoholic and our Catherine-enforced alcohol ban.

'I need all the energy I can get with that lot in there.' I attempt a forced laugh that fades into the night.

The silence hangs between us for a moment.

'How's it going?' I finally ask. *Great Mia – what an enlightened and engaging question.*

'Eh?' He thrusts his hands into the pockets of his combat trousers as he continues to stare at the door from which I recently emerged.

'The centre – since it was re-opened, I mean?' I point at it, lit up like a beacon in the dark.

He shrugs. 'I only volunteer here.'

'I thought you were one of the staff.'

'Nope.' He raises his arm to look at his watch.

More silence.

'Have you seen David?' He nods towards the centre.

'Not since we left the playground. Why?'

'I need to see him.'

I shrug. 'Try his room.'

Catherine must have acted on Leonie's tip-off and prevented David from meeting Harry but I'm not going to tell him this.

He shuffles from foot to foot as though he's unsure whether to follow my advice.

'Shall I tell him you're looking for him, if I see him?'

'Tell him to come to my room.'

'Which is where?'

'SQ4.' He gestures towards a building where a STAFF OF ILKSTONE CRAG ONLY sign is illuminated. 'Well, I'd better be going. I've got things to do.'

As he strides away, I gulp from my can, feeling lonelier than ever. I'll walk the circle of the lake then I might as well try to get some sleep on that rock-hard bed since there's nothing better to do. I get to my feet.

Glancing towards our building again, I can see that Kirsty and Jeanette have emerged from it and are hanging around the main entrance. They're cupping their faces at the windows as though they're trying to watch whatever's going on inside.

Jeanette's wearing a dressing gown and Ugg boots but Kirsty's fully dressed in jeans, a jacket and trainers. She's changed her clothes since I last saw her and I can't help but think that she looks as if she's ready for something.

The way they're stalking around that building, *something* is going on.

I drain my can and throw it in a bin, wondering if I should have hidden it inside a wrapper first. I wouldn't put it past Catherine to start checking the bins, searching for evidence of any perceived wrongdoing.

'What's happening?' I walk towards them.

'Shhh.' Jeanette lifts a perfectly manicured finger to her lips as though she's still leading a group of children. 'We're *watching*, that's all.'

'*Watching for what?*'

In the light from the lamp above the door, I spot a pained expression in Kirsty's eyes. 'I'll tell you what we're watching for, *shall I*? We're waiting for my ex-husband to come back out of Catherine's bedroom.'

'Her *bedroom*? What's he doing in *there*?'

'I'll give you three guesses, shall I?' Jeanette's eyes narrow.

'Nah, I can't see that – really I can't.'

'They looked pretty cosy to me on their way in there.' Kirsty turns back to me with what now looks like tears shining in her eyes. 'So unless we've missed him leaving when we went to check around the back, they've been in there for a while.'

'I'm sure there'll be an explanation. Are you certain it was him? And *her*?'

'I was married to the man, wasn't I?' Kirsty splutters. 'Of course I'm sure. I'd spot him at a thousand paces.'

'What did you mean when you said, *they look cosy*?'

'Willing – comfortable – How should I know? All I *do* know is that Catherine's supposed to be my closest friend.'

In some ways, the prospect of David and Catherine together could be quite exciting. It would put an end to any prospect of him worming his way back into Leonie's bed and also mean David would be more likely to receive the promotion than she would.

'I don't understand it.' Jeanette sinks to the bench at the end of the path to the entrance and wraps her arms around herself. I'd love a cosy dressing gown like the one she's wearing. I don't even own a dressing gown.

'Catherine's dead against relationships between the staff,' I say. 'They can't be.' What I don't say is that if they've got this right, I'll be the only adult female amongst our group that David Naylor hasn't slept with.

'Well the curtains were tightly shut when we went round the other side,' Kirsty says, as if that makes them more guilty. She sits beside Jeanette.

'No wonder Catherine wanted to come on this trip so badly,' adds Jeanette. 'Wait until I tell my mother about all this.'

I contemplate joining them on the bench, but they might be able to smell the alcohol on my breath. Another thing Jeanette could report back to Nancy about.

Bloody hell – now I know why David's been so off with Leonie. Because he's well and truly moved on.

'We should keep a lid on this.' I look from one of them to the other. 'At least until we get back to school.'

'Why should we?' Kirsty's chin juts out in the same way Toby's does when he doesn't want to do something.

'Because all hell will break loose if something *is* going on.'

'Too right it will.'

'What about the kids?' I point in the direction of the dorms. 'We can't spoil it for them.'

'I'm sorry.' Kirsty stares straight at me, her fists clenched in her lap. 'But there's no way I'm keeping quiet about this. People have got the right to know.'

'What is it you're most upset about?' I look from Jeanette to Kirsty. 'Let's say something *is* going on in there.'

'What are you on about now?' Jeanette scowls.

'You're *married* Jeanette, so if you've still got your eye on David, you shouldn't have. And Kirsty, it's not as if the two of you are together anymore.'

'How many relationships have you had Mia? Since you're such an expert.'

A tense stillness hangs between us for a moment.

'Yeah, I suspected as much,' Jeanette says.

Cow. I glance back at the building, unsure what to do next.

'We need to move from here,' I finally say. 'If they notice us when they come out of that room, all there will be is a huge confrontation. Surely that's best to be held off for now.'

'I don't believe it is.' Kirsty sniffs.

'Think of Toby and Jessica then. Do you really want to spoil things for them?'

They look at each other. Thank goodness. Hopefully, I've got through to them.

'I'll have to think about it,' Kirsty replies. 'Actually, I just need to clear my head.' She looks over at the lake, blonde tendrils of her hair fluttering in the breeze down her back. 'Shall we go for a walk?' She turns back to Jeanette. She doesn't look at me which presumably means I'm not invited. Not that I'd want to walk with them anyway.

But that's my own walk around the lake scuppered.

'Nah. I'm not exactly dressed for a walk, am I?' Jeanette smooths her hands down the folds of her dressing gown as she stands from the bench. 'I'm off to see if Jessica's settled down. Plus I need to call my husband.' She pulls a face.

Kirsty heads in the direction I'd planned to go in. I don't fancy following her around the lake like a lost soul *or* crossing her path halfway. Therefore I move to a bench which is more in the shadows than the one they've just vacated.

The door to Catherine's room is just about visible at the end of the corridor through the window nearest to me. I stare at it for a moment, imagining what could be going on behind it. I feel lonelier than ever. No one ever wants *me* in that way.

But never mind how *I'm* feeling – Leonie's going to be gutted when she finds out what's going on between them so it'll be my job to break it to her gently and to help her to feel better.

That's if it's all true, of course – I'm still unconvinced that Catherine would risk her job or her reputation so spectacularly. Still, I'll hang around for a little longer – after all, Catherine's been constantly on at me to take lots of pictures while we're here. She wants plenty of evidence of our trip to share on the school website and in our newsletter.

A time-stamped photo of our dishevelled and, hopefully, half-dressed Year Six teacher leaving our head's bedroom could provide a great talking point.

The other thing I'm considering is the leverage it could provide for me personally. I'm certain Catherine's threats to let me go would cease if I had something like *that* over her. Yes, a photograph could work to my advantage in all sorts of ways. However, I could be waiting here all night to get it.

When I turn back to the lake, Kirsty's disappeared. I look left and right. She can't have just vanished into thin air. Nor can she have walked so fast that she's disappeared behind the trees already. Not unless she ran there.

I pace up and down, the rhythmic movement a futile attempt to quell my unease. I hope Jeanette can keep her mouth shut. If she bumps into Leonie before I do, I'm certain she'll tell her what they suspect and I want her to find out from me.

Scrolling on my phone kills a little time while keeping an eye on the corridor leading from Catherine's door. Suddenly from the corner of my eye, I spot David darting from behind a bush to behind a tree.

So either Kirsty and Jeanette are completely mistaken about him being in Catherine's room in the first place, or he's managed to get out of the building from somewhere around the back.

He runs forwards again and into the doorway of one of the staff-only outbuildings – and it's not the same one Harry went into.

What's he up to?

~

You told me that I couldn't force you to stay
with me,
but you kept on coming back.
And so did my bruises.

THE INVESTIGATION

DI GILBERT

I clear my throat. 'I'm DI Gilbert and this is my colleague Sergeant Parkins,' I say as our next interviewee steps into the staff room. 'We're ready to speak to you now.'

'Our colleagues are currently in the process of informing the family of the deceased,' Chris adds as the seat I gesture to is taken. 'I'm aware that the process of reaching out to the families of the children is also underway.'

The clock on the wall ticks audibly, marking the passing minutes as we navigate through statements. Three more, and our duty in this stifling room will be complete. Hopefully, our colleagues who are also taking statements in the centre office are keeping pace with us.

'Have you any questions before we begin?'

'Can the children go home soon? And us – when we've all spoken to you, I mean?'

'As I'm sure you'll appreciate, it's all going to take some time.' Beads of sweat are forming on my forehead. 'But in answer to your question, we're awaiting extra officers to speak to the children in the presence of their parents as appropriate adults.'

'When we've spoken to them individually,' Chris adds, 'they'll be allowed to leave.'

'What about *us*?' It's a question filled with exasperation. 'When can *we* go?'

'Staff and parent helpers are required to remain here until further notice.' Chris's voice is monotone. He stares straight ahead as though avoiding eye contact.

'For how long exactly?' Exasperation has become impatience.

My frown deepens. 'We'll be here for as long as it takes to find out *exactly* how it happened.' My voice is sterner than Chris's.

'What we need,' I continue, 'is to build a picture of relationships from each perspective that existed between the deceased and everyone else here.'

'We've been led to believe' – Chris looks up from his notebook – 'that several problems existed amongst many of the adults leading this trip.'

'The majority of any *problems* trace back to events in the school about eighteen months ago.' The cryptic words hang in the air, and I can sense there's more beneath the surface.

'What problems?'

'You'd need to read the reports in the media to learn the full extent.'

'Perhaps you could save us the trouble.'

'Almost everyone here has a reason to be aggrieved with someone else.'

The wobble in their voice is intriguing. This, I am *very* interested in hearing.

'Why does this matter *now* anyway?'

'It matters very much.' Hopefully, my gaze has become even more steely.

'You still think the death was an *accident*, don't you?'

I allow a long pause, hopefully, an excruciatingly long pause. 'That's what we're here to establish.'

'Are you saying it might not be an accident?'

'I'm saying that we're keeping an open mind until we know for certain. Until our investigation team has finished up there, we just don't know.'

NINETEEN

LEONIE

A thunderous bang catapults me into alertness, and I draw in a sharp breath, my body tense as I sit upright. *What the hell was that?* I try to be still and listen but all I can hear is the pounding of my own anxiety.

I lie back down and try to steady my breathing, the weight of unease settling over me like a suffocating blanket. I *have* to get some sleep. It took me ages to drop off before whatever it was woke me. Checking my watch, it appears I've only been sleeping for just over an hour.

Closing my eyes, I wish I'd brought my earphones. I could have listened to a guided meditation, some soothing music – anything. There's a quiet that envelops this building, that I don't have at home. Devoid of traffic and other urban sounds, the silence is almost palpable and any noises from within the building seem all the more heightened against it. The vibration of a snore, a door clicking shut, the hack of a cough and then what sounds like a giggle. I can't be sure if it's come from one of the dorms or out in the corridor. I should get up and investigate really. But even though my mind is on high alert, my body is completely exhausted.

. . .

It's no good – I can't sleep. The harder I try, the more my anxiety intensifies. I ram my head onto the lump masquerading as a pillow as I turn over for what feels like the zillionth time. How I'm going to function in the morning and be a responsible adult in charge of so many kids, I don't know.

I can't stop thinking about David and how excited I used to be to see him every day. Somehow the fact that Catherine imposed her ban made the whole thing all the more alluring. When I took over Year Five in September, he was so attentive and always seemed out to impress me. But there was a definite cooling from him after we went to bed for the first time. His attentions have deteriorated more and more ever since.

Something has compelled me to pursue him for longer than I should have done – perhaps I've been chasing what he was like to begin with.

No matter how crappy I feel, I know I'm doing the right thing by taking some control and stepping back from him. If I act like I'm not bothered, perhaps that will pique his interest again. No, I can't think like this. He's bad for my career, bad for my self-esteem, bad for me full stop. Then there's the nagging feeling that's been gradually taking hold of me, especially over the last two or three weeks. The one that's telling me to be very wary about the sort of man David Naylor could *really* be.

My thoughts circle back to a conversation from October, when shadows of doubt had crept in – doubts which had challenged the front he'd presented to me up to that point.

'Who told you that?' he'd asked when I confronted him. He finished wiping his whiteboard and spun around to look at me.

'It's common knowledge.' I sat at the table in front of his desk – the one where he sat children he wanted to keep an eye on. 'It doesn't matter who told me. But what *does* matter is whether you *really* had a relationship with a first-year student on teaching practice placement.'

'Of course I didn't.' He tugged his chair from behind his desk and sat facing me. 'She was eighteen, for God's sake. And had a huge crush on me.'

'Why would she say something was going on then?'

'You know how friendly I am. At least I hope you do.' He fiddled with a pile of paper clips as he spoke. 'She completely misinterpreted the situation, that's all.'

'But you saw her *outside* school. It's no wonder her parents filed a complaint against you.'

'We were going through the children's medium-term plans.' He looked at me with that earnest look he had. The one that said he could do no wrong. 'She saw things that weren't there. The long and short of it was that it all got exaggerated. The whole thing was blown out of all proportion.'

'So you're saying she lied about how far things went between you?'

'Of course she did.'

'What about the two teachers who went off sick? The newly qualified and the—?'

'Again, I was scapegoated. It's not my fault one was so hypersensitive that she couldn't take criticism and the other couldn't take no for an answer.'

'*Bullying* was one of the terms I heard. Sexual harassment was the other.'

'I want to know who your source on all this is. Who's been talking about me?'

'Why? So you can bully them too?' I smiled as I said this, in the hope that my smile would soften my words. However, he didn't smile back. Instead, his whole face darkened.

I hated that we were having a confrontation like that. Even whilst angry, he was so damn good looking and I'd never seen a man look better in a crisp white shirt than he did.

'This is my reputation you're calling into question here Leonie. I'm not a bully, or a harasser, nor someone who'd sleep with an eighteen-year-old.'

'But your reputation for sleeping with staff and parents is built on truth, isn't it?'

'Is that a proposition?' He grinned then which eased my racing heart.

'I don't want to be another notch on your bedpost, thank you very much.'

'Honestly Leonie, just because I'm the only male member of staff for miles, well, until Nick was brought in – it seems that I'm fair game. And you won't even say who's been telling you this stuff.' He looked at me as though he was deeply wounded. Perhaps he thought admitting his feelings might persuade me to reveal who'd informed me about it all. But Mia had made me swear I wouldn't drop her in it. So I didn't.

David withdrew from me for a couple of weeks after my queries into the gossip. It took me a couple more to persuade him that I didn't believe any of it – that I still wanted us to go forwards together.

Of course, Mia was far from happy about this.

The window is open as far as it will go – which isn't far at all. I want to peel my pyjamas off to cool down but that's probably not such a good idea when on a school residential. But I can't just lie here any longer, driving myself demented. I haul myself up and reach for my phone. If I can't sleep, I might as well read.

I let out a long sigh. The silence of the night is heavy to the point of being claustrophobic as I struggle to get back into the book I started when I first came to bed. The intermittent hoot of an owl occasionally breaks it, creating a somewhat eerie feeling within me.

I rub at my stinging eyes as another door clicks closed from somewhere in the building and the low hum of someone's voice reverberates for a moment. It sounds like a woman's voice. Then another giggle and a shush. I strain to listen.

I can hear other noises now. But this time they're coming from outside. Twigs cracking, as though underfoot. I sit statue-still. Who the hell could be out there at half past one in the morning? Ugh – they're retching. *Who on earth is it?* I rise from the bed and head across the room. But I can't see a thing apart from the obscure shapes of trees and rocks silhouetted against the sky.

This is a secure gated facility, with high walls and the best surveillance money can buy – at least that's what the website says. If someone's hanging around out there, it must be one of our lot, or even more likely, it could be one of the staff who works here.

But what if it's Mia? She doesn't drink very often yet seemed keen to carry on when we were together earlier this evening. Maybe she got the taste for those cans? Or perhaps she got friendly with one of the staff here and ended up drinking with them instead? I'd better get out there – check she hasn't made herself ill – after all, she'd do the same for me.

I drag my cardigan over my pyjamas and step into my sandals. Then to prevent it from making a noise after me, I hold the door to my room until it closes. I tiptoe past the doors where the other staff are sleeping, before turning the corner where Catherine's room is. I head along the corridor leading to the door and creep past the boys' dorm towards the main exit.

Finally, I click the door behind me and run in the direction of the trees.

I really didn't think things through before leaving the safety of my room. The owl is far louder out here and the night breeze whispers a ghostly rhythm through the trees. Perhaps I should have woken someone else. After all, there could be *anyone* out here. Each twig beneath my feet echoes through the quiet night, the dense woodland closing in around me as I venture further into it.

Then, as my eyes adjust to the darkness, they fall on a weird shape against the tree. *What is it?* I reach into my pocket for my phone. Now I'm away from the Wi-Fi, I have no signal. But I can use the torch function.

I edge closer.

It looks like a person, slumped against the trunk. I stand for a moment, frozen to the spot. Oh my God. It *is* a person. They could just be sleeping – *but what if they're not?* It could be something far, far worse.

'Hello?'

There doesn't seem to be any movement at all from whoever it is. I swallow. I really should get some help. But that could waste precious time, depending on what is happening here. And I'd better make sure it isn't a drunk Mia first before I wake someone else and get her into trouble.

Shining the light from my phone, I creep towards the tree. As I edge closer and closer, it becomes evident exactly who it is. *And* what has happened.

With her head rolling from side to side and vomit all down herself, it's none other than Kirsty. She's absolutely paralytic.

'What the hell are you playing at?' I poke at her arm. Despite who she is and what she represents, I'm gutted for her. She was doing so well recently, from what I've heard. And I'm also gutted for poor Toby.

'Huh?' She opens an eye into the glare of my phone's light and then closes it again.

'You're here with the school for God's sake.' My voice is a hiss. 'And your son!'

'What about him?' She tries to get up but immediately falls back against the trunk. 'Is he OK?'

'What's Catherine going to say about this?' I look back towards the darkened building; the only light is the soft glow emanating from my window. How I wish I was still tucked up in there and that I'd managed to stay asleep.

'Don't talk to me about *her*.' Though she's slurring, there's a venom in her voice as she spits the word *her* out which is weird, since they're such good friends.

'Get up Kirsty.' I tug at her arm. The one that doesn't seem to be covered in sick. 'Let me help you get to bed.'

'I'll tell you about Catherine.' It's the same again. Utter venom. They must have had some sort of row. If Catherine knows anything about her falling off the wagon, it's little wonder.

'Let's just get you inside, shall we?' I manage to heave her forward but then she collapses straight down again. 'Come on Kirsty – you'll have to help me here.' I shine the light right into her face, hoping it will somehow jolt her to her senses.

She goes some way towards helping me to pull her to her feet now, resting her hand on the tree to steady herself as she rises. I glance back at the building again. Part of me hopes someone will see us and come to our aid. Judging by the state of her, it's going to take me ages to get her to her room. Whether it does or it doesn't, she's going to have to be sent home as soon as she's slept this off – her name shouldn't have been included in that draw in the first place. The moment Mia pulled her name out, I knew it spelt disaster.

David might be a lot of things but at least he puts his son first. Maybe he was telling the truth about Kirsty after all. If this is what she got like when they were married, then it's fair that he got custody of Toby.

I can't believe she's got herself into this state when she's supposed to be supporting her son.

'Let me tell you about Catherine,' she says again as she attempts to point at me. The acrid smell of vomit wafts towards me as she moves.

'You can tell me tomorrow. When you've sobered up.'

'You need to know now.'

'The only thing I need is to get you to your room and to get myself back to bed. Come on Kirsty.'

'Catherine and David,' she slurs. As I continue to shine the light on her face, her stained lips, with what looks like red wine, twist themselves into a smile. 'Together,' she adds, blinking into the glare of the light. 'Turn that thing off, will you?' She raises her hand in front of her face.

'What are you on about?' I drop the phone into my pocket.

'Ask David. And Catherine.'

'You're drunk Kirsty. You're talking rubbish.'

'I'm not. And I'll prove it.'

There's a certainty in her voice. Though I'm convinced she's either mistaken or making it up, another voice nags at me. Perhaps I've got it all wrong about Jeanette. But if, after all the grief Catherine gave me, I find out that *she* and *David* are carrying on, they'll wish they'd never known me.

'Go on then Kirsty. How are you going to prove it?'

But she's too busy being sick again to reply.

~

You relented.
You agreed I'd have to go to hospital.
But warned me not to say a word.

TWENTY

LEONIE

My eyes flutter open to the bright light filtering through the curtains. Sleep must have claimed me at some point during the night. A crick in my neck and the persistent pain in my back serve as unwelcome reminders of the uncomfortable mattress beneath me.

Then it comes to me how I really acquired my pain – from the half-hour strain of steering Kirsty away from that tree, out of the woodland and back to her room. She must have brought a load of booze in with her – either that or some idiot's given it to her.

Today, my mission is clear – I must uncover what or *who* pushed her off the wagon so spectacularly, especially after her year of sobriety. To come back from the clutches of the stuff like she did, and be bone dry for all that time is something to be applauded. But now she's right back to square one.

It might not be any of my business, but *something* or *someone* needs holding to account for the state she was in. I can't help but wonder if it's anything to do with the gossip she divulged to me about Catherine being with David. So today, I *will* find out exactly what's going on. No matter what.

. . .

The crescendo of noise from the children's dorms greets me as I lift my head from the pillow, a symphony of laughter, shrieks and calls echoing through the corridors. I should be going to investigate that they're all doing what they're supposed to be doing but after the meagre amount of sleep I managed, I need coffee before I can face the little darlings.

The proper stuff, that is. I poke around in my rucksack for the packet of filter coffee I've brought with me from home.

Catherine might frown upon me wandering around in pyjamas and a cardigan. Still, if Kirsty's drunken accusations were correct last night, my attire will be the least of Catherine's concerns by the time I've finished.

As I head up the corridor to the staff room, David's voice echoes from inside. As I hear my name, I freeze outside the door.

'You tell Leonie and you'll regret it.'

'Why would you be bothered what *she* thinks? I thought it was all over between you.'

It is Jeanette.

'Because she can make life difficult for me, that's why.'

Something inside me plummets. The giggles and shushing I heard last night *must* have been them. Could Kirsty have got it all wrong about Catherine or is David even more of a philanderer than I ever suspected?

'I'm not going to be just one of your conquests. I'm worth more than that.'

'I don't see what your problem is. You've already got a husband, haven't you?'

'Like I told you last night,' she says in a syrupy voice that makes me want to barge in there and grab her by the throat. 'We lead completely separate lives.'

'And like I told *you* last night – all I'm interested in is a bit of fun.'

Perhaps I should continue to eavesdrop – if only to ensure I'm never tempted to be taken in by him again. It's unlikely, since my newly felt disdain towards him is intensifying with each moment that passes.

But try as I might – I can't bear to just stand here, listening to their conversation. After such a horrendous night with so little sleep, I'm just about ready to explode.

But I won't. I refuse to give them the satisfaction. He's not worth it and she *definitely* isn't.

With as much nonchalance as I can muster, I stride into the kitchen and head towards the kettle as I tighten the cord around my dressing gown. I don't look at either of them as I fill the kettle.

But after a couple of moments of awkward silence, I've *got* to say something.

'That's the line he fed *me* yesterday.' I slam a cup onto the counter. 'The one about wanting a bit of fun.'

'We were having a private conversation actually.' Jeanette storms past me on her way to the sink, her own dressing gown wafting out behind her as she reveals a nightie that she's purposely brought for David's benefit by the looks of it.

'Someone got out of the wrong side of bed this morning.' David's actually grinning at me. It's almost as if he hasn't just dumped me before moving on to what could be two different women last night. Catherine, followed by Jeanette. I'm surprised he didn't turn up at my door as well to try and score himself a hat trick.

He stirs his coffee and tries to pass me his spoon. He's dressed in joggers and a hoodie with his hair spikes pointing all over the place, which reminds me of how he looks on a Sunday morning. I blink the memory away – it will not serve me right now. Besides, I'll never go near him again after he's been anywhere near *Jeanette*. Or Catherine.

'I'll use my own spoon, thank you very much.'

'Come on Leonie – don't be like this with me.'

'I heard your conversation just now. *And* I heard you last night.' I wrench the milk from the fridge before pausing to look from him to her. 'I'll be making sure everyone else knows too.'

'So you've resorted to threatening me now?' David steps towards me. 'Don't you think that's a little pathetic?'

'I've no idea what you're talking about.' The fact that Jeanette has paled beneath yesterday's make-up says otherwise.

'Oh I think you do. And if you think you're the only notch on his bedpost Jeanette, think again.'

'Was it *you* that messaged my mother?' Her voice rises. 'Do you know how much trouble you've caused?'

'Perhaps your *husband's* got a right to know.'

'There's no need for all this.' Her voice rises. 'I know you must—'

'You don't know anything.' I slam the carton on the side. 'But if you're wondering why you're now getting the brush-off from Romeo here, it's because he's had exactly what he wants from you again. You're as much an idiot as I am.'

'Just shut up Leonie,' he says. 'You're making a fool of yourself.'

'Whose turn will it be tonight?' I round on him. 'Will you be returning to giving our headteacher a good seeing to? Or perhaps you'll move on to the centre staff. Just make sure you stay *well* away from *me*.' Leaving him open-mouthed, I snatch my cup, pivot on my heel, and slam out of the room.

Breakfast unfolds as a strained affair, a palpable tension which makes me appreciate the physical distance between us adults at our separate tables.

We largely keep ourselves to ourselves but I occasionally steal glances at the others, wondering who's said what to whom so far. I watch for any sign between Catherine and David to suggest Kirsty was right about last night but they don't even look at each other, let alone speak.

The morning sunlight spills through the windows, casting a glow on the excited faces of the children. I periodically watch the door in case Kirsty emerges, but there's no sign of her yet. I've decided to postpone confronting Catherine about Kirsty's condition and about having David in her room, until at least lunchtime. The children's morning shouldn't bear the weight of adult woes, especially Toby's. Plus I don't trust myself to handle things well at the moment – I still need to calm down.

Whispering during the children's toilet duty, Mia queries, 'What's up with you this morning?'

'I'll tell you shortly,' I reply. And I will. I'll probably talk to Mia before anyone else – as soon as we get a proper chance. Perhaps a sounding board will help me work out how best to approach things.

Or maybe I should just hand my notice in and clear off from Oldale. If I resign before the end of the half-term break, I could leave at the end of the summer term. It's a real shame to even have to contemplate this. I've really enjoyed helping to turn the school around since I started here and I know I had more than an excellent chance at that deputy headship. I'd do a far better job than David.

'Have you seen my mum this morning?' Toby asks as he's washing his hands. 'I tried knocking on her door but it was locked and there was no answer.'

'I gave her a knock too,' I reply. 'She said she'd not slept very well last night but that she'll be along soon.'

The poor kid. Whether the state Kirsty was in last night was a temporary blip or a complete lapse back, Toby doesn't need to find out yet.

'OK.' He grabs a paper towel, his smile fading as he notices David listening in.

'So she's on her way is she?' he asks.

'Don't even talk to me,' I hiss as Toby walks away.

'You're not serious about causing trouble for me, are you? Because I'm telling you right now—'

'Leave me alone.' I head back over to Mia.

'What was all that about?'

'Like I said, I'll tell you soon enough. Make sure you walk with me when we head out to the rocks.'

Stepping outside, my mood lifts slightly as the panorama of towering rocks, trees and the warm morning air envelops me. Mia appears at my side. 'Go on then, spill the beans.'

'Are you OK Leonie?' Catherine asks as we gather at the foot of the rock. The emerald-green top she's wearing brings out her eyes more than usual and her hair is hanging loose around her shoulders for a change. She seems far more relaxed than usual which I can only assume is the *David effect*. 'You don't seem your usual chirpy self this morning.'

'I'm fine,' I reply, not taking my eyes away from Frances, the centre manager, who looks like she's about to speak.

I glance back at Catherine as Frances begins addressing us all. At my rebuttal, her forehead has creased itself into a frown. She's no idea about what I know from Kirsty, by the looks of it. Not yet, anyway.

Kirsty, no matter how drunk she was, was *adamant* that David spent a substantial amount of time in Catherine's room last night. Why would she make up something like that, about one of her closest friends? If she's right, I'm going to create such a stink about it. After all, they will have hardly been playing chess in there. And I really can't believe he's then been in *Jeanette's* room as well. It seems I've had a lucky escape from him.

'Where's my mum?' Toby looks around, with a worried expression this time.

'Yes, where is she?' Catherine asks.

'I saw her in the staff room earlier,' I tell her. 'She's had a really bad night's sleep but said she'll be out here as soon as she's had a shower.'

Hopefully, by lunchtime when we go back in, Kirsty will have emerged from her hangover. Then she can deal with this situation in whatever way she deems fit *herself*.

'OK.' Catherine looks thoughtful. 'I guess we'll just have to redistribute her group until she gets here.'

Toby's face falls, probably at the realisation he's now going to be back with his father.

'Listening ears children.' Catherine's voice bounces around the rocks as she looks pointedly at Jessica, always the loudest of the children and the one the rest of them seem to take their lead from.

Their voices descend into a hush as Frances starts again. 'As you've already been told by Harry,' she says, 'there are three ways to ascend this rock.' She gestures at the rock right behind her as it casts its shadow over us.

'Who knows what ascend means?' Catherine never passes up the chance to ask a question even if it should be addressed to a Year Two class. God, I can't *bear* to be around her this morning.

'Go up Miss.' A chorus of voices rises from the children.

Frances pauses patiently at her interruption, then continues. I can tell from her expression that she's irritated. Catherine's quick enough to admonish the children for talking when someone else is but she has no qualms in doing it herself.

'Some of you might choose to take the footpath up to the

top,' she gestures to the foot of the steep path which winds around the side of the rocks. 'That's the easiest route and should take you about ten minutes depending on how fit you are.'

'I'm very fit,' Toby calls out as he flexes his muscles. David grins at him but Toby doesn't grin back. Instead, he looks around again in the direction of the centre.

'Some of you might want to use the climbing wall.' She points at it. 'And according to Mr Naylor' – she nods in his direction – 'you've already practised having a go at the one at the Yorkshire Climbing Centre.'

'Yesss.' Another buzz rises from amongst them.

'Lastly, some of you might want to join Harry in climbing the rock face.'

'Yesss.' An even more excited buzz goes up.

'We'll go through the training and the equipment we'll be using before we begin and you must listen carefully.'

She sweeps her gaze over the sea of earnest faces gathered before her.

'All of you will be attempting a low-level climb up one of these practice rocks first. Harry?' She nods towards where he's standing with the boxes of harnesses for the children, looking about as enthused about being here as a partygoer at a monastery.

'He's honestly got to be one of the most uninspiring instructors I've ever come across,' Mia whispers with a grin.

'I'm surprised I didn't pick up on it more when we came to carry out the risk assessment,' I reply.

'You'll have been too wrapped up in David to have taken much notice.'

Misery twists in my gut at yet another realisation that those days are over. Being on this trip seems to have ruined everything.

Harry and Frances are busy giving out and securing harnesses onto the children.

'Harry would be better suited to being a funeral director or a grave digger.' Mia giggles.

With his dark, brooding expression, permanently clenched jaw and almost monotone voice, she's probably right.

'At least our group are too excited to be taking much notice of him – or his mood.' I shake my head. 'I'll be putting something on the feedback form at the end though.'

'Good idea. *Someone* needs to remind him that he's working with excitable children and needs to cheer up somewhat.'

I gesture around at the five colleagues gathered around him. 'At least the other staff seem more upbeat and happy to be here.'

'Are you doing the adult climb?' Mia raises her gaze to where the scaffolding has been positioned at the top of the rock. 'I'll probably stay with the children – those who want to use the path.'

'I'll stay with you then. *Unless* we get told otherwise.' I roll my eyes in Catherine's direction.

I remember from when we visited that there are different degrees of difficulty of climbs, abseils and zip wires situated up and down and all around its perimeter.

The highlights of my morning will be riding the zip wire and having a go at the adult abseil. The prospect of both sends a glimmer of light into my dark mood.

I'm not going to let *anyone* spoil the experience I've been looking forward to almost as much as the kids.

~

You told me no one else would ever want me.
But you wanted me even less.

TWENTY-ONE

CATHERINE

'Make sure you record this for Kirsty.' I nudge Mia as Toby reaches the landing point for the children's zip wire. 'It's such a shame she's slept in and isn't able to watch him.'

'Don't let me down son,' David calls out.

'I must give this to someone to look after when it's my turn.' Mia, pink-cheeked with the sun, plucks her phone from her pocket. 'I don't want to damage it on the rocks.'

'I can't believe it's past midday already.' I glance at my watch. 'The children will be keeling over if they don't get some lunch soon.'

'I will too.' She laughs. 'Have they all had a go yet?'

'They've all had a go at climbing, but only half have abseiled so far.'

'Have the *other* half all ridden the zip wire?'

'Yes, Toby's the final one. But we're well behind schedule today. After they've eaten they'll be swapping over.'

'It's been pretty well organised, hasn't it?' Mia smiles.

'They're a great team here.' I raise my face to the sky, savouring the fleeting taste of warmth on my skin, a brief reprieve from the chill that's lingered within me for days.

As I told Nancy, there is nothing whatsoever to worry about – not as far as the children are concerned anyway. As for the adults – they're another matter entirely.

Following the text Leonie sent me, I'm pleased to observe she and David definitely don't appear to even be on speaking terms anymore. I'd love to know what's gone on there but Leonie's being very tight-lipped today.

Until recently, neither of them would heed my repeated requests just to get on with their jobs and channel their efforts purely into the life of the school. But it looks like Leonie's finally seen sense.

I've chosen to abseil, as has Jeanette. Kirsty, David, Leonie and Mia opted yesterday for the full-size zip wire.

I'm starting to have palpitations about what's coming – but it's too late to back out now.

'Kirsty's supposed to be going first on the zip wire,' David says. It's the only time he's spoken to me so far today which has been a relief. After last night, I feel more awkward around him than ever.

'So?'

'Are you not going to find out where she is?'

Harry clears his throat in readiness to speak.

'If you could all listen to Harry please.' I clap my hands three times and the children parrot their three hand claps back. I'm glad to have the excuse *not* to talk to David. 'The quicker you listen, the quicker you'll get your lunch.'

'Alice and Jake here' – Harry gestures to two of his colleagues – 'are going to take you back to the centre while the adults make their way to the top.'

'Awww,' Jessica protests in a loud voice. 'Can't *we* watch you all?'

'You're already late going in for lunch,' Harry replies. 'You'll be able to watch when the activities swap over later.'

'But we all want to watch *now*.' Amelia's voice rises amongst the others. 'Please.'

Harry nods at his colleagues, presumably because he can't be bothered to argue with the children and wants someone to take over with getting them inside. Then he looks down at a crumpled piece of paper in his hands. 'We'll have the two abseilers first.' He points to the bags of safety equipment assigned to each of us at the foot of the rocks where we've already adjusted our harnesses to size.

'Miss Fox.' He gestures to the bag, labelled *Miss Fox* as though I can't read my own name. 'Mrs Smith.' His finger shifts from pointing in Jeanette's direction to the bag next to mine.

'Next, the zip wire riders, Mrs Naylor, Mr Naylor, Miss Johnson and lastly Miss Hudson.'

'Mum's not here yet.' Toby looks sad.

'She can have her turn later.' I pat him on the shoulder. 'Can't she?' I look over at Harry.

'Sure.'

'I'll take her place then.' David pats the bag containing his harness. 'I'll go first. After all, I've got to make sure it's safe for the ladies, haven't I?'

'You've all had your safety briefing,' Frances continues. 'You've been shown how to wear your harnesses, but once we're up there, you'll be double-checked by a member of staff to make sure you've fastened them correctly and that you're safely set up for your ride. Are we all ready?' Her blonde curls bob around in the breeze. She barely looks old enough to be a manager of anything but perhaps that's just me getting older.

The air's filled with the raw scent of the moss-covered rocks. I stare at them, hoping they won't be as menacing as they look. The sooner I get up there, the sooner I can be back down.

Leonie strides confidently along the rugged path that winds its way to the summit, her ponytail swinging from side to side. She's in a very strange mood today – and seems to be purposefully setting herself apart so nobody can keep up with her. Apart from Frances, who's also moving as effortlessly up the incline as a gazelle. She seems to be having no problem keeping pace just a few steps behind.

'Is Leonie alright this morning?' I say to Mia as we huff and blow in unison, the last ones in the line, with the gap between us and those in front increasing all the time.

'Hasn't she had a word with you yet?' Mia asks. 'She said she was going to.'

'About what?' I knew it. I could tell there was something up with her.

'It's not *really* for me to say,' Mia replies, her hesitancy and the emphasis on the word *really* giving me hope that I'll be able to prise whatever it is out of her.

'If you know something Mia, you need to tell me.' I swing around to face her. 'It could be helpful for everyone. There's an awful atmosphere today, don't you think?'

David suddenly turns from his position ahead of us and begins striding back. 'Sorry – I'm going to have to pay a visit.' He thrusts his bag at Mia. 'Since you're going at a tortoise pace, can I give you this? I should be back well before you get to the top.'

She accepts the bag from him. Mia's always the same around David. Like the rest of the teaching assistants. He says *jump* and they say *how high?*

'Pay a visit where?' she asks.

'When you've got to go, you've got to go. I won't be long. Make sure nobody takes my place. Like I said before, *I'm* going first.' He continues back down the rock face, jogging away from us and towards the bottom.

'I think you can manage your own bag, don't you?' I call after him though I don't know why I'm bothering.

'I'll be faster without it,' he calls back over his shoulder. 'I don't want to miss watching you abseil do I Catherine?'

He keeps on running. Mia shrugs and hoists the newly acquired rucksack onto her other shoulder. 'I certainly wouldn't dare take his place!'

'Can you manage both of those?' I nod towards the second one.

'Of course,' she gasps back. 'Have you not noticed how energetic and fit I am?'

Mia's not normally this pleasant towards me – usually I'd describe her as compliant, yet guarded. But I'll drop my line of questioning about Leonie for now. Everything's bound to come out soon enough if Leonie intends to speak to me, like Mia's said.

Instead, we'll focus on staying alive for the next half an hour, or however soon we can get this madness over and done with. That's all I can think about right now.

~

I'd dread you coming home,
but when you didn't
I was tortured by where you might be.

TWENTY-TWO

CATHERINE

'See you at the bottom,' Mia wheezes, as I stop at our designated part of the rock. 'Maybe I should have opted for abseiling too – at least I wouldn't have so far to hike.'

'It's too late now,' I reply. 'You've had all your training for the zip wire. It'll be my turn later. *If* I go through with it. Have fun.'

'You too.' She smiles. It's nice to be getting along with one of the staff for a change.

I gaze into the sky. It's another perfect day, weather-wise anyway. And at least the children are having a brilliant time so far. I look down from the rock to admire the view from up here, cupping my hands around my eyes as I take in the mosaic of trees and fields beneath me.

David is running towards the main building. Oh gosh, what if his real plan is to bother Kirsty? Maybe I should have gone after him – the last thing we need is any more unpleasantness. It's too late now though. I'll just have to get myself down off this rock sharpish – *then* I'll head across.

'Are you ready?' Harry first helps Jeanette and then me as we step into our harnesses.

The straps cinch around me, Harry's hands securing each one. The metal buckles send a shiver through my spine, each a reminder of how much I'm about to depend on them.

'As ready as I'll ever be,' I reply, holding onto his shoulder for balance. 'There's no going back now, is there?' I feel like one of the children as he tugs at my harness before doing the same with Jeanette's.

At least she's dressed more appropriately today – in jeans and a long-sleeved T-shirt like the rest of us. Frances told us yesterday to cover our limbs in preparation for today's activities.

'Where's David?' She peers over the edge.

'In the loo. Why?'

Her cheeks flush. 'No reason. I just wondered.'

She must think I was born yesterday. Nancy has every reason to be upset with how she's putting her marriage in jeopardy.

'Do you recall what was said about when you're coming down?' Harry asks.

'Kind of.'

He looks impatient as if he can't really be bothered going through it all again. 'Start with your feet and knees at a right angle against the rock.' He crouches as if to demonstrate. 'You're on a pulley – and you can lower yourself as quickly or as slowly as you want to.'

'What if I want to go quickly?' Jeanette says as she hugs herself. 'I just want to get it over and done with.'

'When you push away from the rock, let the tension off the slip rope and you will descend on the guide rope. As you've been shown, keep your feet forward to help you either pause or bounce off from the rock as you go.'

'You make it sound so easy.' I stare down at the sea of children's upturned faces. I'd expect a comment like that to elicit a smile from him. But it doesn't.

'Why haven't they been taken in for their lunch yet?' I look at Harry.

'I was just thinking the same thing.'

'Let's just focus on getting down the rock face for now.' Jeanette laughs but it's a nervous laugh.

'You're right. After all, there are plenty of other people down there to take care of the children.'

It seems higher from up here than it looked from below. And the zip wire summit is far higher still. Mia hasn't even reached it yet.

Harry follows my line of vision to the top of the rock. It doesn't look like much is happening up there yet. I believe the plan is to let us go down first.

'What happens if I lose my footing?' Now we're moments away from doing it, Jeanette's voice is trembling.

'You're secured the whole time. Look.' Harry points from the guide rope to where the rope is bolted into the rock. 'The rope's anchored in.'

'Come on Miss Fox.' There's not too much I can do about the fact that the children are still down there and we're running so late. At least it's a cold lunch that's been prepared for us.

The pulse in my chest reverberates like a bass drum as I hang above the world. The walls of my throat have dried up, mirroring the parched surface of the sun-beaten rock face that my trainers are gripping. Elevated a hundred feet above terra firma, I'm clutching the rope for dear life.

A barrage of doubt floods my mind – *what the hell am I doing up here?* My hold on the rope tightens with each passing second.

However, now that I'm in place, I just need to trust the rope and let go. That's what Frances said during the training. *I just need to trust the rope.* That's the hardest part. Nor have I ever been one for *letting go*.

The children might seem excited about watching this but

I'm only too aware that some of the adults here would probably sever this rope, given half a chance. It feels as though they only converse with me to serve their own ends *and* because they have to – even Mia, who's being strangely friendly towards me today. I don't trust anyone and I definitely don't trust this damn rope.

'Let go Miss Fox.' Another voice echoes around the rocks. And then another. 'Go on, we did it.'

Proportionately, the children's descent will have been nearly as scary to them as this is to me. Yes – it was from a far lower summit, but they'll have still felt the same fear and been forced to employ the same amount of trust in the process and in the rope.

'Go on Miss Fox.'

Just a few more seconds then I'll go – I really will. I look down again which I probably shouldn't. Vertigo wraps its icy fingers around my mind, and my head swoons, the world tilting at odd angles.

Paranoia creeps in, and I wonder if David's lurking in the shadows somewhere. After how things finished up last night, he'll be savouring the spectacle of me clinging to this rock like my life depends on it.

Which, at this moment, it does.

OK. I'm going to do it. I'm starting to look foolish here plus, I'm wasting time.

One – two – three.

I finally take a deep breath and let go.

~

You told me I depressed you,
that you hated to be around me,
yet you wouldn't leave me alone.

TWENTY-THREE

MIA

As Catherine lands, a symphony of cheers erupts from the children, echoing through the air. Despite her being so strict, she's definitely more popular with *them* than she is among the staff.

A few minutes later, Jeanette also lands, not to quite the same volume of applause but I guess it's only natural they should reserve more of their enthusiasm for the headteacher. Especially one who's normally so stoic and buttoned-up when we're in school.

It's our turn now for the zip wire. I force myself to look down at the children from our hundred and fifty feet vantage point. My stomach churns. On the fastest part of the descent, it's possible to get up to thirty miles an hour.

'Right I'm going first,' Leonie says. 'Seeing as though David seems to have completely buggered off.'

'You might as well,' I reply. I'm *certainly* not going to volunteer.

'Why does he always get the first shot anyway?' Leonie casts a glance behind her as if expecting David to materialise out of thin air.

'It was actually supposed to be Kirsty.'

'Until he muscled in.' She steps to where the rucksacks containing our harnesses are stacked beside the anchor point. 'Anyway, he's not here to argue, is he?'

There wasn't a great deal of training required for this – there's far more needed for the abseiling. The zip wire, so we've been told, is merely a case of buckle up, sit in the harness and go. By the time we reach the end of it, we'll have slowed right down on the straight and there'll be a centre member waiting there to unclip and release us.

'Where *is* David?' Frances asks, having emerged at our point of descent to help us on our way, now the abseilers are down. 'We won't be able to wait up here for long after the two of you have landed.'

'He's just at the loo, I think,' I tell her as I look to the path up the side as I notice movement out of the corner of my eye. But it's Emma, one of the centre staff, who's on her way up here, rather than David. 'He's been a while though.'

'The kids will be getting antsy down there.' Leonie peers over the edge. 'Not to mention hungry. I know I'm starving.'

'Me too.'

'Oh look.' Leonie points at Jeanette, who's separated herself from the others since she landed. 'What a surprise – Jeanette's texting again.'

'That she's still alive after her abseil.' I laugh as she looks up.

Leonie pulls a face. 'Sadly.' A hint of resentment colours her tone.

'Let's get this show on the road then. Which one's mine?' She glances at Frances. 'I'm sure it had a sticky label on before.'

I bend to the bags and pick mine up. 'Mine's got one.' I slide my harness from inside it.

'It honestly doesn't matter,' Frances says. She tucks a stray curl behind her ear as the rest of them dance in the breeze.

'What doesn't?' I look at her.

'If you end up with a different harness to the one you initially tried on. They only take a moment to readjust.'

'Oh, OK.' Leonie tugs the harness from the bag. 'It doesn't sound like there was much need for the labels then.'

'Not really.'

Frances crouches low enough to allow Leonie to hold onto her shoulder as she steps into the harness.

Emma emerges onto the landing with us, wearing more clothes than she was for judging the raft building yesterday. With her combat trousers and her hair scraped back into a ponytail, she looks more like the rest of us mere mortals today.

'Will you just double-check this for me?' Frances calls to her as she tugs at Leonie's harness.

Leonie looks puzzled.

'We always have two of us to make sure your clips are where they should be.'

'Even us adults?'

'Of course,' Frances replies to her, smiling. 'You're just as important to us as the children.

'Hmm – yep.' Emma slides her phone into her pocket. 'Sorry – it was the kitchen – they've been ready for the kids for ages. I'll phone down to the others to take the kids inside, shall I?'

'Ah, leave them for a moment,' Leonie says. 'They'll be dying to watch us.'

Excitement flutters in my belly. I've so often fantasised about what's about to happen here. However, I couldn't have imagined it would materialise while I'm at work. And I certainly didn't envisage that I'd be getting a chance like this in front of all these observing eyes.

Emma pulls and tugs at several of the straps around Leonie before saying, 'You're good to go.' Wisps of her hair poke beneath her helmet and flutter in the breeze. Even wearing that, she still looks good. Me, I probably look like some kind of insect.

'Aren't you nervous?' I ask her, peering at the expectant ocean of upturned faces below us. David's on his way back – he's broken into a run at the point where the children are gathered. Leonie had better set off quickly. If he gets up here before she does, no doubt he'll try to elbow his way in and be the one to go first. He's probably spitting feathers down there that she's taken his go.

'Nah,' she replies. 'I've done all kinds of stuff like this. I've bungeed, skydived – this is a playground ride compared to the zip wire I rode in Wales. Honestly, that one's like flying.'

'It's not exactly a playground ride.' I shudder as the enormity of what I'm doing dawns on me. The uneven terrain below stretches endlessly, an array of formidable-looking rocks, greenery, winding paths and distant play structures giving depth to the vast drop beneath.

'OK then.' Frances clips the rope attached to Leonie's harness to a cable. 'You can either take a run at it and set off faster or just step off and go. As you become airborne, all you have to do is sit in your harness as we instructed before.'

'Go on Miss Johnson,' several voices chorus from below.

'Here goes nothing.' She grins, breaking into a run before launching herself off the edge.

∽

If I didn't give you what you wanted,
you'd just help yourself.

TWENTY-FOUR

MIA

'What's happening?' Leonie's scream pierces the air. It's only a split second since she went off the edge.

Harry emerges on top of the rock. 'Isn't David supposed to be—'

'Oh my God.' I follow Frances's horrified gaze to the top of Leonie's harness. 'Harry, for God's sake, do something.'

Leonie looks up at the strap which is supposed to hold her weight throughout the ride. 'No. No! Oh my God. Somebody help me!'

Everything seems to go into slow motion as we all stand, rooted to the spot in helplessness. Harry steps closer to the edge, but Leonie's too far from it for anyone to be able to reach her.

For a brief moment, her terrified eyes meet mine, then roll back up to the strap that's holding her. I follow her gaze. Its final threads are already splitting away from each other.

I don't feel safe standing upright anymore. If I were to faint, I might go the same way as Leonie. I drop to my knees as the rope finally gives way, sending her into free fall and hurtling through the air towards the rocks below.

Her descending scream can only be described as bloodcurdling. Then there's nothing, absolutely nothing, any of us can do other than watch as her limbs go from hysterically flailing in a final bid for survival, into twisted and spurting blood as she collides with the ground.

Bile bubbles at the back of my throat. I crawl over to the scaffolding, clinging to it as if what's beneath me is the only solid ground left in the world.

'Has she...? Is she...?' Frances's eyes are scrunched together. She gulps air as she drops into a crouch beside me. 'I can't look.'

'Neither can I.' I watched the impact, the instant gush of blood at the point of collision and the final motion before her body stilled. I can't look again. I'll see what I saw forever as it is.

Harry's face is sheet white. 'There's no way she could have survived that. Nobody could.'

A suffocating hush blankets us, the weight of what just happened sinking in. For a brief moment, we all stand frozen, mirroring Leonie's stillness in our shared shock.

Then the screaming begins, first one child, and then more and more until they're all shrieking and wailing in absolute hysteria. Within seconds the noise has built to a crescendo of grief. I want to shriek and wail too but if I were to try, I'm certain that no sound would leave my mouth.

'Somebody do something.' Catherine's desperate voice reverberates from below.

'Get down there now,' Frances screeches at Harry. 'She needs help. She could still be alive.'

'There's no chance.' He staggers back against the rail next to the anchor point, his voice almost a whisper. 'It's too late. I can tell even from up here that she's dead. Can't you?'

'There's still a chance.' Frances still grips the rail as though her life depends on it. 'There's always a chance. And we have to try.'

'You get down there then.'

'I don't feel too good. I need a moment.'

'Please.' Catherine's voice echoes again from below. 'Some-body, do something.'

Footsteps pound the ground, a rhythmic thud matching the fury in David's bunched fists as he emerges over the top of the rock. 'You said it was safe,' he roars, rushing at Harry. 'Everything is rigorously tested and checked, you said.'

He grabs him by the scruff of the neck, and for a moment, I wonder if he might hurl him over the edge to join Leonie. Instead, he rams him against the scaffolding. 'What have you done to her? What the fuck have you people done?'

'Get off him!' Frances springs forward and grabs David's free arm. 'It's not Harry's fault. It was an accident.'

'She's dead. She's bloody dead. That's slightly more than *an accident*, don't you think?' David's face hardens but he lets Harry go. 'And you're going to bloody pay for it.' He jabs his finger into Harry's shoulder.

'Just stop it will you,' Frances cries. 'Blaming each other isn't going to help anyone right now.'

'Her down there – that could have happened to *any* of us.' He wags his finger from Harry to Frances. 'Do you hear what I'm saying? You. Are. Going. To. Pay.'

A fresh wave of frenzied panic surges from the rocks below. The anguish in their cries will haunt me forever. Guttural and broken. Those children can never unsee what they've just witnessed. 'Miss Johnson,' a lone voice cries from amongst them.

David swings around to face me. 'Go and see to those kids, will you?' It's as if he's only just noticed I'm here.

'But. I can't. I can't do anything. She – she was—'

'Do as you're told! *Now!*'

I stumble away, almost losing my footing as I find myself back on the gravel path. The path which only moments ago, Leonie was also walking on. How can someone so alive only moments ago now be dead?

Without meaning to look, I catch sight of Leonie's mangled body below and bile returns to the back of my throat. The metallic taste of panic floods my mouth as I lean against a rock, my stomach threatening to revolt against the horror below me.

The shrieks and wails of the children are becoming louder. I'm nearly at the bottom and I don't know how I'm going to handle it when I get there.

There's nothing I can do to 'see to those kids' as David put it. Nothing that can take their fear and shock away. They all adored Leonie. But nobody thought of her like I did.

David should be devastated, having been 'with' Leonie for eight months. Yet he's too busy assigning blame and seems almost indifferent to the mangled remains of her body on the rocks. He only seems concerned that it could have happened to *any of us* and who is *going to pay.*

He means it could have happened to *him* of course. Leonie was completely right when she was talking to me last night. David Naylor really only cares about him and himself.

Tears blur my vision as Leonie's smiling face haunts my thoughts.

That was to be one of our final conversations.

I can't believe she's gone. I really, really can't believe it. Nor can I face anybody right at this moment. Not until I've pulled myself together. I drop into a crouch next to one of the ridges near the bottom and let the tears fall.

~

You'd disappear for days on end.
And I'd go to pieces.
I couldn't bear to live with you,
and I couldn't survive without you.

THE INVESTIGATION

DI GILBERT

'Take a seat.' Chris gestures towards one of the sofas and promptly heads towards the other one.

I hitch my trousers as I sit facing the terrified-looking teaching assistant. 'We're merely assembling the facts at this stage but obviously we'll let you know if we need to progress things at the station.'

'At the station?' Her eyes, red and glassy with what looks like tears already cried, widen. 'Why would you need to do that? You don't think I—'

'What my colleague means,' Chris begins, 'is that we'd have to go to the station if we require a recorded interview from you after this conversation.' He takes his place on the sofa next to me.

'We'll start by getting some basic information from you. I'll be asking the questions and Sergeant Parkins here will record everything you say as a statement. We'll end by reading it back to you and then you'll sign it to agree that what we've written is a true account.'

'OK.' She plucks a tissue from the box in between us and

blows her nose. 'I'm sorry. I'll try to keep it together. I'm just really struggling.'

'Understandably so.'

I rattle off the first few questions – name, date of birth and address and watch as Chris writes it at the top of a form and begins writing his first paragraph.

'I, Mia Hudson...' After a few moments, he reads back what he's written so far. '...of 23 Dale End Mews, Oldale, Yorkshire, confirm I have known the deceased Leonie Johnson in my capacity as her teaching assistant in Year Five since—' He stops reading. 'Your headteacher mentioned you'd both started at the school at the same time in September. Is that correct?'

She nods. 'Because we started at the same time and worked so closely together, we became good friends.'

'How good?'

'What do you mean?'

'Did you see one another outside school, for instance?'

She's trembling. She still looks to be in shock. But she's a key witness so we need to speak to her while whatever's happened out there is fresh in her mind. She worked the closest with the deceased *and* she was up there with her when it happened.

'Not really.' She dabs at her eye with the tissue. 'Only when we were working on school stuff.'

'Thank you. What we need from you in this statement,' I say, 'is a detailed account. From your arrival yesterday to the fall from the rock – times, people's placements, any noticeable atmospheres between them.'

'OK.'

'What do you know about the relationship between Mr Naylor and Miss Johnson?'

'They'd finished things as far as I was aware,' she replies. 'If you could even call it a *relationship* in the first place.'

'Why had they finished it?'

'From what I know, it got complicated. Leonie was more invested in him than David was in her – he'd not long since come out of a marriage so there was all the baggage that brought.'

'How well do you know *Mrs* Naylor?'

'Well enough to feel a bit sorry for her,' Mia responds, her gaze distant. 'We both did. Me *and* Leonie.' Her eyes bulge with another onslaught of tears.

'Why's that?'

'Well, she's lost everything, hasn't she? Her son, her marriage, her home. All because of her drinking.'

'Did you see much of her last night?'

'Who Kirsty? No, but I've heard about her getting drunk.'

'Who told you about it?'

'Leonie did when we were walking to the rocks. It's a shame really. I gather she's been off the drink for a year.'

'Have you any idea what might have caused her to relapse?'

Mia nods. 'You might have heard about this already...'

'What?'

'Me, her and Jeanette all saw David going into Catherine's room last night. And *not* coming back out.'

'I see. So you think there could have been something going on there?'

'It certainly looked that way to me.'

'Did Leonie know anything about this?'

She shakes her head. 'Not as far as I know. I was going to break it to her later. She seemed to be struggling enough this morning without me piling any more on her.'

'O-K...' I say slowly, stroking my chin. I wonder why Catherine didn't mention any of this before. Hers was the first statement we took.

'I'm surprised' – Chris fills the pause I've created – 'given the history involved, that Mr Naylor's ex-wife was permitted on this trip in the first place.'

'Is that a question?'

'If you like.'

She hesitates for a moment.

'Were you going to say something Mia?'

She takes a deep breath. 'Mr Naylor's ex-wife is here on this trip because the draw was rigged from the start.'

'How do you know this?'

'Because David Naylor paid me five hundred pounds to make sure her name was drawn.' She looks directly into my eyes. 'As well as Jeanette's.'

TWENTY-FIVE

KIRSTY

Dabbing at my eyes in the mirror, I'm astounded that David had the power to reduce me to tears yet again. But I should have known he'd get me on my own sooner or later.

I'd jumped out of my skin when his footsteps pounded up to my door before throwing it open so it thumped against the wall.

David was the last person I expected to see.

'Why aren't you out there?' he'd demanded, evidently out of breath from running. 'Where you're supposed to be?'

There I was, standing in a towel, as he eyeballed me before wrinkling his nose. 'It stinks in here.' Then he looked at me more closely, his top lip curling into a sneer. 'You're hungover, aren't you?'

'Get out of my room. You've got no right barging in here.'

'You are, aren't you?' He lunged towards me and before I knew it, he had me by my throat against the wall, shedding my towel in the process.

'You're nothing but a fucking disgrace.' His words were laced with venom, each syllable spat out, his spittle landing on my face like drops of acid. For a moment, I thought I was going to be sick again.

'Get off me!' I tried to hook my fingers beneath his. 'Let me get my towel.'

'I don't know what I ever saw in you.' His gaze snaked down my body, and though his tone was filled with disgust, the glint in his eyes and the way he licked his lips spoke of something darker.

Thankfully, he let go of me so I scrambled to retrieve my towel.

'Don't think you're getting anywhere near Toby for the rest of this trip.' He jabbed his finger into my shoulder. 'You're not fit to call yourself his mother.'

I couldn't bring myself to meet his eyes, so my gaze fixated on the floor.

'Where did you get the booze from?'

'I don't know.' I edged away from him.

It's the truth. I have no recollection of wanting a drink, pouring one, accepting one or even drinking one. I still can't understand how I ended up in the state I did.

'I'll ask you again, shall I? Where did you get the booze from?'

'I don't remember.'

'Like hell you don't remember.'

I couldn't bear the way he was looking at me. 'Please – I need you to leave my room. You've no right to be in here.' Tears were stabbing the back of my eyes but I wasn't going to give him the satisfaction of seeing me cry.

Just as I thought he was doing as I'd asked, he pursued me across the room and grabbed hold of my arm. 'Wait until my solicitor hears about this – you can kiss your Sundays with Toby goodbye. He's better off without you anyway.'

'Please, please don't do this to me.' I tried to shake my arm from his grasp. 'I don't even know what happened. Really, I don't.'

'So you're holing yourself up in here all day? You're

supposed to be out there, in charge of your group.' He dug his fingers deeper into my flesh while pointing in the direction of the main exit with his free hand. 'You've ruined everything.' Suddenly dropping my arm, he began backing towards the door.

'What are you talking about now?'

'Don't you worry, I'll be making sure *everybody*, especially Toby, knows *exactly* what you did last night.'

He stormed out of my room and I heaved a sigh of relief as I heard him run back along the corridor and slam out of the exit.

I tilt my head this way and that in the mirror as I blow dry my hair. I feel like death. But then I deserve to. If I can make myself look slightly better on the outside, my insides might start to feel less ravaged.

I couldn't be any more gutted with myself. After nearly a year completely free of drink, I've let myself down so badly. I've been looking forward with every fibre of my being to spending quality time with Toby this week, after being forced to watch him from the fringes for so long. I can only pray that David doesn't carry out his threat and tell our son about the state I was in last night. Why can't he see that he'll be hurting Toby just as much as he's hurting me?

I worry like hell about the fact that Toby's growing up under his influence. He's such a sensitive boy but I torture myself constantly that one of two things could happen – either Toby will eventually copy how his father behaves, or else, as he grows, he'll become a victim of him when he begins to stand up to him more. He's showing signs of that already. And people wonder why I find it so important to be at those school gates as much as I am. I might not be able to collect him after school but at least I can keep an eye on his welfare.

I flick the switch off the hairdryer and reach into my bag for some paracetamol. I can't imagine I've anything left in me now to throw up but I still gag as I try to get the tablets down.

With urgency, I glug the rest of my water down too, feeling the cool liquid rush down my throat, a feeble attempt to wash away the nausea as well as the regret. I spend a few moments trying to steady my breath and hold the water in my stomach.

I wrap the vomit-crusted clothes from last night in a plastic bag and step into clean shorts.

What's all that noise? Screaming, shouting, wailing. The kids should all be out there, taking part in this morning's activities but it certainly doesn't sound as though anyone's enjoying themselves.

I pull the curtain back but can't see a thing through the trees. So, tugging a T-shirt over my head and slipping my sunglasses on, I head from my room towards the main entrance.

The commotion is coming from the rocks. Frances hurries towards me, her expression etched with a kind of horror that forewarns of something terrible.

'What's going on?' My anxiety almost makes me forget the hangover gnawing at my senses.

'I can't stop,' she gasps. 'I need to guide the ambulance in.'

'*Ambulance?* Is my Toby alright?' I call after her. 'Please just tell me that.'

'She's dead,' she shouts back. 'She's bloody dead.'

'*Who is?*'

But Frances continues in the opposite direction.

She?

I break into a run, struggling to catch my breath. As I turn the corner and the children come into view, my eyes rest on Toby before anyone else and I let a long breath out. He's safe.

Catherine, Mia and Jeanette are among the children, comforting them as they guide them away from the rocks. Every single child is weeping and many of them are either clinging to each other or to an adult. Harry follows on, speaking into his phone. However, there's no sign of David. Did Frances make a mistake when she said *she*?

'What happened?' I gasp as I reach Toby. His face is sheet white and his red-rimmed eyes are bulging with tears. 'Tell me.' I grip his shoulders. All I want is for him to hug me back but he's rigid.

'It's Miss Johnson.' His voice trembles as he steps back from me and points upwards. 'She fell from up there.'

'*Miss Johnson.*' My hand flies to my mouth as I follow the direction of his finger up to the top of the rock. 'Is she—'

'You need to come with us Kirsty.' Catherine arrives beside us. Her voice is gentle as she reaches for my arm.

Bits from last night are starting to come back to me. David – going into Catherine's room. It's safe to say that could have been at the root of my drinking. I shake her hand free. Whatever's going on here might be a temporary distraction for now, but I'll never forgive her for what she did last night.

'Her harness broke,' Toby continues, choking back a sob. 'Mum...'

'My poor baby.' I stoop down in a second attempt to hug him. This time he clings to me, just for a moment, before pulling away.

'We've got to go inside now.' He glances around at the rest of the group. I want him to remain clinging to me like Jessica is with Jeanette.

'Where is she now? Miss Johnson, I mean?' Until I see what's happened with my own eyes, I don't think I can quite believe it.

With a quivering finger, Toby points through the huddle of crying children. He closes his eyes as though he can't bear to see whatever it is he's witnessed again.

'Go on with Miss Fox,' I tell him. 'I'll be right behind you.'

As the children disappear around the corner and the sound of their sobbing ebbs away, I edge closer to where David's standing like a statue on the rocks – staring, just staring at Leonie's lifeless form.

Now it's just him and me... and Leonie's mangled body.

I see the blood first – then the angles of her limbs and the twist of her neck. What's in front of me has got to be the most horrific thing I've ever seen. No wonder Toby's in shock. No wonder the children are so inconsolable.

My body responds in what's become its all-too-familiar way to what I'm seeing and the water I've just drunk makes a sudden reappearance.

David swings around, disgust etched across his face.

'At least *you'll* be happy now, won't you?'

~

I begged you to stop treating me so badly.
Or to just let me go.
So you laughed.

TWENTY-SIX

KIRSTY

'What are you still doing here?' Harry yells as he approaches us. I've no idea where he's come from – I assumed he'd gone with the others.

'You don't get to speak to me,' David yells back at him. 'Not after the negligence *you've* demonstrated. I'll make sure you're finished after this, do you hear me? *Finished.*'

We turn to Leonie's sprawled body, her hair fluttering from beneath her helmet. I observed her yesterday as she paddled with the children, and then as she landed in the water with her group – all full of laughter when their raft capsized. It's inconceivable that she's dead.

Another realisation floods my mind. Leonie was the one who helped me into my bed last night. Who knows where I might have ended up if it wasn't for her finding me? But what happened between me watching Catherine's door and her helping me in from the woods? It's all a complete blur.

I only started paying any attention to Leonie when I found out from Toby that she was sneaking in and out of my former home – clearly when she thought he'd be asleep. It was only natural that I became concerned for her. After all, I know exactly what David's capable of.

'It was an accident,' Harry replies, looking to be as in shock as everyone else. 'We don't know what—'

'But we're sure as hell going to find out, aren't we Harry?'

My attention flits to David's eyes. They're bone dry – he's never been one for expressing any emotions, showing care for others, but I'd expect there to be something, *anything*, after what's happened here. He's obviously moved on completely from Leonie.

To Catherine.

'Did you see what happened?' I direct the question at Harry, knowing David won't be the one sharing any useful information.

'I was halfway up the rock when she fell.' Harry begins to speak, but his words are devoured by the roar of engines and the blare of a siren.

'I don't know why they're sending ambulances.' David raises his voice over them. 'It's not as though they can do anything to help her.'

'Why are they sending police as well?' Shielding my eyes from the sun, I watch as they all screech to a halt, parking as close as they're able to get to us. There's a collective slamming of doors as paramedics and police officers begin to make their way over the rocks.

'Of course they can't help her.' Harry's voice is flat as the siren is silenced. 'But they'll certainly have questions to ask.'

'Too bloody right they will,' David replies. 'You'd better get looking for somewhere else to *volunteer* – that's if you don't get sent down for criminal negligence after this.'

'Just shut it, will you?' Harry rounds on him. 'After what—'

'I don't know what's going on here, but you two can cool it immediately.' A police officer arrives between David and Harry and takes hold of each of their shoulders in his hands.

Two paramedics are right behind him. 'Is it a single casual-ty?' one says, as the other heads straight towards Leonie. 'Was anyone else involved?'

'Is one not enough for you?' David's face contorts into that awful almost-smirk, an expression I used to know so well. The paramedic gives him a strange look and hurries to join his colleague.

He never fails, my ex-husband. Ever.

'Who's in charge here?' A second police officer approaches us. 'I'm DI Bradley Gilbert,' he says, 'and this is my colleague Sergeant Chris Parkins.' He gestures to the officer who tried to put David and Harry in their place.

'Frances is,' Harry says. 'I'm just a volunteer instructor.'

'And your name is...'

'Harry Douglas.'

'What happened?'

'All we know so far' – Harry closes his eyes momentarily – 'is that the harness gave way.'

He points up to where the broken strap is just about visible – still waving in the air.

'It *gave way*?'

I feel a knot tighten in my stomach as the DI's eyes narrow. I have a good idea of what he's thinking.

He exchanges glances with his colleague. 'Were you super-vising the activity?'

'Kind of.' Harry looks pained. 'Along with my colleagues.'

'And you're going to pay for it,' David snarls.

The officer gives him a look as if to say *shut it*. 'I gather from the phone call we received that the person in question was one of the teachers?'

'That's correct.' David stands up straighter.

'There were children present too?'

'Thirty-six of them,' I reply. David glares at me as if to say *who permitted you to start answering their questions?*

'And you are?'

'Kirsty Naylor, I'm one of the mums – I'm helping here.'

'Did *you* see what happened?'

'No, I was inside – I didn't see a thing. I'm sorry.' They aren't to know that I've been laid up all morning, nursing a staunching hangover. All this has certainly taken my mind off it, as well as everything else from last night.

'We'll need to speak to you *all* shortly and get a statement from everybody – the children as well. Can I ask how old they are?'

'Nine to eleven,' I reply.

His colleague shakes his head. Something in his eyes tells me he's a parent too. 'Is anyone still up there?'

'No.' Harry's voice is barely audible as he stares at the ground.

'Has anyone been back up since it happened?'

'No.' He slowly raises his eyes and shakes his head.

'Right.' The DI gestures to some other police officers who've arrived and are scrambling over the rocks towards us. 'Get this entire area cordoned off, ready for the forensic team.' He gestures to the far corner where the rocks end and the woods begin. 'Where are the children now?'

'They're all inside.' David nods towards the centre where only the roof is visible from behind the trees.

'And your name is?'

'David Naylor. I'm the Year Six teacher.'

'Naylor?' He looks from David to me. 'I take it you're—?'

'Divorced,' David says quickly. His tone of voice suggests he would add *thank God* if he could.

'So you're a parent helper here?' He slides a notebook and pen from his top pocket and writes something. 'So you're a volunteer instructor.' He waves his pencil from Harry to David. 'You're the Year Six teacher and there's thirty-six kids inside. Who else have we got here please?'

'The children are with one of the teaching assistants, Mia Hudson,' I begin.

'I'll do the talking if you don't mind.' David glares at me and I resist the urge to tell him that he can no longer order me around.

'I really don't mind *who* does the talking.' DI Gilbert glares back at him.

'There's another parent helper in there called Jeanette Smith,' David says, 'and the headteacher is Catherine Fox.' I watch him closely as he says Catherine's name but he's giving nothing away.

'Can you tell me more about the person who's fallen please?'

'Her name's Leonie Johnson,' David says as he glances over at her. As the paramedics drape the sheet over her lifeless body, I can almost feel the weight of the fabric, a final, chilling curtain signalling the end.

Tears well up. I can't help but feel a surge of empathy. I'll see her broken body each time I close my eyes – probably for the rest of my life. I watch as the two paramedics shuffle away from her. Despite the heat of the day, I shiver.

'How old was she?'

'Thirty-one, I think,' David replies, not taking his eyes off her either.

'She's – *was* – the Year Five teacher,' I add, as if what class she taught matters anymore.

'Our colleagues will escort you to be with the rest of your group.' DI Gilbert nods at two more police officers who've now joined us.

'But not you.' His tone changes slightly as he turns his attention to Harry. 'We need you to show us where things are. Were there any other centre staff members involved in what's happened today?'

'There were two on the ground, Alice and Jake. Frances and Emma were up there.'

'Where might we find them all?'

'They've gone inside with the children.'

'Where were you when it happened?'

Harry glances up again. 'I reached the top just as she jumped from the edge.'

As we walk away from the rocks, it's difficult to put my finger on the emotions that are coursing through me. Once I was envious of the access Leonie had to Toby but now, all I feel is an overwhelming sorrow for her.

～

I'd have asked someone to help me.
But you'd cut me off from everyone who'd once mattered.

TWENTY-SEVEN

CATHERINE

I push my plate away. There's no way I can eat a thing. The sight of Leonie sprawled on those rocks is all I can think about.

It must be even worse for the children. They'll be haunted by what they've seen today.

My trembling hand reaches for the too-sweet tea, a feeble attempt to drown the lingering echoes of that scream.

'It'll help with the shock,' one of the kitchen staff had said in a matronly way as she'd placed it beside me – as though anything really could.

My gaze sweeps the dining room, capturing the silent grief mirrored in the children's eyes. The air hangs heavy, each child and adult grappling with the enormity of the tragedy.

Hardly anyone else is eating either. Children showing signs of shock have been checked over by the paramedics. I've been told which ones to keep the closest eye on. Many are still weeping. I'll be glad when we can start getting some of the parents here to take over with them. Right now, I feel out of my depth.

Another of the Year Five girls on my table pushes her plate away and drops her head into her hands. Amelia, who's sitting next to her, immediately reaches to comfort her. Reacting to this

sort of tragedy certainly hasn't been dealt with on any of the
training courses I've attended, both when I was starting out as a
teacher, or any time since. I'm at a complete loss as to what to do
or say – it's not as though there's anything I *can* do or say that
can help anyone to feel better.

'Poor Miss Johnson,' wails Jessica. Jeanette immediately
shifts her chair right beside her and draws her closer. Two of the
other girls on their table haven't stopped crying since we came
back in.

Yet I'm all too aware that this is the calm before the storm, a
prelude to decisions I must make – contacting Leonie's next of
kin, breaking the news to all the parents, then confronting questions from the governors and the media.

The governors. I glance back at Jeanette, who's still
comforting Jessica. Her phone's next to her plate. I push my
chair out with a scrape and head towards her.

'Have you been in touch with anyone?' I point to her phone.
'It's just that we need to contact Leonie's family before anyone
else is told.'

At the mention of her name, the girls on Jeanette's table
break into a fresh round of sobbing.

'Like who?' Jeanette's face flushes. That isn't a good sign.

'Like your *mother*.'

'What do you mean?'

'Please leave it for me to contact her, if you don't mind
Jeanette.'

'She's already on her way here.' At least she has the grace to
look sheepish about it.

'Absolutely marvellous.'

The way things are going, what's happened is going to be all
over the media before Leonie's family has even been told – I
can't let that happen.

Jeanette's voice trails after me. 'My mum's the chair of
governors. She had a right to know.'

I walk away, biting back the words that are threatening to escape me. This is not the time for confrontation.

Two more police officers catch my eye as they approach the door of the building with Kirsty and David in tow. Having quizzed Mia while we walked back here, at least I now know about Kirsty having fallen off the wagon again. However, I can't think about *that* yet – there'll be time to confront it later.

No doubt David's hanging around the police to be in on the action – to be seen to be helping the police with their enquiries whilst inflating his own sense of self-importance.

For someone who seems to have spent an inordinate amount of time in bed with Leonie, I'd expect him to be far more upset than he appears to be. The man's a heartless brute. It's not just because of what Kirsty's told me about him and the bruising I've often suspected him of causing to her. I've also seen and heard enough of what he's like for myself.

Toby, at the sight of his parents, jumps to his feet and rushes to the dining room door ahead of me.

'If Mr Naylor had done the zip wire first,' I hear one of his friends say as I pass them, 'it would have been *him* dead now.'

'Or any of them.'

'Boys.' I pause at their table. 'We'll have none of that please – it's not helpful at all.'

Toby flings himself at Kirsty the moment he steps into the foyer.

'Toby, get here now please.' David steps towards them and grips hold of his shoulder.

'Leave them be, for God's sake,' I mutter.

He turns and gives me a scowl that says it all.

'Are *you* alright?' I step towards Kirsty as Toby lets her go and allows himself to be steered to David's side.

She scowls at me too.

'Kirsty?'

I was intending to suggest that she went home when she'd slept her hangover off but there's no need for any of that now – we'll all be returning to Oldale soon enough.

She turns away. It must be to do with how drunk she was last night.

As soon as I know what procedures the police need to follow, I'll begin contacting parents to come to collect their children. That's the best thing for them now – to be back at home in their familiar surroundings after what's happened here. I glance over my shoulder. The kindly member of kitchen staff has her arm around two of them and many of them are still consoling one another.

'We need to speak to the headteacher,' one of the police officers says to no one in particular. I guess that in my jeans and trainers, I look less like a headteacher today than I normally do.

'That's me. Catherine Fox.' I step towards him.

'I'm DI Bradley Gilbert. I'm in charge of the investigation into what's happened, and this is my colleague Sergeant Chris Parkins.'

'Right. Well, you just tell us what you need, and we'll do whatever we can to help you.' I'm relieved to have someone else taking charge here.

'I'm sorry for what's happened to your colleague out there. It must be a very difficult time for you all.'

'Yes.' I glance back at the children again. 'We're just trying to keep it together for the children right now. We adults can fall apart later. Just bear with me one moment.' I turn to Kirsty. 'Do you want to take Toby back in with the others? I'll let you know what's happening as soon as I can.'

As Kirsty steps towards him without replying to me, David rests his hand on Toby's shoulder. 'He's staying with me.'

'Please Dad. I want to go with Mum.' Fresh tears fill his eyes.

'For God's sake David. This isn't the time to assert your so-called authority,' I hiss.

'Is there a problem here?' Sergeant Parkins frowns.

We all look at one another for a moment.

'I want to go with my mum,' Toby says again, staring straight at the sergeant.

'Off you go then.'

I silently dare David to pursue his argument. Thankfully, he lifts his hand from Toby's shoulder, glaring at me the whole time. We all watch as the two of them head through the door to join the others.

'At this stage, we'll be starting to piece together exactly what happened,' DI Gilbert continues, tilting his head in the direction of the rocks. 'So clearly, we'll need everyone's cooperation with that.'

'Like I said, we'll help in any way we can.'

I glance from the window where an intermittent blue flash in the distance, and the sight of white-suited figures on the rock, tells me their investigation into what happened is very much underway.

'Were you present throughout the entire incident Miss Fox?'

'Yes – I was watching from the ground with the children. It's been a terrible shock for them, as you might imagine. For us all.'

'How about you Mr Naylor?'

'I was on my way back from the toilet at the time but yes, I saw her fall.'

'The scene and the equipment involved are currently being examined so before too long, we should have a clearer idea about exactly what went wrong up there.'

'Tell me what you need from us.'

'While we're waiting for the preliminary findings, we need

to take statements from all the adults – the ones with your school and the adults based here at the centre.'

'Can that be done here?'

'Initially – yes,' he replies. 'Although just to let you know, we may need to instigate further *recorded* interviews at the station. It all depends on the outcome of our initial investigation.'

'I understand.'

'We'll also need to ask a few questions of each of the children,' his colleague adds.

'Is that really necessary?' I turn to face the dining room where the soft glow of sunlight filters through the closed curtains, casting a warm but sombre atmosphere over the children watching our interaction. 'To be questioning the children, I mean? Surely they're all going to say the same thing.'

'We'll keep it as brief as possible.' He follows my gaze. 'But even if we get a *shred* of something useful from talking to them, it'll be more than worth it.'

'I understand.' I nod. 'To begin with, though, I think we need to make sure that Leonie's family have been informed. I'd hate for the news of her death to reach them through the media.'

'I completely agree.'

'Where's the trip file David?' I turn to him. 'You've got all the next of kin details in there, haven't you?'

'I'll go and get it.' He turns away, seeming pleased to have been given a purpose instead of just hanging around.

'I'll come with you.' Sergeant Parkins strides after him.

DI Gilbert turns back to me. 'Would you like to break the news yourself, or—'

'I think it might come better from yourselves,' I say quickly. If I can pass on the responsibility of this awful task, I will.

'No problem. Our officers are trained in breaking news of this magnitude. Not that it ever gets any easier. I'll get a couple of them on to it right away.'

'Thank you.'

I've never been good at giving bad news, especially when face-to-face, which something like this will surely have to be. I have an anxious tic that causes me to almost smile when I'm delivering awful news – it's most inappropriate.

And I can't think of anything worse than having to let Leonie's parents know that their daughter's dead. She ought to have been as safeguarded as the children up there.

One thing's for certain – this place will be getting closed down faster than a takeaway with an infestation of rats, and God only knows what's going to happen to our school after this. I can't imagine after the further negative press it's about to receive that we'll be allowed to stay open for much longer either.

Nancy's impending arrival hangs in the air, a reminder that beyond the walls of this centre, the outside world is about to intrude on our bubble of shared grief.

∾

I thought us having a baby
would stop you from hurting me.

TWENTY-EIGHT

CATHERINE

'If you could just excuse me for a moment.' My phone buzzes inside my handbag. I know who it will be before I even look at the screen.

'Nancy,' I say. 'I'm aware you've heard what's happened.'

'Is that all you can say?' she shrieks. 'And why did I have to hear the news from my daughter instead of from *you*?'

'As I'm sure you can appreciate, we've got a lot on here at the moment.'

'Which is why I've driven over,' she replies. 'But the officers at the gate won't let me in.'

'Of course they won't. They're not letting *anyone* in or out yet.'

'So what am I supposed to do?'

'Please Nancy, just go back home for now. I'll let you know when the police have finished their investigations here at the centre.'

'Can I ask who you're speaking to?' DI Gilbert steps closer to me.

'Nancy Giles. She's our chair of governors.'

'Who's that?' Her voice rises again.

'It's the Detective Inspector Nancy. Look, I'll have to go. Just go home – there's nothing you can do that isn't already being done.'

I end the call before she can say anything else. What she thinks she can do here, I have no idea.

'How do you want to organise speaking to the children?' I ask.

'Well, given their age, they will all need an appropriate adult present.' DI Gilbert gestures towards them and I notice how pristine his white shirt is. It's strange, what details are noticed in a situation as grave as something like this.

'Should that be one of us, or do we need to call their parents in?'

'I think these children, given what they've been forced to witness today, need a parent with them as soon as possible.' DI Gilbert nods at the open door into the dining hall where they're all still watching us intently. I've never, ever known our children to be so quiet. 'We're just waiting for a couple more units to arrive and then we'll get on with it.'

David returns to the foyer with Sergeant Parkins, who's clutching the emergency contacts folder.

My heart breaks for Leonie's poor parents. She often mentioned them in the staff room and it was obvious they were close. Within the next half an hour, their whole world is going to be blown apart.

'I'll start ringing around the parents then,' I say. 'It will be good to do something useful, to be honest.'

'Don't give them *any* specific information over the telephone,' replies DI Gilbert. 'All they need to know at this stage is that there's been an incident and they need to collect their son or daughter as soon as possible.'

'An *incident*?' The word doesn't feel anywhere near appropriate.

'Just so they're assured of their own child's safety,' he says.

Sergeant Parkins looks up from his notepad, his heavy eyebrows knitted in concentration. 'It will also give our colleagues time to break the news to Leonie's family before the children's parents start arriving here.' Beads of sweat are breaking on his forehead in the glare of the sunshine which has moved around to the floor-length windows.

'We've got parents to two of the children already here – Kirsty, as you know, is Toby Naylor's mum and Jeanette, sitting by the window, is Jessica Smith's mum.'

My gaze catches Kirsty's but she looks away. Despite what's happened, I don't want her to feel any more ashamed about last night than she will already. No doubt David will milk her falling off the wagon to his full advantage, but as far as I'm concerned, it's just a monumental setback for her, but something she'll hopefully allow me to support her with.

By sitting with Toby whilst he answers their questions, Kirsty might start to feel better about herself.

'In that case, my colleagues will start with them. The adults will need to remain at the centre until we've taken all the statements, but we'll start releasing the children once we've spoken to them.'

'Can I tell them what's going on now?'

'Yes of course. I'll come in with you in case there are any questions.'

As I walk back into the dining room, the silent stares of the children fixate on me, their eyes reflecting a mix of confusion and sorrow. There's no need for me to do my three-clap signal to quieten them. What happened out there is going to take some serious getting through. We're going to have to organise a hefty programme of counselling to have any chance of helping them.

'Children,' I begin, hoping the correct thing to say will find me. 'Words cannot begin to describe the terrible tragedy that took place earlier today.'

'Poor Miss Johnson,' sobs a small voice.

'Not only are we all horrified by what's happened to Miss Johnson,' I continue. 'We teachers are also extremely upset that you all unfortunately had to see it.'

'What's going to happen to us now?'

'As you'll have noticed, the police are here to help us. They're going to find out exactly what caused Miss Johnson's accident and they're going to need your help.'

'Is she *really* dead?' one of the boys from my group asks.

'I'm afraid she is.' I lower my gaze to the floor. It doesn't feel appropriate to go on. They need another moment for the finality to sink in.

A single grief-stricken wail echoes from the table in the far corner. I nod towards Mia to go over and look after the girl. She hurries straight over, wiping at tears of her own.

Considering they were so friendly, Mia seems to be coping extremely well with Leonie's death, but it probably hasn't sunk in fully with her yet.

As for David, who I can see out of the corner of my eye, still talking to Sergeant Parkins, he's a colder fish than I ever gave him credit for.

Anxiety tightens its grip on my gut, and my fingers instinctively knot together. Slowly, the noise level rises.

'If you could just all listen to me for a little longer please children.'

They settle down again.

'We're shortly going to be calling your parents and carers to come and collect you,' I begin. 'But before you leave, some of the police officers need to ask each of you a few questions about what happened.'

'Can't we stay until tomorrow anymore?' one of the Year Six boys calls out.

'I'm afraid not,' I reply. 'The police have lots of investigating to do here.'

'Do we have to stay here now?'

'Yes – while you're waiting for your grown-ups to arrive, you must all wait in here.'

A buzz of conversation rises among the children again.

'There are some colouring pens and board games in the corner for them.' The woman who brought me the tea is now creeping around clearing the tables. She points at a trolley in the corner.

'Children, there are some things on that trolley to keep you busy.' I nod towards it. 'Thank you.' I try to smile at the woman.

'I don't want to do *anything*,' Amelia says. 'I just want Miss Johnson to be here again.'

'Me too,' another child echoes.

'We all wish that,' I say. 'Very, very much. But for now, all we can do is look after each other until we come to terms with this terrible shock.'

I turn to DI Gilbert. 'Do you need to add anything to what I said?'

'No – I think you covered it. If you could get on with those phone calls, I'll start getting everyone's statements along with my colleague.' He gestures to Sergeant Parkins. 'And hopefully, we'll hear from the investigative team shortly.'

I turn to the window into the foyer where Sergeant Parkins is handing a piece of paper to another two officers. Grim-faced, they exit the building and head to a police car at the end of the path. It's parked in the same spot as our coach was just over twenty-four hours ago. It feels like a very, very long time has passed since then.

DI Gilbert strides away, and David immediately approaches me. 'About last night—'

I glance around to make sure nobody's listening. 'Your behaviour was wholly inappropriate.'

'I'm aware of that now. Perhaps I was just—'

'I really don't want to discuss it. Especially at a time like this.'

'I wanted to apologise, that's all.' He looks at me with the earnest expression that seems to win so many others over. But it's fake. He's only apologising to remain in the running for the deputy headship.

'Let's just pretend it never happened, shall we? It's not as if anyone saw you coming into my room.'

He nods, then, pointing to the window at the retreating police car, he says, 'They've gone to break the news to Leonie's parents. Poor sods.'

'Who? The police, or her parents?' I stare at him. I've got to say something here. 'You seem remarkably unflustered by what's happened.'

'What's that supposed to mean?'

'I'm well aware that there was still something going on between you and Leonie – at least until recently.'

'We all have our ways of reacting to things.' He frowns. 'You've no idea what I'm thinking *or* feeling Catherine.' His eyes darken. 'So leave it out with the psychoanalysis, if you don't mind.'

I really can't put my finger on how nonchalant he is. Anyone would think we were in the aftermath of a fire drill, the way he's behaving.

Instead, we're stuck in the middle of a nightmare which is about as dramatic as it gets for a school trip. And this is probably only the start.

∽

***You told me I'd be a useless mother,
and you hoped the baby wouldn't take after me.***

TWENTY-NINE

MIA

I said I was going to the loo, but I'm lingering in the staff room like a lost soul, the uncertainty of what's to come tightening the knots in my stomach. No doubt all hell will break loose when the parents begin to arrive. Catherine's busy calling them so at least she won't realise that I've been hiding in here for the last twenty minutes.

I just want to leave this place. I want to be at home, however poky my flat is – just to be in comfort and familiarity, away from this environment that now feels so alien. I don't know how I'm ever going to face walking back into our classroom again. Leonie practically lived in it – she'd be there at half past seven every morning and would often stay until the caretaker threw her out at half past six in the evening.

Me, I saunter in at quarter to nine and I'm out as soon as possible when the bell goes at half past three, straight after I've seen the kids off.

Leonie probably only spent so many hours at the school to be around David. And look where that got her...

Speak of the devil. He's heading up the corridor, looking somewhat troubled for the first time since she died. It's always difficult to work out what could be going on in his head and that's the case more than ever today. *Since she died.* I can hardly believe I'm thinking these words. The realisation that she's gone, forever, feels like a lead weight pressing on my chest.

'What is it?' I say as he reaches me. His expression is a stark departure from the composed façade he usually has, and my heart races at the sight of it. Surely nothing else has happened?

'I should be Toby's appropriate adult while the police talk to him – not *her*. I'm the one with the custody order.'

'Is that it? I thought something else must have—'

'What do you mean, *is that it?*' I don't like the way he's looking at me. 'You've no idea about what goes on in the real world, have you Mia?'

'Why don't I make you a drink?' I move to take a mug from the cupboard. I can't take anyone having a go at me. Perhaps he won't take his bad mood out on me if I'm offering to make him a drink.

'No – no I don't want one.' He paces from one end of the room to the other, grabbing a fistful of his fringe as he comes to a stop at the water fountain in the corner.

The air's thick with tension, every sound echoing around the bare walls, making me want to run away. But I've started making myself a drink and I'll look like I'm scared of him if I leave now. Besides, I'm curious to see what's bothering him.

'Stupid bloody woman – it's all gone totally wrong.'

'Who?' Surely he doesn't mean *Leonie*.

'My ex-wife, that's who.'

'She's hardly to blame for what happened.' I drop a teabag into my mug.

'Haven't you heard? Trouble follows my ex-wife around like a bad smell.'

I glance at him. The Superman T-shirt he's still wearing is completely at odds with how everything's turned out here today.

'What do you mean?' I brush my fringe from my eyes. This would be a first – David Naylor confiding in *me*.

'I'm just so done in with it all.' He throws himself onto one of the sofas. 'It's one thing after another.'

'What's happened to Leonie out there is more than *a thing*, don't you think?'

'You'd only known her five minutes,' he retorts with an edge to his voice that's bordering on a sneer. 'Anyone could see you had some sort of obsession with her.'

'*What?*'

'You should have heard what she used to say about *you*.'

I want to clamp my hands over my ears, having heard more than enough yesterday. I don't want to know what else she might have said – I only want to remember her sitting opposite me last night, drinking gin in a tin with me. I want to remember our in-jokes when we worked together in the classroom. And all the times when I enjoyed watching her from one of the group tables as she led a lesson at the front.

'Just leave it, will you?'

'You totally got on her nerves, do you know that?' He steps closer to me. 'Following her about, copying her, asking your nosy questions all the time.'

'Just leave me alone, will you?' A sob catches in my throat.

He stares at me. 'You couldn't stand me and her seeing each other, could you?'

Then suddenly feeling braver, I say, 'She saw sense in the end though, didn't she?' I stare back at him. 'You and Catherine deserve each other.'

'Me and *Catherine*?' A strange look crosses his face. Then it morphs into something else.

'I saw you last night. We all did.'

'So what?' He shrugs. 'There's no law against it.'

'You really are an arsehole aren't you?' An utter dislike for him washes over me. Suddenly I'm seeing him like I never really have before. 'You walk around that school like you own the place,' I continue. 'I can't believe I used to think you were alright. But now, all I see is a nasty, chauvinistic, rotten-to-the-core piece of shit.'

I can't believe I've just said what I've said. I certainly didn't plan to. But now as I watch his face, I can tell I've gone too far.

'What did you say?' He stiffens and for a moment, I fear he's going to fly at me. If he does, I'll just yell for help; it's not as though the police are very far away.

'And if you think I'm going to keep quiet about you black-mailing me to go along with that draw, you've got another thing coming.'

He lurches across the room and grabs the scruff of my T-shirt. '*You* of all people don't get to talk to me like that.'

'What Leonie said about you last night was spot on.'

'Why, what did she say?' My neckline tightens as he pulls it harder.

'Let me go,' I yell out as loudly as I can. I just hope someone hears me.

He puts his hand across my mouth, so tightly I can smell the sweat on his fingers. There's nothing else I can do other than sink my teeth into his fingers.

'You *vicious* little bitch.'

'Get away from me,' I shriek as he releases his grip on my face.

'Get away from her *right now*.' David jumps at the voice and twists around to see where it's coming from. We both look at the two police officers standing in the doorway with Kirsty and I can honestly say that I've never felt more relieved in my life.

'What the hell's going on in here?'

'Nothing. Alright? Emotions are just running high, that's all.' David thrusts his hands into his pockets and heads towards the doorway. 'Can I get past please?'

'You most certainly can't. Not until we find out what's been going on here.' The police officer's stern voice reverberates through the staff room.

'It's nothing to do with what's happened to Leonie if that's what you're getting at,' he retorts. 'It was just a private disagreement between myself and Mia.'

'Take a seat Mr Naylor.' DI Gilbert's voice has an edge to it. 'We'll speak to you next.'

'Then we'll talk to *you* Mia – in a few minutes,' says Sergeant Parkins.

'Why? I've already spoken to you.'

'We'd like to find out more about what's just happened.'

'Are you alright Mia?' Kirsty grabs my arm as the door closes behind us.

'I'm fine, I think.'

It's a complete lie. I'm shaking from head to foot, the adrenaline coursing through me like an electric shock. But it's the knowledge that Leonie has bad-mouthed me to David at other times that has upset me as much as him grabbing me.

'What was it all about?'

'He told me things Leonie's supposed to have said about me. Nasty things. I guess I just flipped and told him what I thought of him. So he completely lost it with me.'

'You need to report him. No matter what you were saying to each other, no one's got the right to attack you like that.'

'I know.'

I should probably report him to Catherine but perhaps, in the circumstances, she won't even do anything. And do I really want to stir even more chaos today?

'Make sure you tell the police you want to press charges for assault when you go back in there.'

'I'll think about it.'

'Never mind *you'll think about it.* That's what I had to live with month in, month out.' Kirsty points back to the staff room door. 'Only Catherine knew how bad things were for me at home and look what *she's* gone and done with him.'

'I take it Leonie told you?' Kirsty's voice dips.

I nod. 'I can hardly believe it.'

~

*Some women bloom when they're pregnant.
I withered into nothingness.*

THIRTY

MIA

'I'll come back in there in a few minutes,' I tell Kirsty. 'I'm just going to wash my face.'

'Will you be alright?'

'I'll be fine.'

I lean against the wall in the corridor, as she disappears back into the dining room while lifting my eyes to the freshly painted ceiling.

My face is still smarting from where he squeezed it. Thank God the police and Kirsty turned up when they did. What worries me now, if he's grabbed me like that *here*, he might try to do something similar again – like when we're back at school. And perhaps there'll be nobody on hand to help me next time.

'Where's Naylor?' Harry appears at the side of me.

As if I haven't heard enough of that name for one day. 'David or Kirsty?' I swing around to face him, still rubbing at my jaw.

'*Him*. Where is he?'

'Talking to the police.' I jerk my head in the direction of the staff room. 'Why are you calling him *that* anyway? I thought you were his friend?'

'He's no *friend* of mine,' he says as he storms away, leaving me staring after him.

I can't bear to join the others just yet. I need to get myself back together first. Slipping into the staff toilets, I press against the sink, releasing a heavy breath. Exhaustion weighs me down. I need to get out of this suffocating place and go home.

'Yeah, she's still here. What happened has probably sobered her up a bit.' Jeanette's voice resonates from within one of the cubicles.

I hold my breath. I probably shouldn't be listening but I can't help myself.

'How should I know who she was drinking with? Who's to say she was drinking with someone else anyway? She might have been on her own.'

'I know.'

'Well, you were there when our names were drawn. It was all fair and square.'

In the silence of the room, I can hear Nancy's voice though I can only pick out snippets of what she's saying. *Leonie – How I'd cope – Her poor parents.* I lean closer to the cubicle door.

'I know Mum but it *wasn't* me, was it? To be honest, we're all still in shock.' Her words bounce around the tiled walls.

'I hope you're staying well away from David Naylor today.'

I catch that line loud and clear.

'I erm, well, yes of-of course I am.'

'Because if I hear any more—'

'Look Mum, I really should be getting back to Jessica.'

'OK. But you haven't heard the last of this from me, do you understand?'

'Mum I've really got to go. I'm in the toilet, for goodness' sake.'

'How she's doing? Jessica, I mean.'

'Catherine's sitting with her. She's taken it really badly.'

'You get back to her then.'

I'd better get myself out of here. I don't want her to know I've been eavesdropping. As she flushes the toilet, I dart to the exit. Then the cubicle door bangs. I wasn't quick enough.

Jeanette startles upon seeing me. 'How long have you been standing there?'

'Oh erm, just a minute. I couldn't face going back in there just yet.'

'My mum rang while I was in the loo.' She looks sheepish as she runs water over her hands.

'So I gathered.'

'How are you doing?' She looks at me through the mirror as she rubs her hands together.

'It's been one of the worst days of my life.'

'I could tell you were good friends.' She shakes her hands over the sink.

I let go of the door handle and drop my arms to my sides. It's the friendliest Jeanette's ever been towards me and I need someone to be nice to me at the moment.

'I'm really struggling, to be honest.' Tears fill my eyes, regrettably not for the first time today. 'And to make things even worse, I've just had David set about me in the staff room.'

'David did?' A strange look enters her eyes as if she doesn't believe me.

'Kirsty and the police came in and stopped him. If it wasn't for them...' My voice fades away.

'What do you mean, *set about you*?' She shakes her mane of dark hair down her back as her eyes move to herself in the mirror.

'I said something he didn't like.' I brush a tear away. 'So he grabbed me around the face.'

'He did *what*?' She dries her hands on the edge of the towel and leans against the sink. 'What on earth did you say to him?'

'Does it really matter? The man's nothing but a controlling bully.'

She looks back at me as though deliberating what she's going to say next.

'What is it?'

'Nothing.' She opens her handbag and begins rummaging in it. Surely she's not looking to apply lipstick, or something. Surely she's not *that* shallow.

'Go on. There's something up, I can tell. Is it about *David?*'

'I'm not saying.'

'Leonie told me about the two of you. Is it true?'

Jeanette's silence says it all.

'But me, you and Kirsty were outside together. David was in *Catherine's* room.

She looks down at the floor.

'You have, haven't you? That means he's slept with *two* women in the same night! Ugh!'

'He assured me that nothing happened with Catherine.'

'That's *not* what he just told me.'

Her face falls even more. 'What exactly *did* he tell you?'

'When I accused him of having slept with Catherine, he replied, "There's no law against it, is there?" You know, with the nasty smug expression he has.'

Jeanette's hand flies to her throat which she massages as though trying to comfort herself.

'Are you OK?'

She closes her eyes. 'I guess so.'

'You slept with him, I take it?'

She nods. 'I know. I've been a complete idiot. I fall for his patter every time.'

'How long have the two of you—'

'It's been on and off for ages,' she cuts in. 'Ever since my eldest daughter was in his class. Why do you think Leonie hated me so much?'

'What about your husband?'

'Just – don't. I don't know *what* I'm going to do. Especially now my mother's found out. She thinks he's disgusting.'

'Well she's right. If you think you're going to get a happy-ever-after with David Naylor, you're going to be in for a shock. Even Leonie had seen the light.'

'He told me *he'd* ended it all between them.'

'It sounds like he's told you everything you might have wanted to hear so he could get into your—'

'Alright,' she snaps. 'I've been stupid. *Stupid. Stupid. Stupid.*' She kicks the bottom of the sink.

'At least you're still here.' I slide down against the door. 'Think about poor Leonie.'

'I can't,' she replies. 'I can't get my head around it all.'

'I wonder if her family have been told yet,' I say. 'The poor sods.'

'They must have been. My mum said it's been on the news.' Jeanette reaches into her pocket and taps a few buttons on her phone.

I watch her as she reads – the dusting of freckles covering her nose, the perfectly curled eyelashes. What was she *thinking* of – with David? She *knew* there was something between him and Leonie. She'd also *seen* him go into Catherine's room. Then there was the presence of his ex-wife to throw into the mix as well as Jeanette being married herself. What an idiot.

She thrusts it at me. 'Here, have a read.'

Teacher in Adventure Trip Tragedy Zip Wire Plunge

What should have been an exhilarating three-day trip for thirty-six primary school pupils today turned to tragedy after a thirty-one-year-old teacher plunged to her death from a hundred and fifty feet.

Horrified children from Oldale Primary School in North Yorkshire watched as the safety harness worn by Year Five teacher Leonie Johnson suddenly malfunctioned, sending her hurtling to the rocks below.

Investigations are underway at the recently refurbished and reopened Ilkstone Crag from which staff declined to comment when our reporter made contact with them.

Miss Johnson's family have been informed and enquiries into her death are ongoing. We will bring you more on this story as it comes in.

'Come on, we'd better go back.' I pass the phone back to her. I don't really know what else I can say to her.

~

You'd tell me how ugly I looked –
that it was no wonder
you were sleeping with other women.

THE INVESTIGATION

DI GILBERT

'Do you want to tell me what made you grab Mia Hudson around her face?'

David shuffles in his seat. 'She'd made some crass comment about Leonie. She could probably tell how gutted I am, and yet she just couldn't leave it alone. I'd go as far as saying she was trying to goad me.'

'What exactly did she say to you?'

'That Leonie was better off dead than being with *me*.' He points to himself. The corner of his eye twitches as he replies. I've interviewed enough people in my time to be able to tell when someone's making things up.

'Clearly, we'll be speaking to Mia about what just happened.'

'And she may well decide to press charges,' Chris adds in a harsher tone than the one I've managed to adopt.

'Would your altercation have had anything to do with the draw that was carried out?'

'What draw?' His expression is one of the most nonchalant I've ever seen. But he's not fooling me.

'The one where both Kirsty *and* Jeanette *won* their places on this trip. The one you paid Mia Hudson to assist you with.'

'I did no such thing.'

'It would be in your interests to admit if you did *now*.'

'How's this even relevant to what happened to Leonie?'

'I'm not saying it is. But if you're not telling the truth here, it will be easy enough to check transactions on bank statements.'

'I'm not saying anything else about that without a solicitor present.'

The guy's got guilt written all over him. I make a mental note to ask Mia to log into her bank as one of my next jobs. Then we'll take it from there.

'Tell us about your relationship with Leonie,' I say.

'Leonie wanted far more than I did.' He relaxes into his seat, probably relieved for the emphasis to be taken away from Mia Hudson. 'So while what we had was fun, it became necessary to put a stop to things once and for all. It was only last year that my marriage broke up, and I wanted my focus to remain on my son.'

'When did you call things off with her?'

'Yesterday.'

'I see. Was there any reason you waited until you were away like this on your school trip rather than breaking it to her before or afterwards?'

'Not really. It's just – she was piling the pressure on.'

'In what way?'

'For us to sneak off together or get together in the middle of the night, that sort of thing.' He rakes his fingers through his hair. 'But I'd already made my mind up that I wanted to cool things.'

'And how did she take your decision?'

He looks straight into my eyes. 'Not very well, if I'm honest.'

'Forgive me for making this observation David but you don't seem as upset by her death as I'd expect you to be – given that you *were* in any sort of a relationship.'

I'm not keen on this man at all. His smooth talk might work wonders on the ladies, but I'm impervious to his charms. The disdain mirrored on Chris's face reveals he shares my sentiments.

'Of course I'm upset.' He shifts his gaze from me to Chris. 'I just don't go around weeping and wailing like some people might.'

'Might that be because you've already moved on to someone else?'

'What do you mean by that?'

'You tell us?'

'What have people been saying?'

'If you could just answer the question please David. Are you less upset about Leonie Johnson's death because you've already moved on to someone else?'

'I take it she's told you then?' He shakes his head.

'Who?'

'Jeanette.' He presses his lips together.

'Actually, I meant Catherine Fox. Since you were seen entering her room last night – and *not* leaving it.'

Blimey, he's quite the philanderer, this man. He might look the part with his floppy fringe and his muscles in all the right places but beauty, in this case, is definitely only skin deep. And we haven't even got started on the things we've heard about how he treated his ex-wife.

'Nothing happened with Catherine Fox.' There's a trace of a smirk on his face. I exchange glances again with Chris.

'OK. We'll park that for a moment. Let's move on to the risk assessment procedures for this trip. I gather you were in charge of them?'

'Yes. Leonie oversaw the process with me. Though the safety of the actual ride is the centre's responsibility, as I'm sure you'll appreciate.'

'So as far as you were concerned, David, the risk assessment procedures were robust, and every detail had been meticulously followed?'

'Of course.'

'Who was your contact here when you were setting up the trip?'

'Harry Douglas. He invited us to be the first primary school to try the centre out.'

'He volunteers here, so I'm told.'

'That's correct.' There's an arrogance in his voice that gets right under my skin. After what I walked in on before though, there's little he could do to worm into my favour anyway.

'Why would he invite *your* school when there are other primary schools that are much closer?'

'We used to know each other.'

'Used to?'

'I dated his sister, many moons ago.'

'I see. So you and he have kept in touch?'

'Not exactly – but he must have looked me up or kept tabs on me over the years. We were supposed to catch up over a beer last night but it didn't happen.'

'How do you mean?'

'He'd invited me out for a drink, for old times' sake.'

'But you didn't go – is that what you're saying?'

'Catherine intercepted me on my way out so no, we didn't end up being able to go.'

'Is that what led you to end up in her room?'

He opens his mouth to respond, but we're interrupted by a knock at the door and a man poking his head into the room. 'I'm sorry to interrupt—'

'This is our colleague, DI Rhodes,' I explain to David.

'I need to speak to both of you outside,' he continues. '*Straightaway* please.'

THIRTY-ONE

KIRSTY

'Can I come to your house if Dad doesn't come back?' Toby puts his pen down and looks up as the door squeaks. From the expression on his face, he's definitely hoping he *won't* come back. I follow his gaze, half expecting to see David, but instead, it's Catherine, returning after seeing the last of the parents out.

'We'll see sweetheart.' I squeeze his arm. I wish more than anything in the world that I was taking him home with me.

Dusk will fall in a couple of hours and the sun will set on the final day of Leonie's life. The image of her lifeless body sprawled on those rocks spins back into my mind. I wonder if she's still lying out there or whether they've moved her somewhere else. Or what's left of her, given the state she was in.

'Just hang on a minute.' I rise to my feet. It's a good opportunity to finally confront Catherine with what I saw last night while she's on her own. 'You carry on with your picture – I won't be long.'

My head throbs with each step I take towards Catherine. It's as if tiny hammers are relentless in their assault on me. This hangover is the worst I've ever had and I'm still struggling to recall how I ever got into this state. That's the worst thing about it. It's not as though I knowingly got drunk – but the more I try to recall the exact order of last night's events, the more they blur into a disorienting haze.

I recall bumping into Harry by the lake, but the details remain elusive, like fragments of a fractured mirror that I'm struggling to piece together. The most important bits came back to me soon enough – while the rest of it remains a blur.

'Can we talk Catherine?' My head pounds harder still as I nod towards the far corner of the room – hopefully well away from prying eyes and curious ears.

As we reach the corner, I spin around to face her, the movement making my head swoon even more. 'Why was my ex-husband in your bedroom last night?' For a moment, she seems to be searching for the right words. Guilt, perhaps? 'Don't even try to deny it. I saw you both with my own eyes.'

'We were *talking*, that's all.' She leans against a cupboard and looks straight at me. She looks exhausted.

'*Talking?* In your bedroom?'

'*Nothing* happened Kirsty.' She closes her eyes for a moment. '*As if it ever would.*'

I glance around to make sure no one's listening. Jeanette and Mia are watching us. No doubt they'll be grilling me about this. 'Why can't you just be honest with me Catherine? I've heard enough lies to last me a lifetime.'

'I *am* being honest with you,' she hisses back at me. 'He was in my room for all of five minutes. If you must know, I threw him out when he overstepped the mark.'

'What do you mean?'

'Oh, you know what he's like. Yes, he started making lewd remarks. When I tried to throw him out, he became nasty.'

'When I checked around the back of the building, your curtains couldn't have been more tightly closed.'

'They were already closed before I let him in. Come on Kirsty – how long have you known me? We're friends, aren't we?'

'Why the hell would you allow someone like *him* into your *bedroom* of all places, if nothing's going on?'

'He said he wanted a private word – there *was* nowhere private so yes, I made a very poor error of judgement.' She clasps her hands together and lets out a long breath. Catherine's voice is shaking but her eyes don't leave mine.

The fluorescent lighting in here is making my head pound even harder.

'Surely you wouldn't believe him over me if that's what this is going to boil down to?'

'I don't want to but it's not as if either of you can prove anything. If he was to say something happened while you say it didn't, it just ends up being your word against his.'

'Why the *hell* did I allow him into my room?' Catherine shakes her head. 'Even for one minute was too long. It certainly hasn't been one of my better decisions.'

'Too right. If what you're saying is true, he could bring you down with this. Mia and Jeanette saw him going in there too, you know. And no one saw him leaving again.'

'*Mia and Jeanette?*' She glances over at them. 'Neither of them have said anything to me. Anyway, it's what *you* think that I'm more bothered about. I wouldn't touch David if he was the last man on earth. I know better than anyone what sort of misogynistic arsehole he is.'

It's not a word Catherine would use lightly so I'm more inclined to believe her – which is a huge relief. I want to believe her – of course I do.

'Is this why you got so drunk last night?' She rests her hand on my arm. 'Because you got the wrong end of the stick?'

'The truth is, I'm not even sure what happened last night.' I look down at my feet. 'I bumped into Harry by the lake and he said something about David letting him down. I remember that he seemed agitated. But after that, it's a complete blur.'

'So you were drinking with *Harry*?'

'I only said I bumped into him.' I scrunch my eyes together. 'I'm trying to think.'

'And then what?'

'I *think* I remember being in his room.'

'In the staff quarters? You shouldn't have been in there any more than I should have agreed to talk to David in *my* room.'

'Probably not.'

'Did *he* give you all the drink?' She thrusts her hands into the pockets of her jeans.

'Just a Coke, as far as...'

My words fade away as two officers I was speaking with earlier, along with a third, *and* David appear in the doorway of the dining room.

'DI Rhodes would like to speak to you all in the foyer,' Sergeant Parkins announces. 'Would you mind bringing the other two staff members out here for us please?'

'Of course.' Catherine looks worried as she beckons towards Jeanette and Mia. 'Toby and Jessica,' she calls across the room, 'can you keep each other company for a few minutes while we have a quick word with the police?'

They nod and move closer to each other. Now it's just them left, they've been allowed to turn their phones on so they're busy playing some game against each other. He's such a lovely lad, my Toby. Being here with him has brought home even more just how much I'm missing out on.

The four of us follow each other to the door and convene in the foyer opposite the officers. Their faces suggest that whatever they're about to say could change things here.

'What is it?' Catherine asks.

'Our initial examination of the scene has now been conclud-ed,' the detective inspector begins, his voice sharp and his eyes marble-hard. He looks around us all. 'And our investigation into Leonie Johnson's death has considerably shifted.'

Considerably shifted. What's that supposed to mean? I don't like the tone of his voice one bit. He also said *the scene*, rather than *the scene of the accident.*

'Our colleagues...' Clasping his hands across his portly stom-ach, he rolls his thumbs around and around each other. '...have reported their findings concerning the safety harness which should have secured Leonie to the main wire.'

'And?' Even David looks worried for a change. It's the expressions on their faces. This isn't going to be good.

'It would appear that her harness was tampered with.'

An audible exclamation of shock ripples through everyone.

'It can't have been,' David begins before he's drowned out.

'Therefore this investigation has become a murder inquiry.' DI Gilbert's tone is even sterner than his colleague's. 'We will shortly be escorting everybody to Yorkshire police station to conduct formal recorded interviews under caution.'

'Tampered with? But how?'

'How can you tell?' David asks. 'Surely it could have just snapped? How would you know the difference?'

'It *has* been tampered with,' DI Rhodes says again. 'There is evidence of cutting. The centre's CCTV as well as some fibre samples are currently being more closely analysed so we'll have more conclusive results at the station shortly.' His words hang in the air. 'I really can't say any more than that for now.'

We all look around at one another, the weight of the phrase 'murder inquiry' casting a shadow over the room.

No one says the words we're possibly all thinking. *One of us is a murderer.*

∾

When I made threats to end it all,
you laughed.
You even told me that no one would even miss me.

THIRTY-TWO

KIRSTY

For several moments, a stunned shock continues to hang over the foyer. The expressions of the officers seem to suggest they are thinking along similar lines – any one of us could be involved. After all, every single one of us in this room could be said to have a motive.

Finally, Mia breaks the silence. 'I just can't believe this. I'm sorry but I need to get some air. I need to—' Tears are running down her face but DI Gilbert steps in front of her to prevent her from getting to the door.

'I'm sorry but you must wait here.'

'I was her friend you know. I hope nobody thinks it could ever be—'

'Just shut up Mia.' David looks at her with the look of disdain we all know so well.

'Nobody is to leave this building until more officers arrive,' DI Rhodes says. 'Then we'll begin your transfer to the station.'

'But what about those of us with children here?' I glance around to look at Jeanette, seeking solidarity from her.

'Toby is *not* your concern,' David hisses.

'Mum, can I go to the toilet?' Right on cue, he emerges from the dining room. I can't help but feel smug that it's *me* he's asking, rather than David.

'*I'll* take him.' He lunges towards us and grabs hold of Toby's hand.

'But I want Mum to take me.'

I look from Catherine to DI Gilbert, willing them to override the situation.

'Be quick,' DI Gilbert says, shifting his gaze from Toby to me. '*You* can go with him.' He nods towards me. 'And then meet us straight back here.'

I loiter for a moment, just in case he has anything else to tell us about what they think could have happened with Leonie. However, he probably won't say anything further in front of Toby.

'I'm desperate Mum.' Toby hops from foot to foot. *Typical.*

'Come on then.' I'm sure I'll find out more about what's going on soon enough.

'You're not coming *into* the toilets with me are you?' he says as we get to the door of the cloakroom. 'I'm old enough to go on my own.'

'I know you are.' I force a smile. 'I'll wait just here for you.'

He disappears through the cloakroom and into the toilets. I close my eyes and roll my head from side to side against the chill of the metal doorframe trying to relieve the constant thrum of pain inside. I've managed sobriety for nearly twelve months, yet right now, twelve hours since I had my last drink, it's as though I'm back at the foot of the mountain I thought I'd climbed. I can't believe what I've done to myself.

'Is it true what I've just bloody heard?'

I open my eyes to see Harry, his fists clenched at his sides and what looks like a storm brewing in his eyes.

'What?'

'That we've *all* got to go to the station?'

'Surely you wouldn't expect *not* to have to go after what they've just said to us.'

'It's *Naylor* they should be pinning all this on. He's got away with *everything* he's ever done.'

I jump as he barges past me. 'Hey – you'll have to wait,' I call after him. 'Toby's in there.'

'If I want to use the toilet, I hardly need *your* permission,' he snaps back without even looking at me.

Given the mood Harry's in, I'd better send David in after all. I'm not having Toby left on his own in there with him.

Or am I overreacting here? After all, Harry will have been thoroughly vetted to work with children. Glancing back at the door into the cloakroom, I hesitate for a moment. But an instinct deep in my gut is prodding at me. Yes – I *should* send David in there.

He's talking to Sergeant Parkins as I rush up behind them.

'David?' They both swing around. I hate even saying his name and I hate even more having to ask for *his* help like this but I can hardly go into the toilets myself. Harry, standing at a urinal, is a sight I can do without.

'Can't you see I'm talking?' David looks as irritated as he always does when he's forced to deal with me.

'It's just...'

Catherine's eyes flit along the corridor. 'Is Toby still in the toilet?'

'Yes, that's what I wanted *him* for. Harry's just gone in after him and he seemed in a strange mood. I could hardly stop him – nor was I going in after him. But shouldn't he be using the staff toilets, not the boys'?'

'I wouldn't *expect* you to go after him.' Catherine starts towards the door then pauses and gestures towards David without looking him in the eye. 'Actually, can *you* take a look in there?' Her tone towards him is every bit as icy as I'd expect it to be after what she's told me. I *do* believe her now.

'Is there a problem?' DI Gilbert raises an eyebrow.

'Our school policy doesn't allow *unaccompanied* children to be in toilets when they're not on our school premises. Not with someone who's not been checked by *us*.'

'I see.'

I sink onto a chair, expecting to hear raised voices echoing from the toilets at any moment. But all I hear are Harry's words bouncing around inside my head.

They should be pinning this on Naylor.

An image of Harry's face as he handed me the glass of Coke last night pushes into my mind.

David emerges from the cloakroom, panic etched across his face. 'There's no one in there.'

Dread clings to me as I rise from the chair and rush towards him. 'I watched them both go in.'

Catherine appears behind me. 'They *must* be in there. They definitely haven't come back out yet.'

A chill creeps over me as I recall the clench of Harry's jaw and the snarl in his voice.

'They can't have just disappeared.' Catherine pushes past David into the cloakroom.

'You bloody idiot!' David rounds on me with a sneer. 'You should *never* have left him.' His words hit me hard, stirring the familiar self-blame that he's always managed to provoke in me.

'Are you just going to stand there, all of you, or are you going to get after them?' David bellows. The two officers that were standing at the door have joined the others in the foyer and David's actually right for once. None of them seem to be doing a thing.

'What's happening?' Jessica creeps from the dining room and heads to Jeanette's side. 'Where's Toby?'

'He'll be back in a minute,' I reply, desperate to believe that's the truth.

'Come on, let's get you back in there.' Jeanette ushers her away.

'Sierra Oscar Four One Seven One.' DI Gilbert lifts his radio from his lapel to his chin. 'Request further units to attend at Ilkstone Crag. We need a traffic patrol for a ten-mile radius.'

'Does Harry Douglas drive?' He looks at me as though I'm supposed to know.

'I haven't a clue,' I reply. My voice is strangled – I've got an awful, awful sense of foreboding about all this. As if I didn't feel sick enough before.

'We have a white male, aged approximately thirty-five years old and...' He looks at David now.

'His name's Toby,' he yells sending spittle in all directions. 'Toby Naylor. He was only going to the toilets. *You* should have been bloody watching him.' He spins around and jabs his finger in my direction.

Mia flies to my side. 'Maybe *you* should have been watching him.' She looks straight at David. 'He's your son as well.'

As David steps towards her, I lunge between them. I'm not going to allow him to have another pop at her. I might be used to being grabbed and shoved around but she shouldn't have to be.

'How old is he?' DI Gilbert asks.

'He's eleven.' It's like time has slowed and I almost feel as though I'm shutting down. One minute my son was heading into the toilet and the next, he's vanished into thin air.

'We're looking for a Toby Naylor, an eleven-year-old pupil at Oldale Primary School, last seen going into the boys' toilets at Ilkstone Crag.'

'Is he *definitely* with Harry?'

'He-he must be,' Mia says. 'Unless he's hiding somewhere.'

'He wouldn't do that.' David glares at her.

A voice comes back over the radio. 'How long have they been missing?'

DI Gilbert looks at me.

'I don't know.' I glance at my watch, taking deep breaths to try and stay calm. 'For just a few minutes.'

'If anything happens to him because of *you*...'

'I know how stressed you must be.' Sergeant Parkins puts a hand on David's arm. 'But taking it all out on your wife—'

'Ex-wife,' he snaps.

'Why would he take him?' Tears are rolling down Mia's face. 'There's no reason for it, is there?'

I can't just stand here like this – I need to be doing something. 'I'm going to check his bed, just in case.' I head towards the door leading to the boys' dorm. Perhaps in my hungover state, I've somehow allowed him to get past me.

But there's no sign. The space so full of bustling activity just hours ago is now eerily deserted.

I'm sorry for them all that their trip has turned into such a nightmare and desperately sorry for what's happened to Leonie, but right now, I just need to find Toby. His bag's on his bed and Fred Bear, who he's had since he was a baby, is tucked up against his pillow. I choke on a sob at the sight of it.

'Where's his jacket?' I swing around to where Catherine's followed me in.

'It could be in the cloakroom.' She rushes off and I head after her. If Harry had something terrible in mind, he wouldn't have gone to the trouble of making sure Toby was wearing his jacket – he'd have just taken off with him. Or was he already wearing it? I can't think straight.

'It's not there.' Catherine comes back shaking her head.

'I'll take a look around the outside of the building.' Sergeant Parkins heads towards the door. I wish I'd thought of doing that myself.

'Can I get a description of Toby's jacket please?' DI Gilbert looks at me.

I'm horrified to realise that I can't describe it. I didn't even buy it for him – David ensured I was stripped of that right. He's ensured I'm stripped of *every* right.

'It's royal blue with a white stripe around it.' David looks almost smug as he glances at me. Our bloody son has been taken and all he can think about is getting one up on me. I can't believe I once felt *any* love towards this man.

'And a description of Toby as well please?'

'He's about this high.' I put the edge of my hand against my chest. 'He's got spiky strawberry-blonde hair and blue eyes.' Tears fill my own eyes. I can't really imagine Harry would hurt him, but then I couldn't have imagined that he'd be capable of taking him in the first place. That's if he has – we still don't know for sure.

'What was he wearing?'

This, I can also answer.

'Blue jeans, a red and black T-shirt and white Nike train-ers.' Sadness claws at my chest again at the realisation that these are more clothes that *David* has bought. Even when I do buy things for him, David never lets him wear them.

'If we could now have a description of the adult who's believed to have taken him please.'

I listen peripherally as David describes Harry, and then DI Gilbert relays this to his control room. Sergeant Parkins returns from the courtyard.

'There's no sign of them.'

My chest tightens to the point where I feel winded. Not only has an innocent woman died here today, but my son is also at risk. I can't believe this is happening.

'You stupid, *stupid* bitch.' David marches towards me and for a moment, I think he's about to go for me in front of all these people. 'Because of *you*, Harry bloody Douglas has taken my son.'

'*You* can stop that right now.' Sergeant Parkins stretches his arm out to guide him away from me.

～

I didn't want to get out of bed.
I didn't want to live.
I was in the darkest place a human could be.

THIRTY-THREE

CATHERINE

'Have you got a recent photograph of Toby?' DI Gilbert asks. Kirsty and David reach for their phones at the same time but David beats her to it.

'Hang on.' His face darkens as he presses his phone screen. 'I've had a message from Douglas. Fifteen minutes ago.'

'What does it say?' DI Gilbert cranes his neck towards it, as does DI Rhodes.

It's your turn to know how it feels to lose someone you love.

David's face twists into an expression that's a cross between terror and fury.

The hand of fear around my chest tightens its grip. I've got a good idea of what he could be meaning.

'Let me get through. I mean it,' David hollers at the officer who has returned to guarding the door. 'You can't stop me from getting out there to find my son. You lot aren't exactly doing a very good job of it, are you?'

'You've been asked to wait in here.' The officer presses a

hand against his shoulder to move him back. 'My colleagues are *everywhere* out there, searching for them.'

'David, just listen to him,' I tell him.

'If you don't move out of my way...' David dodges around the officer's arm as though it doesn't exist. 'I won't be responsible for my actions. Have you got that?'

'You're not helping matters Mr Naylor.' We all turn to where DI Gilbert and Sergeant Parkins dart in front of him with another two officers behind them, looking as though they're ready to intervene.

'Keeping us like prisoners in here isn't going to bring Leonie back, is it?' He shrugs off the two pairs of hands which have landed on his shoulders. 'Whereas my son still has a chance. So *get out there* and find him, will you?' He backs away from the officers but at least he's stepping further back into the foyer.

'Calm down David.' Jeanette reaches out for his arm but he shakes her hand away as though a wasp has just landed on it.

'Get off me.'

'Why don't you give it a rest David.' Kirsty paces the floor. 'Toby's out there, God knows where and you're acting like an absolute idiot again.' She finally settles against the door into the dining room.

'Come and sit down Kirsty.' DI Gilbert ushers her into the room, away from the others and I follow them in. He's doing the right thing by forcing some distance between her and David.

'What *are* you going to do to find him?' she asks. She seems to be handling this pretty admirably, considering. It's probably not sunk in with her properly yet. But at least she's not yelling her head off at the police like David is.

'We're beginning with a thorough search of the site and the immediate area around it. If that proves futile, we'll keep widening the search until we find them.' DI Gilbert's tone is filled with confidence. At least he's saying *until* we find them.

'What can I do to help? I can't just sit in *here*.' Kirsty

gestures around the hall. 'I'd like to get out there with you too, if that's OK?'

He shakes his head. 'I'm sorry. Even if there *wasn't* the matter of us needing to interview you all at the station, you'd be better waiting right here,' DI Gilbert replies. 'While we're out there looking, there's every chance Harry could decide to bring Toby back. I'm sure his mum will be the first person he'll want to see.'

She brushes a tear away. I want to tell her that it's alright to cry. In fact, given the circumstances, I'm surprised she's not in floods. But then, she's always bottled it all up.

'I'm right here with you.' I reach out and rest my hand on her shoulder.

'We've also got a family liaison officer on the way. She'll support you and update you as we keep up the search for them.'

Fear clouds Kirsty's eyes. 'Does that mean you don't expect to find them *quickly*?'

'We're hoping we will, and of course, we'll do everything we can, but she's on her way just in case. It's just procedure.'

'But what about that message he sent? What if—'

'We're just in the process of triangulating that message.'

'What does that mean?'

'We'll soon be able to pinpoint exactly where it came from. As well as whether they'd already left the grounds when Harry sent it. If that's the case, we'll be able to ascertain the direction in which they've headed.'

Kirsty glances at the clock. 'It's been nearly half an hour already. He could have got a long way in that time. Especially if he's driving. Have you found out about that yet?'

'We believe they're on foot.' He nods.

Relief rips through me – it's probably too early for that but if they're on foot, at least they're unlikely to get far without someone seeing them. Unless they're hiding, that is.

'Their descriptions have been circulated to the media and

around all the local forces.' His voice is filled with reassurance. 'And we'll keep you posted when we confirm the location of his phone.'

His radio beeps and crackles.

'This might be it.' He raises it from the lapel of his jacket to his chin. 'DI Gilbert.'

'The suspect's mobile phone has been located by the perimeter fencing,' says the voice. 'It's sustained significant damage and the SIM has been removed.'

DI Gilbert moves away from us and backs out into the corridor.

'What does that mean?' Kirsty calls after him.

'Just wait here. I'll be back with you in a few moments.'

'He's going to get his own back.' Kirsty's voice is full of anguish as she sinks to one of the chairs. 'He's taken the only thing he knows he can hurt *him* with.' She jabs her thumb in David's direction. 'A poor, innocent child. *My* poor, innocent child. And there's nothing I can do about it but sit here and bloody *wait*.'

'His own back, for *what* exactly?' I try to look into her face. However, it remains turned to the floor while her hair falls all around her shoulders. She seems to have gone into some kind of trance as she rocks herself backwards and forwards on the chair. 'What's happened Kirsty? Just tell me.'

She's squeezing her hands together in her lap so tightly that her knuckles are whitening. 'Kirsty!' I raise my voice, trying to snap her out of it.

Eventually, she looks at me. 'Chloe killed herself.'

'Who's *Chloe*?'

'She was Harry's twin sister.'

'What happened? When?'

'It was an overdose. Harry was the one who discovered her but it was too late by then. She died on her way to the hospital.'

'What's all this got to do with anything going on here today?'

'It was before he met me.' Her voice is flat. 'David was Chloe's boyfriend at the time.' She raises her eyes to meet mine. 'The one who drove her to it.'

'Why have you never told me?' There's *no way* I'd have okayed this trip if I'd been made aware of any history between David and Harry.

A man still heartbroken about his sister's suicide invites the ex-boyfriend he holds responsible to the top of a hundred-and-fifty-foot rock.

This is insane.

'*Why* didn't you tell me?' I repeat my question.

'I don't know. I've been too focused on my *own* survival, I guess.'

From what I've learnt from Kirsty over the years, *survival* is the right word. And because of what I *do* know, I don't need to ask for any specifics of how David will have treated Chloe when they were younger.

While they were still married, I allowed Kirsty to stay with me so many times, I lost count. She'd turn up at all hours of the night saying, *he's kicked me out again.* Or, *he's being so nasty, I couldn't take it anymore.* But whenever she was forced to find refuge with me, he'd never allow her to take Toby from their house. He's always been possessive of his son – the trophy son he always wanted – a so-called extension of himself.

His social media page is stuffed with pictures of them together along with declarations of *my son this – my son that.* Harry could have viewed them all and known Toby would be the one thing he could use to hurt David.

Everything's starting to slot into place. Apart from what happened to Leonie. I can't see how that slots in at all. But I guess we'll know more soon.

Hopefully, the threat of 'loss' hinted at in Harry's text is an empty one. I'm still convinced he's just hiding with Toby some-where. Perhaps he's trying to teach David some sort of warped lesson after what it sounds like he went through with his sister. At least, I pray that's all it is.

What I know for definite is that the governing body at Oldale Primary will wipe the floor with me after what's happened here over the last couple of days.

We've got one dead teacher, a sociopathic one, a vengeful activities instructor and a missing eleven-year-old. Not only that, but we've also got thirty-five other utterly traumatised chil-dren and a parent helper who got so drunk she had to be put to bed.

Things can't get any worse.

Finally, sirens wail in the distance. Kirsty looks up from where she's been slumped on a seat in the corner with her head in her hands.

'I know it's a really stupid question but are you alright?' I sit beside her and rest my hand on her arm. She's shaking. It could be because of Toby – or it could be the drink with-drawal. I still can't believe she fell off the wagon so stupendously.

At least she's not telling me to get lost after what she suspected me of earlier. I expect her concern for Toby's well-being has outpaced any ridiculous suspicions she had about me and her ex-husband. And if David thinks he's heard the last of it after his smutty remarks and initial refusal to leave my room when I asked him, he can think again.

'If he harms a hair on his head...' She shrugs my hand off and gets back to her feet. She looks like she doesn't know what to do with herself.

'They'll find them, you know.' I follow her to the window. 'I'm convinced, I really am, that Harry wouldn't do anything to put Toby in any danger. He's police checked to work with children, after all. There's a line most people won't cross.'

'I wish I had your faith Catherine.' Kirsty pulls the curtain to one side. But there's nothing much to see now the police have finished what they were doing on the rocks.

'How well do you actually know him? Has he had anything to do with Toby over the years?'

'I've had little to do with him apart from when he once tried to warn me off David.' She continues staring out at the rocks. 'The only other time was when he messaged me on Facebook. It was after we'd split up – he wanted to tell me I'd had a lucky escape.' She looks back at me over her shoulder as she clutches onto the windowsill.

'Harry clearly knew what he was doing when he invited our school on this trip by the looks of it.'

'I've no idea. I didn't know he was even here to be honest.' She keeps her back to me and her shoulders are shaking. 'I was pretty shocked to have been allowed to come in the first place.'

'I was glad at the time. For Toby's sake. And for *mine*.'

'I need a drink. Don't worry—'

My face probably belies what I'm thinking.

'I don't mean *alcohol*. Or maybe I do,' she mutters as she strides towards the sink in the far corner of the room to fill a glass of water. She's been like this every time she gives up drinking. Holding a glass of *anything* seems to give her some comfort.

'What *did* cause you to drink last night Kirsty? You were doing so well.'

'To be honest, I'm struggling to think of much else apart from where Toby is right now.' Tears flood her eyes as she gulps at her water. 'Just leave me be for a few minutes, will you? I just need to get myself together.'

'I'll just be over there.' I point across the room. 'I'm going to make sure Jessica's alright.'

I was exhausted this morning after a shocking night's sleep

but I'm now flooded with so much adrenaline that I wonder if I'll ever sleep again. I head over to where Jeanette and Mia are sitting with Jessica.

'I've rung Jessica's dad to collect her,' Jeanette says. 'Will he be allowed in here to get her?'

'You'd better have a word with *them*.' I nod towards the growing police presence spilling out of the foyer and into the seated area outside. At least it's her husband she's called to collect Jessica and *not* her mother. I can't think of anything worse than facing Nancy at this moment.

'How are *you* doing Mia?'

'I can't wrap my head around it all. I mean, who'd do something like—'

'Catherine, can you come with me – I don't think I can do this on my own.'

I take a sharp inhale of breath as I swivel around to face Kirsty. 'You can't do what?'

She seems to be frozen to the spot. 'I've just remembered something,' she begins. 'Something Harry told me last night.'

~

I should have been preparing for a new beginning.
Instead I was planning the end.
(Chloe Douglas)

THIRTY-FOUR

CATHERINE

'Hey – are you OK?' My hand instinctively reaches for her arm, my fingers tightening around it. A surge of concern ripples through me as she leans against a pillar. 'Look at me.' Her lips are drained of colour and her eyes are glazed over as if she might pass out. 'Kirsty, sit down, for goodness' sake.'

'I need to speak to the police,' she says. Her face is even paler than it was before.

'Why, what's up?'

'I've remembered something important.'

'I've brought her some water.'

DI Rhodes nods as he sits at the table. I can feel his eyes on me as I cross the centre office to sit beside Kirsty. At least he's allowed me in while she speaks to him.

'Are you OK?' I reach for her hand.

She shakes her head. 'Of course I'm not. I won't be until they find Toby.'

'We're doing everything in our power to find them, you know.' DI Rhodes emanates the strain of the day with his underarm sweat patches and shadow of a beard across his chin.

'I know you are.' Kirsty's voice is small.

'There's every chance,' he adds, leaning forward, his eyes still fixed on Kirsty, 'that Harry's just hiding out with Toby somewhere, playing some kind of game.'

'That's what I said.'

'What did you want to speak about?' The inspector's eyes are kind which I'm grateful for. Kirsty's got enough to deal with.

'I've remembered more about last night.' She tugs her hand away from mine.

'OK?'

'I *was* with Harry. When I was speaking to the other officers before, they said I'd been seen entering the staff building. But I didn't remember anything then.'

'She was drinking last night,' I add. 'And it sounds like she had some sort of blackout with it.'

'I see.' He sits up straighter in his seat. 'But now you *do* remember – is that what you're saying?'

She nods.

'Go on.'

'I thought I was drinking Coke at the time, really I did.' Her voice rises. 'But he must have added vodka to it.'

'Who? Harry?'

She nods. 'I didn't realise I was drinking alcohol until it was far too late and by then, I remember deciding I'd had already had so much drink that I might as well carry on.' Fresh tears fill her eyes. 'I'm so ashamed of myself.' She lowers her voice as if those final few words are only meant for me to hear.

'It's OK.' I squeeze her arm. And then to DI Rhodes, I say, 'Kirsty's a recovering alcoholic.'

At least I've found out that she didn't *voluntarily* return to the bottle. Rather, she was plied with the stuff by the sounds of it.

He nods, giving me the impression that he already knows this.

'Harry must have piled the booze into me to mix me up, to confuse me, to put me out of action, or whatever, whilst he—'

'Whilst he what?'

'He said he'd been planning to go out for a drink with David. But that he'd let him down.'

'Is there anything unusual about that?' DI Rhodes shifts in his seat. 'From what I gathered from my colleagues who are currently speaking to David, the two of them were once friends, weren't they? Harry invited him to bring his class here.'

She shakes her head. 'They're *not* friends. David might be under the illusion that all might have been forgiven but he couldn't be any further from the truth.'

'All *what* might have been forgiven?'

Kirsty dabs her eyes on the sleeve of her cardigan. 'David used to be in a relationship with Harry's twin sister.'

A flicker of interest seems to enter his eyes.

'I honestly thought it was ancient history between them,' Kirsty says. 'Harry and David, I mean. And Harry's sister Chloe.'

'*Chloe.*' He writes something down. 'Carry on.'

'Well I don't know the exact details about it,' she continues. 'Other than that David devastated her. And if his treatment of Chloe was anything like his treatment of me...'

'What happened?'

'She ended up taking her own life. Because of *him*. And I, for one, can totally understand how he'd have driven her to do that.'

Now I think about it, Kirsty had once mentioned a story about a former girlfriend of David's with this sort of outcome but I didn't realise that she'd actually *died* and I'd never have known in a million years that he was once with *Harry's* sister.

'How long ago was this exactly?' DI Rhodes's voice is gentle and I'm grateful to him for going easy on her.

'Like I said, it was well before he met me – he was in his late teens. From what I've found out over the years, he took every scrap of dignity Chloe had at the time – exactly like he did with me.'

I shake my head. That man has so much to answer for.

'There was only one thing stopping me from doing the same thing when I was with him.'

'Toby,' I say, following her gaze to the floor.

'And now, because I was too drunk last night to remember what Harry told me, Toby could be anywhere out there and in all kinds of danger.'

'What exactly *did* Harry tell you last night?'

'That his initial plan had been to drag a confession out of David while they were in the pub together. He wanted him to admit to the abuse out loud and acknowledge that he was the person wholly responsible for Chloe's death.'

'I see.'

'I told him he'd be best leaving all that pain in the past and that he was only destroying *himself* by continuing to rake it all up.'

'What would dragging a confession from him have achieved anyway?' I say. DI Rhodes frowns at me as though I shouldn't be the person asking the questions. But it *is* a fair question.

'He was planning to record what David said,' she replies. 'Then he was going to bring the recording to *you*. He said he'd lived for too many years not being able to get justice for his sister and if he could somehow get him fired from teaching, he'd be happy with that.'

'Until I prevented David from leaving the building,' I say, recalling the smirk on his face when I caught him at the door.

'Harry wasn't happy when I was trying to talk him out of it all.' Kirsty clasps her hands in her lap. 'So he told me something else. Something which he thought might convince me of his way of thinking. Or rather he *showed* me something else.'

'What was that?'

'You've got to believe me when I say this.' Her voice bears an edge of desperation. 'If I'd not blacked out with the drink – if I'd only remembered before, I'd have come straight to you – I promise I would. Leonie might still be here then.' Her face crumples and she drops her head into her hands.

Leonie might still be here! What the hell is she about to say?

'It's OK Kirsty.' I pass her a tissue and drape my arm around her shaking shoulders. 'I'm right here.'

'Tell us what he showed you,' says DI Rhodes.

'If only I'd remembered before. I could have done something.'

'Just tell us.' I squeeze her shoulder and my eyes meet with the grave expression in DI Rhodes's.

'The rucksack.' She raises her head and dabs at her eyes with the tissue. 'The one labelled with *my* name.'

'*What* rucksack?'

'The one containing my safety harness – it was all ready for the zip wire. I'd been fitted for it before we went in for dinner. We all had.'

He pushes his glasses back up his nose. 'What are you saying here?'

'It should have been me.' Her voice is small and for a moment, I wonder if I'm hearing things.

'What do you mean, *it should have been you?*'

'Are you telling us,' asks DI Rhodes, 'that the safety harness that *Leonie* was wearing at the time of her death was meant for *you?*'

'That's exactly what I'm telling you.'

'I can't believe this.' My face probably mirrors the expressions on his at this moment. What the hell is going on here?

'Why would *Harry* have your harness in his possession? In his room?'

'He'd caught David hanging around in the equipment store.'

'Really?'

'While everyone was still at the playground last night.'

'Are you absolutely sure about this?' He fiddles with the corner of his notepad. 'And this is what Harry told you?'

'I think so. Though I still don't *quite* trust myself with what I'm saying. It still might all be a blur in my head. I'm not even sure how much I had to drink last night.'

'We can now safely say that Harry has a definite motive for taking Toby.' DI Rhodes massages the bridge of his nose.

'To get back at David in any way he can,' I add.

'But what I still don't understand,' DI Rhodes continues, 'is if Harry intercepted a harness that David was planning for *you* to use, why it *still* ended up being available for use by Leonie this morning. It's not as if Harry had a grievance with Leonie. Did he?'

The question hangs in the air, adding yet another layer to it all. If he did, I can't imagine what it would be.

DI Rhodes clicks his pen for a moment while looking thoughtful. Then we all jump as there's a loud knocking at the door.

'Come in.'

Sergeant Parkins pokes his head around it. 'We need a word with you sir.'

'Just bear with me a moment please.' DI Rhodes rises to his feet.

What the hell's going on now?

Kirsty jumps up and starts after him. I follow.

'If you could both wait here please.' He turns, blocking Kirsty's path to the exit. 'I'll be back in a moment to let you know what's happening.'

I collapse back into my seat. 'I can't believe David got you here to *kill* you. No wonder you blocked it out of your head for a while. We should know by now that the man's capable of *anything*.' I reach for her hand again, feeling the cool tremor of her fingers against my palm.

'And now Toby's caught up in it all.' Her entire body shakes with the force of her sobs.

∿

Karma will prevail, I often told myself.
But I knew I wouldn't be around to see it.
(Chloe Douglas)

THIRTY-FIVE

MIA

'I keep thinking about Miss Johnson and it's making me really sad.' Jessica shuffles her chair towards her mother.

'I know. We all feel sad.' Jeanette puts her arm around her and their long, dark hair merges.

'When's Toby coming back?' Jessica chews at the corner of a sandwich Frances brought for her earlier, her doe eyes flitting between me and Jeanette. 'Where is he anyway?'

'It shouldn't be too long now,' I say. Even if she's picked up any snippets of Toby being with Harry, she'll just see Harry as a staff member here at the centre and therefore a trustworthy adult.

I'm still not sure why he's taken Toby, only that from the tone of that text message, there seems to be some dark history between him and David. Nothing would surprise me about *him*.

Jessica's mother and I seem to have struck up something of an allegiance since our conversation in the toilets. But I still can't believe what she did with David last night.

I'd often noticed Jeanette staring at Leonie with an expression I now recognise only too well. Envy for her confidence, for who she was and all she achieved. But most of all, the envy was probably for the fact that she had taken David's attention away from her. At least for a time.

Since he's been in with the police, I've been terrified in case he's saying anything about me. His words swim back to me, *anyone could see you had some sort of obsession with her. You got on her nerves, following her about, copying her, asking her nosy questions all the time.*

What if they think it was something more sinister? What if they think it was *me* who did something to her harness?

'Why don't you put that phone down and find a board game for us to play?' Jeanette says to Jessica, her voice suddenly cutting into my paranoia.

'I wonder why Kirsty and Catherine went back in with that inspector before.' I follow Jeanette's glance to the door as Jessica heads towards the games trolley. 'I saw her whisper something to one of them, then away they went.'

'It's quite an unlikely friendship, don't you think?' says Jeanette.

'Who? Catherine and Kirsty?'

'Yeah. The revered headmistress and the recovering alcoholic who's not allowed to have her son living with her.'

'That sounds terrible.' I pull a face at her. I feel so sorry for Kirsty at the moment that I don't want to listen if Jeanette's planning to tear her to bits. 'Anyway, they've been friends for years – Kirsty encouraged Catherine to apply for the headship in the first place.'

'I bet you all loved her for that.' Jeanette's laugh is almost a cackle. Even Jessica glances over from where she's looking at the games and puzzles.

'We call Catherine "the new broom" at school,' I say, glancing around to make sure she doesn't suddenly appear behind me. She's very good at that. Which is probably why my contract is often under threat.

'So I've heard.'

'But she's shown she *can* be more human while we've been here.' I think back to when we were walking up the rock earlier. Gosh, if only I could turn the time back to then. 'But in school,' I continue, 'everything has to be done to her exacting require-ments and if your face doesn't fit – well you're on borrowed time.'

'And does *your* face fit Mia? Oh Jessica, pick it up.'

Jessica bends to collect the pieces of her jigsaw which she's dropped on her way back to our table.

'All this with Toby has taken the focus off what happened to Leonie though, hasn't it?' I say.

'This is a nightmare.'

'It's been well over an hour now.' Jeanette glances from the clock to the window where the curtains have been left slightly open.

'I just hope he's alright.' I follow her gaze. 'The alternative doesn't bear thinking about.'

Jeanette glances at Jessica. 'Are you OK love?' She's still picking up jigsaw pieces from the floor. I can imagine what's going through Jeanette's mind. *I'm so glad it wasn't you he took.*

Suddenly, I shiver. If there's any truth in that expression *someone's walked over my grave*, I've just experienced it.

Leonie returns to my mind again. Just a few hours ago, she'd never have suspected in a million years that she'd shortly be heading towards her own grave.

I drop my head into my hands.

～

One of the hardest things was knowing
that even after I'd gone,
you'd be free to inflict your pain on other
unsuspecting women.
(Chloe Douglas)

THIRTY-SIX

MIA

'I need to go to the toilet Mum.'

'I'll go with you.' Jeanette rises to her feet and reaches for her hand.

I can see in her eyes what she's thinking, *no way are you going in there on your own after what's happened to Toby*.

I let a long breath out. This has been an utterly endless day. And it still seems to be far from over. Catherine and Kirsty must have finished speaking to DI Rhodes as they're back in the foyer. The other two must have finished with David as well as I can hear him yelling again. He's right to be beside himself with worry, but shouting and bawling at the police officers like they're all beneath him isn't going to do anybody any favours. Least of all *him*.

He barges into the dining room, a whirlwind of anger and desperation. 'I'm going nowhere,' he yells back at the two officers who are pursuing him. 'Not until my son's been found.'

As he reaches one of the tables, he pulls his ringing phone from his pocket and his expression suddenly changes. 'It's Toby.'

A sudden hush sweeps over everyone as he glances at the two officers who are now flanking him at either side.

'Put it on speakerphone.' DI Gilbert slams his palm onto the table. 'And everyone else is to keep silent.' He sweeps a stern gaze over us all.

The air is thick with tension, a collective anxiety uniting everyone.

David presses his screen and lays the phone on the table in front of us all as I creep towards them. 'Toby!' he cries. 'Where are you?'

We all lean forward, listening for a moment which feels eternal. Then, just as I'm starting to think there's nobody on the line, someone speaks.

'So now you know how it feels, you *bastard.*' I hold my breath as I wait for what might come next.

'Where's – my – son?' David grabs a fistful of his hair.

'If you don't mind, I'd prefer to talk about *my* sister.' Harry's voice is low but filled with sarcasm.

'Your *sister*? Look – get my son back here and we can talk about whatever you like.'

'I hardly think you're in a position to be calling the shots here Naylor.'

Kirsty rushes from the door towards the table. But before she has a chance to speak she's stopped short by DI Gilbert, who raises a finger to his lips. He pulls a notepad from his top pocket and scribbles something. As he pushes it next to where David's phone is resting on the table, I crane my neck to read what he's written.

Keep him talking.

He then appears to note down the number on David's screen and darts towards the door into the foyer, closing it behind him.

'I never *did* get an apology, or even a *shred* of remorse from you for what you did to Chloe, did I? You should be in prison for it.'

'Look Harry, that was all years ago. I've changed since then.'

I would have expected Kirsty to jump in by now but evidently she's leaving this call for David to handle, possibly because she realises it's *him* Harry bears the grudge against.

'Like hell you have,' he says. 'Have you ever even given a second thought to what you put her through? After what you drove her to do to herself?' The pain is clear in his voice.

'What she did was *her* responsibility.' David's suddenly adopted a tone he would use when trying to convince others of his opinion in a staff meeting.

He should be trying to pacify Harry. He's got Toby, after all. David should be saying *anything* that might convince him to bring him back.

'How can you say that after what you did to her? And what you've done to me. It's wrecked *my* life too, knowing the pain she was in.'

'I want my son returning to me *immediately*. Don't make things any worse than they already are.'

Kirsty elbows him. I would too. Threatening Harry is only going to make him angrier and potentially more volatile.

'This is *entirely* your fault Naylor. You treated my sister like she was a piece of shit. She told me everything, you know – *everything*. From all the nasty names you called her, the punches and kicks, the time you abandoned her in the middle of nowhere on her own.'

'We were eighteen years old, for God's sake. She wanted something more serious than I did, that's all. How was I to know she'd—'

'And then, after you forced her not to go through with her own pregnancy, you got someone else pregnant, didn't you? Bastard.'

David remains quiet but his hands have curled into fists. I wonder if Harry's referring to Kirsty as the *someone else*.

I look across to the doorway, watching as DI Gilbert puts his hand up to prevent Jeanette and Jessica from re-entering the room as he tilts his radio towards his face.

'But even after that,' Harry continues, 'you still couldn't leave my poor sister alone, could you? Reeling her in and throwing her back out all the time like she was a worthless piece of rubbish.'

'She wouldn't leave me alone.'

'Then there was the time you forced yourself on her. She'd started to see the light with you and had asked you to leave. But you took what you wanted anyway. That's because you're nothing but an evil bastard.'

David's staring at the phone as if he's afraid to make eye contact with the rest of us. Toby's probably at Harry's side throughout all this, hearing every word Harry's saying. I can only hope he doesn't fully understand.

'That's not true.'

'If it's a choice between believing *you* and what my sister told me, I—'

Kirsty steps forward. I'm shocked she's managed to hold herself back so far.

'Harry, it's Kirsty.' Her voice is wobbling. 'Please just bring Toby back to me. *Please!* He'll be so scared. I'm so sorry about your sister, you know that. But Toby hasn't done anything to deserve any of this.' Her hands are trembling too.

'Like I told him before, it's *Naylor's* turn to lose someone now.' He spits the word *Naylor* out like it's a glob of phlegm.

As if Kirsty wasn't pale enough before, she appears to pale even more. It's probably the word 'lose' that's done it. 'OK, so you've got a grudge with David,' she says. 'I don't blame you one bit for that.' Her hair falls over the phone as she speaks into it. 'But Toby's just a kid.'

'He's Naylor's kid.'

'He's my child too – and I've suffered more than you can imagine from David's behaviour too. Do what you want with David, but please, I'm begging you, please let Toby go.'

'Do you know how many years I've wanted to hear him grovel for what he drove my sister to do?' His voice hardens some more.

'You're not going to get much further with this.' David elbows his way back in front of the phone. 'You might as well give yourself up now.'

'It should have been *you* on those rocks this morning *Naylor*.'

I gasp. And so does everyone else. There it is. It was *Harry* who killed Leonie. And by the sounds of it, he didn't even mean to.

The revelation crashes into me but is swiftly replaced by a pang of guilt. Selfish, maybe, but the truth gnaws at the edges of my mind – it could have even been me dangling from that wire before plunging to my death. I was up there with her and it was only because she was braver and so full of excitement that she went first.

On the ride that was meant for David.

'Put Toby on the phone Harry. I need to know he's alright.' Tears are rolling down Kirsty's cheeks as she pushes her way back in. 'He isn't just David's son. He's *mine* too.'

'Do you really think I care about *you*?' Harry's voice is a snarl. 'Besides, you wanted Naylor punished as much as I did. That's what you were saying last night.'

Bloody hell. Harry really meant what he said before. It should have been David. And he's making it sound as though Kirsty already knew about it. She glances up and her eyes meet Catherine's. She quickly looks away.

'Don't you think I've been punished enough?' Kirsty cries.

'We both know it should have been *me* wearing that harness and it would have been if you hadn't warned me.'

My hand flies to my mouth. It's getting worse and worse. *The harness was initially meant for Kirsty! And tampered with by David.*

I can't believe all this. And I can't forget that even I'm implicated. There's the five hundred quid hush money I got for keeping quiet and helping David with the rigging of that draw. Without that, Kirsty *and* Jeanette wouldn't have been here in the first place. But I had no idea what David was planning to do to Kirsty. How could I have done?

Poor Leonie. Poor, poor Leonie. Talk about being in the wrong place at the wrong time. Fresh tears stab at my eyes.

'Just bring Toby back to me. Please Harry.'

'I didn't want any of this, you know that.'

I hold my breath. Harry seems to be softening.

'I wanted him to admit what he'd done, that's all. I wanted some closure at last. Or to get something I could take to the police. But he couldn't even be bothered turning up to have it out with me.'

'I understand all that, but it's got *nothing* to do with Toby. Please just let him go.'

'It should have been Naylor who fell from that bloody wire.' His voice cracks. 'It was *supposed* to be Naylor.'

My gaze shifts to DI Rhodes, whose attention is divided between the phone and the doorway. I catch DI Gilbert giving a quick thumbs up, hopefully signalling their success in their station having traced the call. I can't imagine it means anything else.

'I'll call you back in a few minutes.' Harry's voice slices through the air with an unsettling finality. Each word feels like a countdown, an impending dread of what these next few minutes might hold. 'I'll give you the chance to say your final goodbyes.'

'No!' Kirsty cries. 'Wait! Please!'
But he's already gone.

~

Some day.
You'll hurt as much as you hurt me.
(Chloe Douglas)

THIRTY-SEVEN

KIRSTY

I stare in horror at DI Rhodes. 'Please – you've got to do something. You heard what he just said. He's going to hurt my boy!'

DI Gilbert bursts back into the room. 'We've managed to trace Toby's phone,' he blurts. 'They're still here, somewhere in the grounds. Leaving the other phone at the exit was clearly a decoy.'

'The man's bloody deranged.' Tears stream down my face, the weight in my chest tightening as we all pursue each other from the room. However, I've allowed a glimmer of hope in after that call. At least he hasn't gone on the run with him. *They're still here in the grounds.*

'We'll find them Kirsty.' I feel the weight of DI Rhodes's hand on my shoulder. 'The dog units have just got here and the helicopter's on its way up. It's just a matter of time.'

I glance from the window to a distant rumble of noise. I can't see anything happening out there – only the familiar rhythmic flash of blue lights in the distance.

'You wait here with Jessica,' Catherine says to Jeanette as we reach the foyer.

'You should all wait here too.' DI Rhodes turns to me and Catherine. 'Once we locate them, depending on where they are and on Harry's state of mind, it could be a delicate operation to retrieve Toby from him.'

But David lunges towards the exit, his eyes ablaze with a feral intensity before disappearing around the corner. I could have predicted he would take off. I'm surprised he hasn't been arrested yet, with what they now know but I expect it's just a matter of time. The police officer who was standing here before and might have tried to prevent David from leaving the building has disappeared, presumably to join in with the search.

'I'm not waiting here either. I might still be able to reason with Harry.' I dart after David.

'You must try to stay calm.' Catherine catches me up. 'I honestly don't believe Harry's got it in him to hurt Toby. He's just trying to hurt David.'

'But who knows, not now he's been backed into a corner like this.' I look in all directions. 'Where did he go? David, I mean?'

Catherine's eyes dart around too. 'I've no idea. But if Harry's phone was found near the exit, maybe they're hiding near there.' She starts in that direction. 'Come on.'

'Toby,' I shout. 'Toby, where are you?'

Catherine shoots me a look. 'I wouldn't do that,' she says. 'If we *are* closing in on Harry and you being nearby spooks him, well he's already shown how unpredictable he is, hasn't he?'

We approach the perimeter walls, both panting for breath.

'We can't go any further.' Catherine catches my arm. 'Can't you hear them all out there?'

I glance around. The gates are tightly closed and there's no way Toby would be able to get over walls as high as these are. The police must be right. They're somewhere in the grounds. But there's nowhere to hide around here.

'The woods,' I gasp. 'That's where they could be. If he hurts a hair on my boy's head...'

'I don't think he will Kirsty. You heard what he said. He didn't mean to kill Leonie. This is him panicking. He'll see sense – I'm certain of it.'

'I completely disagree,' I say over my shoulder. 'He'll be going to prison after all this so won't be bothered what *else* he does now.'

It will start getting dark before much longer. Toby's always been scared of the dark. Some of the other kids were laughing at him last night for having brought his nightlight to plug in at the side of his bunk. But they'd all brought their bears and one had even brought a picture of his dog. They're all back in their homes now, I think with a pang. They're safe and sound but my poor boy. He's—

'Find!' A voice echoes from the far side of the lake. Catherine and I exchange glances as we break into a run.

Oh my God, oh my God, oh my God. *What* have they found? My heart is in my mouth as we approach the officer holding something aloft. The closer we get, the more the dread collects in my stomach. The item he's holding in the air becomes visible as we get nearer to him. It looks like Toby's mobile phone.

'No, no, no.' My gaze sweeps over the surface of the lake, so innocently bathed in evening sunlight. 'What if they've – what if he's...' I drop to my knees, unable to get the words out.

'It's OK, it's OK.' Catherine drops down beside me. 'Remember what Frances said yesterday. The lake's only deep to chest height.'

'That's at the edges,' I cry. 'Not at the centre.' I scramble to my feet. I need to do something.

'Over here.' A further voice echoes from the woods, making me unsure which way to turn. To stay here with Toby's phone or to see what they've found now.

Officers seem to emerge from all directions, most of them

heading towards the trees. I can't cope with this. They've got to find him. He's got to be OK.

Running from the lake to the woods feels like running through treacle. I want to get there yet at the same time I don't. What have they found? What on earth have they found?

Fighting for breath, Catherine and I rush towards several officers who are now gathered at the centre of the woods. I tunnel my way between two of them. I have to find out what they're looking at. I *need* to find out.

'It's Toby's jacket,' I blurt as a renewed sickness rises in me.

'You really should be waiting back inside.' DI Gilbert gestures to me and Catherine.

'Where would *you* be if it was your son?' *What will I do if Harry hurts him? How will I go on?* I'd swap places with Toby right this instant. Harry can do what he wants with me, but not with my innocent boy who we've already put through more than enough in his eleven short years. I slide down a tree trunk into a crouch. There's no way they're sending me inside, not until I know my boy is safe.

He's not only seen David pinning me against walls time and time again and throwing me to the ground, but in the later years before we finally spilt up, he frequently saw me so out of my head on drink, I couldn't put *myself* to bed, let alone him.

I'd do anything to turn back the clock. I'd read him ten stories every night. I'd sit beside him and watch as he falls asleep. I was a rubbish mother for a long time. But looking back, all I was doing was trying to anaesthetise the pain I was experiencing in my marriage with alcohol. I'd give anything to have the chance to make it up to him.

'If only I could swap places with him.'

'I know.' Catherine's reassuring touch finds my hand, squeezing it in silent solidarity. In the chaos, her presence is an anchor and a reminder that we're in this nightmare together.

A threat towards me wouldn't be revenge in Harry's eyes. After all, David wouldn't bat an eyelid if anything happened to me. But his world will be turned upside down and inside out if anything were to happen to Toby. Personally, I wouldn't be able to go on without him.

'Up there!' Another voice rings out. I leap back to my feet and, frantically scanning our surroundings, I strain to look through the branches that are cloaking us. Desperation claws at me, turning every tree trunk into a potential threat as I rush towards the voice.

'I can see them,' Catherine gasps, pointing. There, silhou-etted on the top of the rock stand two figures, one tall, one short. My breath catches. As far as I can tell, they're in exactly the same spot that Leonie must have been in before she plunged to her death.

'No!' I scream. My footsteps pound the forest floor, the urgency echoing through the trees as I sprint towards my son. 'No-no-no!'

'Kirsty! Get back here!' shouts Catherine.

As I tear away from the rest of the group, Toby's life unfolds like a rapid slideshow, from the day he entered this world to his tentative first steps. Images of his innocence, his school uniform engulfing him, his arms around my neck, his gap-toothed grin, all intensifying my desperation. *Please God, please God, keep him safe. Don't let anything happen to him.*

I've got to bring Toby down safely and I'll push Harry off that rock myself if that's what it takes to do that.

Commands pierce the air from behind, urging me to stop. But my legs move with a will of their own, fuelled by a mother's determination. Each step echoes a silent promise to reach my boy. I've lost more than enough at the hands of David Naylor already and I'm not prepared to lose Toby.

Perhaps this is all I deserve after what I've had a hand in

causing. After all, I haven't been entirely honest about my recollection of events leading up to Leonie's death.

~

No one is safe around you.
And there was only one way I could leave.
(Chloe Douglas)

THIRTY-EIGHT

KIRSTY

I can't afford to let my thoughts wander. Every step is a heartbeat, every breath a prayer – just get to Toby, bring him back down to safety.

As I reach the path at the foot of the rocks, there's a pounding of footsteps behind me. I can't look around, I can't stop, I just need to get myself up there.

'Go back to the others.' David seizes my shoulder, tugging me to a stop. 'You're going to put him in even more danger.'

'It's *you* who put him in danger in the first place.' I try to shake his hand off but his fingers are digging into my flesh like hooks.

'Do as I say – do you hear me?' He shakes me. 'This is between me and Douglas. It's got *nothing* to do with you.'

'He's *my* son – do you hear me? So get your hands off me.' I bring my elbow forward and drive it back into his ribs as hard as I can.

'Toby's *my* responsibility, you stupid bitch.' He shoves me to the side, sending me sprawling to the ground as he carries on running, while rubbing at the area where I elbowed him. 'Go back to your vodka,' he calls back over his shoulder. 'It's all you're—'

His voice is drowned out by the helicopter as it moves around to this side of the rocks and begins backing away in the direction of the building. Now that they've been located, a helicopter might only complicate things with its presence and its noise.

My palms scrape against the rocky surface as I scramble back to my feet, the harsh grit cutting into my skin. As I lurch after him, I look up again, hoping for another glimpse of Toby to reassure me he's still OK. I can't see either of them. All I can do is pray that Harry hasn't yet spotted either me or David making our way towards them.

My breath catches, and a surge of panic tightens my chest as he sprints further ahead, leaving me struggling to keep up.

This *could* be a really bad idea. Being suddenly confronted by *anyone* might spook Harry to the point where he could suddenly hurl both himself *and* Toby from the top. But if David gets there first it might be even worse.

The air roars in my ears as my feet continue to thump their way up the side of the rock. I've got to get there. I've just got to get to him.

As my sandals pound against the gravel, a vision of Leonie's twisted and bloodied body floods my senses. *Please don't let that be my son.* This thought is enough to send a renewed energy through my body that propels me on – faster and faster.

Before I know it, I'm gaining on David.

'I told you to go back.' He twists his neck in response to my footsteps crunching up the path behind him.

'Please let me handle this,' I hiss as I get alongside him. 'For once in your life, just listen to me.'

'What part of "he's my responsibility" are you struggling to understand?' His eyes are ablaze with anger as he rounds on me.

An amplified voice echoes from the rocks below, cutting

through the chaos. 'Stand away from the child.' I steal a glance downward at the officers fumbling with reflective vests. 'Get down on your knees and put your hands behind your head.'

'Please David.' I tug on the back of his jacket as he sets off again. 'If *you* confront him, you'll anger him more than I will. He's more likely to do something terrible.'

Against all the odds, he stops, a fleeting moment where my voice seems to break through his rage. It's as if, for the first time, he's actually hearing me.

'I can get through to Harry. I have a far better chance than *you* have.'

'You'd bloody well better.' He shoves me forward so hard that he nearly sends me sprawling again. 'If anything happens to my boy, it's on *you*.'

It must be the first time he's ever listened to me. It'll be because he'll want *me* to take the risk of being pushed from the top of that rock, rather than *him*.

I lurch forward, the gravel beneath my sandals biting into my soles. I can barely breathe as I ascend to the final summit. *Please, please, please,* I repeat in my head as the top comes into sight.

Then I see him. *Toby.* Harry's gripping one of his arms and they've got their backs to me.

I pause for a second to gather myself. This is the moment where I either inflame everything – or the moment where I manage to talk Harry down and lead my son back to safety.

A sudden panic grips me. Perhaps I should be letting the police deal with this. They'll be right behind me and trained to negotiate in these sorts of situations. And they haven't got skin in the game like I have. *My own son.* I'm probably going to be in big trouble for taking matters into my own hands. But Toby's my boy – my only child. *Any* mother would be up here, doing what I'm doing.

Before I know it, we're all facing each other next to the scaffolding that secures the zip wire. 'Please Harry.' My voice is shaking more than ever. 'Please just give him to me.'

Toby cowers behind him, literally three feet from death. 'Mummy.' He hasn't called me mummy for years.

'He hasn't done anything wrong,' I plead. 'Your argument's with *David*, not an innocent child. Just give him to me and I'll send David up here to face you.'

'It's all gone totally wrong.' Harry's voice falters. Even in those few words, he sounds broken. Completely broken. 'It was never supposed to be Leonie who died – it was meant to be *Naylor* – you know it was. It was only supposed to be *him*.'

'I know.' At least we've established some sort of a dialogue.

He won't have any idea yet about how much I've divulged to the police about him so if I just stick to what's between him and David, he might let Toby go.

'The other kids weren't supposed to be watching,' he continues. 'They were supposed to be inside. I tried to get them inside but...' His voice trails away as he peers over the edge of the rock.

His remorse gives me hope. I can get through to him – I know I can.

'Look, what's done is done Harry. You can't change anything that's happened.' I follow his gaze. The crowd below is a long, long way down. 'But you can stop all this from becoming even more tragic than it already is.' My voice is hoarse from all the crying I've done.

'If I roll over now, I'm going to prison anyway.'

'Not necessarily.'

'I couldn't hack it in prison – no way.'

'You can plead extenuating circumstances. When you tell them about Chloe.'

It's as if I've just sworn at him. The expression on his face completely changes and he steps back, dragging Toby with him. 'Don't you even say her name!' Now they're only two feet from the edge.

'Please.' I step towards them. 'Come away from there. I didn't mean to upset you even more.'

'It was supposed to look like an accident,' he says. 'For *Naylor*. But then they'll probably know it all anyway, won't they?' He raises his voice some more as he jerks his head towards the people gathered below before looking back at me.

'I haven't said a thing.'

'Like hell. Do you really think I trust a word you say?'

'Just give me my son – then we can talk about all this. I won't tell them anything, I promise. *Please!*'

'I want to hurt *him* like he hurt my sister.'

I should never have mentioned Chloe. He was beginning to soften before I brought her into it.

'Mum!' Toby stretches his arm out at me, eyes bulging with fear. Somehow, I've got to get to him.

I daren't edge any closer in case Harry steps even further backwards. There's hardly any room left as it is.

'If I'm going down, he's coming with me.' He draws Toby closer to his side.

'Let him go. Please Harry – I'm begging you.'

'Naylor,' he shouts. 'You might as well say your goodbyes.'

'Come here son.' My teeth are chattering. We're all precariously close to the edge now. But Toby's the nearest. One wrong move and it's all over.

I'm close enough that Harry could lunge at me and grab me with his other hand and drag me over with them too. He might as well. If he jumps with Toby, my life is over anyway. I'll probably jump after them.

I hear voices. David's and what must be the officers. I can't imagine they'll just storm up here. Not while everything's literally hanging by a thread.

'I've lost *everything* while Naylor's just going to carry on – living his cushy life – shagging everything that moves,' Harry snarls. 'Even after all this, he'll still come up smelling of fucking roses.'

'He won't. I've already told the police what he was planning to do to me. *See*, he's far more likely to get sent to prison than *you* are.'

'But I've *killed* someone.' He sounds like a wounded animal. 'Maybe I can't live with that.'

'So why would you want to kill an innocent boy as well?'

Harry points beyond me. 'Stay where you are, do you hear me?'

We all look to the crunching at the other edge of the rock. It's Catherine. She suddenly freezes.

With his attention now on her, Harry must momentarily loosen his grip on Toby for he manages to break away from him. He bolts towards Catherine and Harry lunges after him. I stick my leg out, causing Harry to stumble forward.

'You *bitch* – you're going to regret that.'

'Get him away from here,' I shout as Harry scrambles back to his feet.

'*Mum!*'

Catherine manoeuvres Toby around and behind her back. David and the police appear behind her.

'Please Catherine. Take him down. Get him away.'

'Nowhere to run now is there Douglas?' David steps forward, grinning. He's actually *grinning*.

Harry's gaze flits from our newly gathered audience to the rock edge. Toby's now completely safe and out of his reach but I'm still fair game. Plus I'm on the wrong side of him – literally as well as figuratively. Somehow I have to get past him and back to safety. I hold my breath. Is he going to give himself up here?

Or is he going to jump, taking me with him?

As two police officers edge closer to us, I've no idea which direction I'm going in. All I know is that I'm either going over the edge of that rock or by some miracle, I'll be hauled back to safety.

I close my eyes. It's all out of my control. Hands grip my shoulder. Then my arm. Then my leg.

The police have got me. I'm safe.

Just as Harry leaps from the top of the rock with a final anguished howl.

∾

You're as dark as the night.
One day it will devour you.
(Chloe Douglas)

THIRTY-NINE

CATHERINE

Time stands still as I turn Toby into me. I wait for the crunch of flesh and bone into rock for the second time today. At least there are no children other than Toby to witness it this time.

The weight of Leonie's death is unbearable, and now etched into my soul. The image of our children seeing such a horror is a cross I'll always carry, a haunting burden that I'll never be able to let go of.

I can only pray that the officers still down there managed to get clear of Harry's fall in time.

A voice roars into the air. 'We've got him.'

With Toby's hand in mine, we rush to the other side of the path, joining three of the police officers. Peering cautiously around the edge of the rock, I hold my breath. I can't believe it. They've caught Harry in a large net at the bottom.

Toby looks up at me. 'Are they going to arrest him Miss Fox?'

'Yes. I should think he'll be going to prison for a long, long time after what he's done today.'

Harry's squirming in the net like a beached eel as the police lower it to the ground and scramble towards him. It takes three of them to pin him face down to the rocks as a fourth officer handcuffs him.

I'm so relieved he hasn't died. Now, at least, he'll have to face justice for everything he's done. Not only has he ended Leonie's life, whether he meant to or not – but he's also terrified the living daylights out of Toby.

'I just want to go down now.' Toby's shaking from head to foot and clinging to my arm. I slide my cardigan off and wrap it around his shoulders. 'I want my mum.'

'We'll go down now.'

'But where's my mum?'

'Let's just get *you* down, shall we? We can see her at the bottom.' I look back through the officers who are behind us but I can't see Kirsty or David. 'They'll still be with the other policemen. The ones who pulled your mum back to safety.'

'Is she alright?'

'Of course she is. You both are. We'll just need to get you checked over.' I take his clammy hand in mine. My only concern at this moment is getting this boy back onto lower ground.

'She was lucky that policeman got to her, wasn't she?' His teeth are chattering as I begin guiding him down the path.

'Hold onto me Toby. Yes, she *was* lucky. *Very* lucky.'

'And I was too.'

With every footstep that we take back towards the bottom, I feel an increasing sense of relief. Harry's finally in handcuffs and I feel certain David will be in them by now as well. It's something I'd prefer Toby not to have to see but that might be beyond my control.

He's *bound* to get sent to prison for his initial plans to sabotage Kirsty's zip wire ride. I knew I'd get him out of Oldale sooner or later but had no idea as to how dramatic it would become. I'll no doubt get hauled over the coals for everything that's happened here over the last couple of days but I'll fight on. Those children need me to.

'Where are they?' Toby looks back over his shoulder.

As far as I can tell, the same number of police officers seem to be following us back down as came up. But there's no sign of David *or* Kirsty.

They're hardly likely to be walking back down *together*. Something feels wrong. Very wrong.

One of the younger officers peers back over his shoulder as well. 'They were right behind us a moment ago, I'm sure of it.'

I hear the commotion before I see it.

'What's going on Miss Fox?' Toby grips my arm.

'Get off me!' Kirsty's shriek pierces the air.

'Mum!' The urgency in Toby's cry echoes his mother's distress.

This is an absolute nightmare. The police should have been accompanying them back down, every second of the way, surely? Whatever's happening between them is not quite as high as they were before but they're still at least a hundred feet up.

Boots pound on the path away from us as the officers set off back up the rock. Shrieks and shouts bounce all around us as Kirsty and David push and tussle with one another. *At the top of a rock.*

This isn't going to end well. I move my hands to Toby's ears as he burrows himself into me.

'Get off. Let me go.'

Their altercation has taken itself right to the edge. I can only pray they've got that safety net ready down there again.

Oh my God. The rock they're on forms a peculiar angle with another jutting out several feet beneath it. If David gets the better of Kirsty up there, she's likely to hit that on the way down. No safety net can help her then.

If it's him that goes over, then so be it. All I can do is try to shield Toby from the horror show that's become of his parents.

I can't look. There's no way I can watch the inevitable. Nor can I seem to move. Judging from the screams and yells emanating from above, one of them is moments away from their death.

≈

When it was the end,
I expected my life to flash before my eyes.
But all I saw was you.
(Chloe Douglas)

FORTY

KIRSTY

My breath catches. David's fingers close around my T-shirt, a desperate grasp that pulls me even nearer to the edge. I gasp, helpless, as the world tilts below me.

'It's time to go Kirsty.' As I try shifting myself in the other direction, he turns me around and begins bumping me even closer to where it will all be over. 'Since this was meant for you in the first place. It should be *you* in that morgue. It *will* be you.'

'Don't be so stupid,' I gasp. 'You'll do life in prison. What about—'

'You've already told the police about me.' His grip on my T-shirt remains as tight as ever. 'I heard what you said to Douglas up there. I'm doing time anyway. So I might as well have the pleasure of knowing *you're* not around anymore.'

'No!' I drop to my knees. But this doesn't stop him. He grips my shoulder as he drags me right to the edge. I really *am* going to be hurled to my death in front of Toby.

I've survived so much already over the last decade that I'm not ready to die. All I want to do is fight on – to never drink a drop of alcohol ever again and to get my son back with me where he belongs.

'Think of Toby. He'll never forgive you if you kill me David. You'll lose him forever.'

'He'd never forgive me if I were to leave an old soak like *you* to bring him up. No chance.'

'Mum! No!' Toby's distraught voice slices through the air.

'Surely you don't want to put him through *this*. We should both be with him after what he's—'

The drumming of boots is closing in. Can I really be rescued for a *second* time?

'Nooooo.' I screech as the ground swims below me. I grip onto David as tightly as he's gripping onto me. 'Please David. Don't do this to me.'

'I want you out of his life, once and for all.'

'Help me! Someone! Please!' The breeze blows in my hair for the very last time. *This is it.* Even going to prison for my knowledge about Harry's plans would be preferable to being dead.

I close my eyes. Brace myself for the inevitable. Hopefully, my heart will just stop on the way down.

My son's scream is the last thing I hear as I'm released into the air. I wait for death to rescue me.

'Get down on your knees,' somebody shouts above me.

And my world turns black.

～

I'm not sure of the point my life ended.
The moment we met or the moment I died.
(Chloe Douglas)

EPILOGUE

KIRSTY

Ten months later

'I can hardly believe we're doing this,' I whisper to Catherine as we stand in line to book ourselves in.

'Remind me why we are again.' She pulls a face.

'Closure,' I reply. 'But now we're here, suddenly I'm not so sure either.'

'Is this your first time?' the officious-looking woman behind the desk demands. I can only hope for her sake that she doesn't have a keen sense of smell, spending all afternoon in here. The smell of body odour mixed with disinfectant is not a good one.

We both nod.

'Stand there. We need your photograph and then your fingerprint. Both of you.'

'You'd think *we* were the criminals,' Catherine mutters as she steps forwards to where the officer is pointing. 'I feel like telling her that I'm a perfectly respectable headteacher of a school.'

'I *am* a criminal, aren't I?' I say as I stand behind her, pointing down at my ankle. 'Kind of.'

At least my alcohol tag isn't visible beneath the bootleg jeans I'm wearing, though I'm sure it will set the alarms off when I go through the scanner. I'm only just able to wear my jeans again after having the pins removed from my other leg.

The courts, as part of my sentence, didn't need to shove this tag on me. Drink nearly cost me *everything*. I'll never touch a drop again.

The flash of the camera momentarily blinds me and the fingerprinting scanner feels cool and slightly sticky beneath my fingertips.

Standing in the cold, sterile line for the second stage of booking in, the stark white walls of the processing area feel like they're closing in on me.

'It'd be easier to get into Buckingham Palace.' Catherine slides her feet back into her shoes. 'I can't believe what they've subjected us to. 'Do we really look like we'd be smuggling drugs in our mouths or down our blouses?'

I pull a face. 'There's just the dog search to go now.' I nod towards where a cute-looking spaniel is waiting with yet another officer.

'Sit on the chairs and keep your hands in your lap,' we are ordered. 'And don't make contact with the dog.'

'Table number seven.' There are no pleases or thank yous in this place. Our fingerprints are checked again as we head into a huge dimly lit room. It reveals tired faces, some holding hands, others consoling children. Who'd bring kids into a place like this?

My heart is thumping as I glance around. Then I spot him in the far corner.

'What still annoys me,' I say, 'are the paltry sentences they hand down. He'll be out in a few years and you watch – they'll probably give him a new identity or something.'

'You heard what the judge said.' Catherine squeezes my shoulder as she walks behind me. 'They gave him the maximum sentence they could.'

'Thanks for coming.' Harry nods at us as we sit facing him. His prison-issue shirt and jeans look to be hanging from his once-muscular frame. But I can't feel sorry for him. How can I after what he did to Toby?

'How's Toby?' It's as if he's read my mind. Anger bubbles within me at his mention of him. I want to retort that he's got no right to ask, but the din of voices around us stifles my own voice. How dare he even utter my son's name after what he did to him? Luckily, Catherine answers for me.

'He's needing a lot of counselling. But he's doing OK.'

Harry's face relaxes slightly. 'Have you got him back with you?'

'Why do you want to know?' Tension throbs in my face. Is this the only reason he's got us here? To assuage his conscience over what he did to us?

'It's just...' His head droops. 'If I could know that *one* good thing's come out of all this, it would make everything more bearable.'

I'm struggling to hear him above the racket of everyone in here, all competing to be heard. And we're not even in the thick of the room.

'Yes, I've got custody of Toby.'

'Thank God.' His shoulders sag. 'Your ex should never have been granted it in the first place. Not after everything he did.'

'I think we're all on the same page there.' Catherine looks around, her eyes falling on the snack bar. Harry follows her gaze and then looks at me. If he thinks we're staying here to have a cosy cuppa with him, he's very much mistaken. I want to hear what he's got to say and then get out of here as quickly as possible.

'I asked you here,' Harry sighs, then continues, 'mainly

because I wanted to say how sorry I am for what I did to Toby. Taking him like I did was an absolute moment of madness.'

'You didn't just *take* him, though, did you?' I lean forward in my seat. 'You *terrorised* him. Up on that rock. Do you know the nightmares that child has had because of *you*?'

He shakes his head. 'I'm just so, so sorry. I've been doing lots of work on myself since I got in here. Group work, counselling, that sort of thing.'

'And has it done any good?' Catherine crosses one denim-clad leg over the other.

'It's a shame it took me being in *here* to start addressing it all.' He clasps his hands together. 'I've carried the trauma of what my sister did for years – and the hatred towards...' His voice trails off. It's as if he can't bear to say his name.

I know how he feels.

'But I stopped him from meeting you for a drink,' Catherine says, raising her voice again above the ever-rising noise. 'What was all that about?'

'I'm not so sure anymore.' Harry looks her straight in the eye. It's the first time he's done that with either of us since we sat down. 'At the time I wanted to get him talking – to hear him admit to what he put Chloe through out loud. That *might* have been enough for me at the time. Or I might have recorded him on my phone as evidence – I just don't know. I wasn't thinking straight. I just thought that if I could get a couple of drinks down him, he'd talk – if only to gloat about getting away with everything he did to her.'

'You managed to prevent what he was planning to do to Kirsty. Despite everything else, that speaks volumes to me.'

Catherine's often said this to me. If Harry *hadn't* caught David in the equipment room. If he *hadn't* inspected the harness labelled with my name, what the outcome might have been for *me* then.

'Yeah but what did I do? I tried to turn what he'd planned

around on *him*, but instead, an innocent woman with her life ahead of her fell to her death.' He drops his gaze again. 'Then I took Toby because—'

'I think we all know the reasons why,' I snap. I can't bear hearing it all again. 'You told us all that night when you were on the run. You talked about it in court. But what doesn't—'

'I know what you're going to say. It's unforgivable what I did next. I can barely forgive *myself* so I'd hardly expect *you* to be able to. All I can say is that I was in an extremely dark place last year. The doctors here have said I was in some kind of breakdown state at the time.'

'I take it you're on medication now?' Catherine's voice is soft but Harry still manages to hear her.

He nods. 'I'm on much more of an even keel. I'm not trying to excuse what I did but I've let David Naylor wreck *my* life as much as he's wrecked the lives of others.' He gives me a knowing look. He means mine too.

'Why did you ply me with all that vodka? I've never really got my head around that.'

'When I told you he'd set the trap for *you* and I'd decided to swap things around to trap *him* instead, you threatened to go to the police – don't you remember?'

I glance at Catherine. 'Vaguely.'

'I only wanted to stop you. I knew once I'd got a couple of drinks down you and you had the taste for it again, you'd keep drinking. I wanted you to be unsure of your own mind so I could just deny it all.'

'You did that alright. Because of you, I was in bed for the entire morning when I could have done something to change things.'

'I'm sorry. It's only since I got in here that I've been able to process what I did.'

'Which is?' Catherine raises an eyebrow.

'I killed Leonie. And I'd give anything to turn the clock

back.' His voice wobbles. 'In some ways, I should have been given a greater sentence than *he* was given.'

'You had mitigating circumstances.'

'*Catherine!*' She almost sounds like *she's* forgiving him. I know she's got a reputation for being a hard-faced 'new broom' as they call her at school, but I know the *real* side of her. She's got a heart of gold really.

They can't call her a *new* broom anymore. She's been in charge for nearly two years now and has completely turned the place around.

Catherine glances over at the snack bar again. I give her a look as if to say, *we are* not *going there*. It will only prolong things. I just want to get out of here, go home and shower this place off me. I plan never to step foot inside a prison again.

'I can't believe *you* got punished as well Kirsty – you should know that was *never* my intention.'

'Don't remind me.' Now my leg's on the mend, and my collarbone which was also badly fractured when David pushed me from that rock, I've still got a hefty dose of community service to face for *perverting the course of justice.* According to the judge, being *drunk* is not an adequate defence.

Others might not agree. But I know, deep down, that I *more than* deserve to be punished.

'It could have so easily been me in there,' I say as we reach the final set of doors. I look back to see where the officer who was leading us has dropped back to. It's taken nearly as long to get out of the place as it took us to get in.

'You are *not* a criminal.' Catherine lowers her voice. 'It isn't your fault you were comatose with vodka, and it's not as if you didn't tell the police what you knew *as soon* as you remembered it all.'

The rattle of keys in the lock reaffirms what a lucky escape I've had – in so many ways.

But what *nobody* knows still is just how much I wanted my ex-husband dead in the cold light of day.

However, there's definitely one person with more than an inkling.

I wanted David dead probably more than Harry did. So yes, I was drunk and had, initially, wanted to involve the police, like Harry said back there.

However, there was *nothing* wrong with my memory the next day.

It was an endless morning, just lying in bed staring at the sun seeping around the edges of the curtains as I waited for the news of David's 'accident'. I had little doubt that Harry would take care of the necessary details and do everything in his power to make it happen.

So it came as a hell of a shock when David burst into my room, larger than life to have a go at me. If Catherine had known he was heading to me while I was on my own in the building, she'd have tried to stop him, surely?

After he'd stormed out again, the only conclusion I could draw was that Harry couldn't have noticed David going off anywhere.

So the next thing that hit me was, *what if that harness has been accidentally made available for someone else?*

I'd already heard the distant shrieks and shouts coming from the rocks from the children, and knew from the itinerary that the adults' turn was running late. I had time to do something.

So I texted Jeanette.

THERE'S A PROBLEM WITH THE ZIP WIRE! MAKE SURE NO ONE GOES ON IT!

At first, I thought she couldn't have seen the message in time. But if that had been the case, she'd have shown it to the police – after all, it would have been a vital piece of evidence.

So I can only conclude she'd been watching Leonie as she got ready to go from the top of the rock. Leonie – her main rival for David's attention – and the rest. David – whose room I later discovered Jeanette had been in for much of the night.

It seems Jeanette had her *own* moment of madness in the short time where she could have done something to prevent Leonie's death but chose not to.

We've never spoken about it. And now Toby's at one high school and Jessica's going to another, perhaps our paths will never need to cross again.

At least, I hope not.

The cool breeze as we return to the car park carries the welcome sense of freedom. I look back at the sprawling prison, trying not to think about the thin line between this outside world, in which I've managed to remain, and the reality within those prison walls – an existence which could so easily have been mine.

I smile at Catherine as I slide into the passenger seat. I've had more than a lucky escape. And I've got my son to collect in an hour.

A LETTER FROM MARIA FRANKLAND

Dear reader,

I want to say a huge thank you for choosing to read *The Taken Child*. If you did enjoy it, and want to keep up to date with all my latest releases, just sign up at the following link. Your email address will never be shared and you can unsubscribe at any time.

www.bookouture.com/maria-frankland

It was my ten-year-old niece who sparked the idea for this novel when she was telling me all about the school residential she was counting the days down to go on. She went on to tell me more about the activity centre and all its fantastic activities, adding that teachers and parent helpers were so desperate to be a part of it that their names were going into a draw to decide who would go.

This got me thinking then, that if the wrong names were drawn, perhaps of people who didn't get along or with an axe to grind with one another, to be thrust into such proximity *and* amongst such hazardous pursuits might well be a recipe for disaster...

I really enjoyed the research required for this particular novel, especially the trip to Go Ape, which was necessary for me to make sure I knew my stuff about the mechanics of a zip wire. The instructor raised more than an eyebrow when I asked him about how and where a safety harness might be tampered with!

I'd love to know your thoughts on the story and would hugely appreciate a review on Amazon or Goodreads, or both if you're feeling generous. Or even better, come and find me at one of the following places:

www.mariafrankland.co.uk

 facebook.com/writermariafrank

instagram.com/writermaria_f

BOOK DISCUSSION QUESTIONS

1. How does the use of alternating viewpoints contribute to your understanding of the characters and the unfolding of the story?
2. Discuss the theme of responsibility in the novel. How did different characters grapple with their responsibilities towards the children, each other, and the truth?
3. Were there any characters you empathised with or felt conflicted about due to their actions and decisions?
4. Discuss the various relationships among the characters in the story and the effect of them.
5. The outdoor activity centre plays a significant role in the story. How did the setting contribute to the overall atmosphere and suspense of the novel?
6. Explore the moral dilemmas faced by the characters, such as David's choices and Kirsty's struggles with addiction. How did these dilemmas add depth to the story?
7. How did Catherine's strict policy against staff relationships impact the characters' decisions and behaviours?
8. Discuss the theme of betrayal in the novel. Which characters experienced betrayal, and how did it affect their actions?

9. What ethical questions arise from the actions of the characters and the outcomes of the story?
10. How did the characters evolve throughout the story? Did any of them change significantly, inwardly or outwardly, from the beginning to the end?
11. Were you surprised by the identity of the person responsible for the tragedy at the outdoor activity centre? How was this reveal built up to?
12. Did you find the resolution satisfying, or were there loose ends you wish had been tied up differently?

ACKNOWLEDGEMENTS

Thank you, as always, to my amazing husband, Michael. He's my first reader, and his opinion is vital to my editing process for each of my novels. His belief in me means more than I can say.

My next huge thank you goes to Susannah Hamilton, my editor at Bookouture, who is a joy to work with. I love bouncing ideas around with her and what she doesn't know about the psychological thriller genre isn't worth knowing! I'd like to also acknowledge the hard work of Laura, my copyeditor, and Becca, my proofreader, as well as David Grogan at Head Design for his amazing cover design.

A special acknowledgement goes to my existing community of wonderful readers, especially those in my FrankFans reader group, who give me so much support and encouragement.

I will always be grateful to Leeds Trinity University and my MA in Creative Writing Tutors there, Martyn, Amina and Oz. My Master's degree in 2015 was the springboard to being able to write as a profession.

And thanks especially to you, the reader. Whether you are new to my work or have read every book, thank you for taking the time to read this story. I really hope you enjoyed it.

PUBLISHING TEAM

Turning a manuscript into a book requires the efforts of many people. The publishing team at Bookouture would like to acknowledge everyone who contributed to this publication.

Audio
Alba Proko
Sinead O'Connor
Melissa Tran

Commercial
Lauren Morrissette
Hannah Richmond
Imogen Allport

Cover design
Head Design Ltd.

Data and analysis
Mark Alder
Mohamed Bussuri

Editorial
Susannah Hamilton
Nadia Michael

Made in United States
North Haven, CT
07 July 2024

54495085R00168